The Christmas Fake

RACHEL KAYE

To my Writer Mama besties—thank you for your constant support and encouragement. This book would not exist without you.

And to Tom—the hero of this story has a beard. I'm not saying it's because of you, but it's not <u>not</u> because of you. I love you endlessly.

Content Note

The Christmas Fake is the first book in *The Greyport Series,* a series of interconnected stand-alone romance novels set in the fictional small town of Greyport. This book is an open-door romance featuring on-page sexual content.

Though *The Christmas Fake* is a light-hearted read, there may be some topics that lead to discomfort. Please treat yourself kindly.

Detailed discussion of a motor-vehicle accident and associated injury/medical trauma. Not depicted on page.

On-page depiction of grounding techniques in relation to trauma. Minor workplace injury.

Parental abandonment. Briefly mentioned, not depicted on page.

On-page depiction of complicated family dynamics.

Detailed discussion of illness and death of a parent and associated caregiver role. Not depicted on page.

On-page misogynistic comments from side characters.

Negative self-talk from main character regarding a past injury and associated body changes.

Intense sipping...you've been warned.

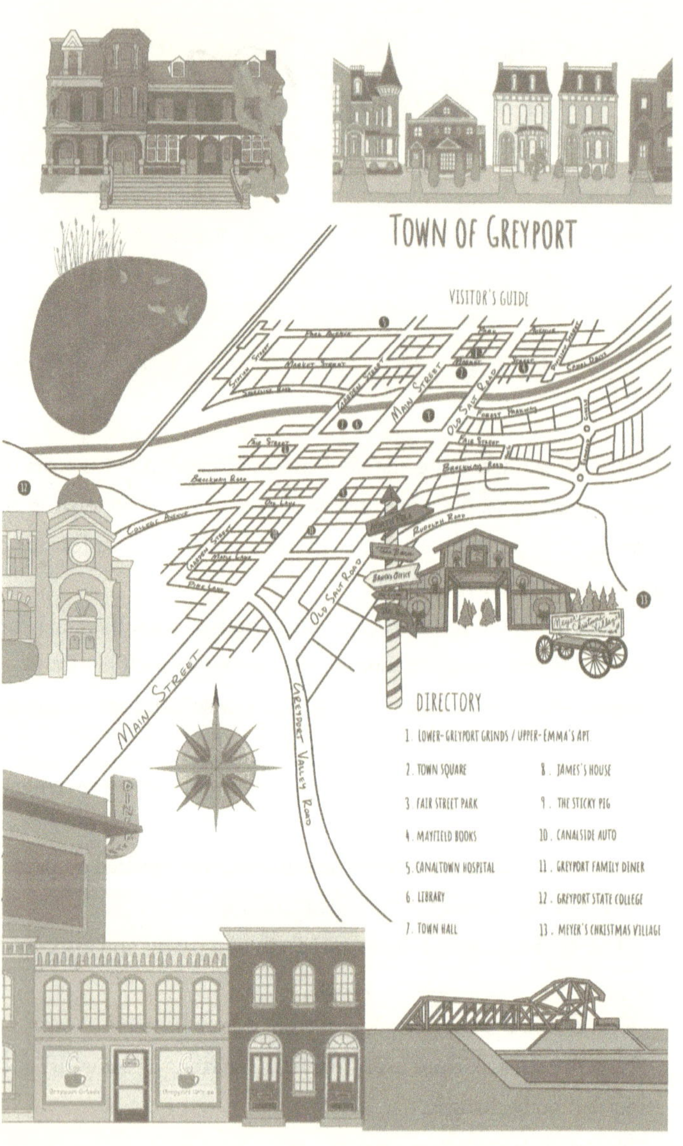

TOWN OF GREYPORT
VISITOR'S GUIDE
MAIN STREET
GREYPORT VALLEY ROAD
OLD SALT ROAD
COLLEGE AVENUE
MARKET STREET
FAIR STREET
BROCKWAY ROAD
FOREST PARKWAY
RUDOLPH ROAD

DIRECTORY
1. LOWER - GREYPORT GRINDS / UPPER - EMMA'S APT
2. TOWN SQUARE
3. FAIR STREET PARK
4. MAYFIELD BOOKS
5. CANALTOWN HOSPITAL
6. LIBRARY
7. TOWN HALL
8. JAMES'S HOUSE
9. THE STICKY PIG
10. CANALSIDE AUTO
11. GREYPORT FAMILY DINER
12. GREYPORT STATE COLLEGE
13. MEYER'S CHRISTMAS VILLAGE

CHAPTER ONE

Emma

"Come sit on Santa's lap like the dirty girl I know you are. Or else someone's going on the naughty list..."

My car door flew open, and the crude words echoed through the garage.

"Shit, shit, shit," I said as I rushed to silence the car's speaker.

I could hear my heart pounding in my ears as I intentionally ignored the mechanic's knowing smirk.

Maybe it wasn't too late to move back home—an echo of my mother's familiar refrain. I'd been living in Greyport for three months and probably heard Linda Hartwell, Queen of the Guilt Trip, repeat it at least twice a day, along with a heaping helping of, 'Who takes a job in a tiny library across the state,' and, 'That junky car of yours won't last a week in the snow.'

Granted, she hadn't been far off on the car subject, hence the visit to the local repair shop, Canalside Auto. I was desperately hoping they took walk-ins and offered steep discounts to new-ish Greyport residents.

"That the noise you said it was making when you turned on the heater?"

Of course, the mechanic was funny besides being sexy as hell—tall with dark hair and the barest hint of stubble that would probably feel amazing rasping along my skin. I wasn't normally into the blue-collar kind of guy—not that I had much time for any sort of guy these days—but this one might have me considering an exception.

Plus, I was supposed to be all about stepping out of my comfort zone nowadays. Branching out, meeting new people. Not that I'd had much success as of late, but still, I was committed. Mom might not understand it, but looking mortality straight in the eye tended to leave its mark on a person.

"It's an audiobook, that's all." I fumbled for an explanation, praying he wouldn't notice my flushed cheeks. "A, uh...friend borrowed my car last night, and she must have left it playing."

"Weren't you the one who drove here?" he called me out on the white lie. Didn't he know the unspoken rule to ignore that sort of thing, save a girl the embarrassment?

"Uh...yeah." There was no use covering with another fib, not when the erotic Santa audiobook was clearly synced to my phone. Truly, the most laughable part of that line of fiction was the idea that I had any friends in Greyport at all, let alone any close enough to drive my beater of a car. Hell, my closest confidant in this town was a run-down park bench.

"You doing anything after this?"

My head flew up, and I met the mechanic's gaze.

"Are you asking me out right now?" I was a hot mess, frizzy hair flying and sweat building up under the thick layers of my striped sweater. Not exactly dressed to kill.

"Trying to," he said with a shrug before shoving the driver's seat back to make room for his long legs.

"Do you even know my name?" I had given it at the front desk when I checked in, but he hadn't seemed too interested. He looked up from the seat and grinned, the right side of his mouth twitching up a tad higher than the left.

The new-and-improved version of Emma could envision herself kissing that mouth.

"Wanna tell me?"

"Huh?"

He looked at me for a beat, waiting.

Oh. He wanted my name. "It's Emma."

"Well, Emma, I'm Harrison. What do you say? You let me take a look at this, and maybe later we can see if I can learn any new skills from your...friend's...book."

With that, he jabbed the power button on the car radio, and the sounds of my audiobook filled the air again.

New Emma might be in over her head here.

I PARKED MY NOW-FIXED car opposite a faded-blue Victorian home as my phone's GPS verified my arrival at the address Harrison gave me. He'd quickly sourced and repaired the mysterious car noise before we'd exchanged numbers and agreed to a nine o'clock meeting.

The late hour only confirmed what we both knew—this was not a date. I had to admit to thinking there would be more wooing before we got to the go-home-together stage. Though I was supposed to be trying new things, checking items off my list, the disappointment still lingered.

I delved into the pocket of my thin coat, running my fingers over the scrap of lined notebook paper hidden inside before pulling it out.

The familiar page was delicate from frequent folding and unfolding. It was written in a wine haze the first night in my apartment when I'd been without internet or TV, only my potential regrets to keep me company.

I traced my ring finger down the words written in smeared ink.

HOW TO MAKE FRIENDS

BEFRIEND YOUR COWORKERS.

JOIN A GROUP.

JOIN A SPORTS LEAGUE.

JOIN A GYM.

GET A DOG.

STROLL LOCAL MARKET.

GO ON A HIKE.

SAY YES TO EVERYTHING.

I had finished approximately none of the tasks, but I hoped tonight would be a good starting point. I hadn't made the list intending to have a random hookup, but if I squinted hard, it fit into the *Say YES to everything* category.

And perhaps Harrison had some friends he was willing to share.

A message notification came through on my phone, from my mom, but I swiped it away without opening it. I was afraid any distraction would tear me from my path.

With a bracing inhale, I tossed the list back on the dash, hopped out of the car, and penguin-walked my way up the well-plowed driveway. The glass-paneled door rattled under my knuckles as I tapped on the wood, ripping off the metaphorical Band-Aid. Harry answered my knock almost immediately, already shirtless and wasting no time.

Apparently, only one of us had been having an internal crisis.

With a brief greeting and a tug of his clammy hand, he hauled me inside.

The sudden pressure of his mouth on mine sent a jolt through my body. Were all one-night stands this...abrupt? His lips were chilled and slightly chapped. And that was...a lot of tongue. Still, not the worst first kiss overall. I could work with it.

With Harrison leading, I silently repeated the *Say Yes* mantra as we made our way up a flight of stairs to a bedroom.

Or maybe it was his murder lair. I didn't know him, after all. I should have done that thing other women apparently did and sent a of photo his license plate or address to a friend. Outside of books and movies, I'd never known anyone to do this, but surely it was a trope for a reason.

I couldn't think of a single friend I would even send something like that to. Most of the friends I still had back home had firmly attached themselves to the same men or women since high school or college, with very few anonymous hookups along the way. The idea of murder by a one-night stand likely didn't cross their minds. But I might be poised to become the outlier.

The sharp edge of the bed pressed against the backs of my knees, giving me pause.

"Wait." I braced my forearms against Harrison's broad shoulders as he leaned down to scoop my hips up onto the mattress.

"Yeah?" He puffed the words past full, shiny lips. His kissing skills might not mesh well with mine, but the boy had a pretty mouth.

"You're not, like, a serial killer or something, right?"

"Not the last time I checked," he said with a laugh, abs flexing with the movement. He must work out. I'd have to ask for suggestions on the best gym in Greyport—to check that task off my list. Despite a few local gym chains offering deals, the most affordable option was still out of my budget. Medical bills and moving expenses ate up most of my savings. And the Greyport Public Library didn't exactly pay a fortune for someone to run their community outreach and programming.

I swallowed down a shiver of self-consciousness as I pulled my shirt up and over my head, sending the soft knit sailing toward Harrison's hamper. He had clearly been interested enough to ask me out. My jeans and sweater weren't hiding that I wasn't a dedicated fitness buff.

"Emma."

I dragged my attention back to the half-naked man standing in front of me.

"Get out of your head, okay? This is meant to be fun, yeah?"

I nodded, determined to exist in the moment as I brought his head down to mine and let the touch of skin on skin carry me away.

Chapter Two

Emma

T HE SHEETS SENT AN itch across my skin as I woke beside a still sleeping Harrison. I turned my head toward the red LED lights of his clock to check the time.

Three a.m.

I had drifted off after the second round of sex. It hadn't been bad as far as first-time hookups were concerned. Harrison was hot and skilled in the lovemaking department. Still, I had very little desire to repeat the experience, and I got the impression he felt the same. There was no explosion of chemistry, no pressing need for a repeat.

My shift at the library didn't start until nine, and though Harrison had said I could spend the night, the idea of staying until morning didn't sit right.

I slipped from under his arm—he was a cuddler too—and began the quiet scramble for my clothes. Harrison had closed his bedroom door in the night, but a faint stream of light filtered in from the hallway, illuminating the room while I searched.

I fought off a shiver as my bare feet hit the hardwood. Thankfully, I found my socks first, just under the frame of the bed. In short order, I collected my sneakers, gripping the canvas sides between my fingers as I located my purse with my other hand.

Harrison didn't stir as I opened the door just enough to slip through. Closing it behind me, I tiptoed down the flight of stairs to the front entry.

"Who the fuck are you, and what are you doing in my house?"

My shoes and purse went flying, miscellaneous contents going airborne and clattering as they hit the floor. A portrait of an older brunette—dressed in a pale pink sweater with a thin gold necklace around her neck—tilted, nearly falling from the wall.

The shadow of a tall, broad-shouldered man loomed over me. He stood to the left of the door, blocking my only point of exit.

The taste of adrenaline filled my mouth as I stood frozen in place.

Had I escaped unscathed from my one-night stand only to be unwittingly serial-killed by a home invader?

"I'll repeat, what are you doing in my house?" the shadow man said in a growl.

Okay, not an intruder, apparently. Now this man thought *I* was the criminal.

"Um." I looked up toward the top of the stairs, willing Harrison to appear so he could explain to this stranger that I hadn't broken in.

Wait, was Harrison *married* to this guy? Did completing the first task on my list brand me a home-wrecker?

"Your response is, 'Um?' Really? You can stop looking for him to rescue you. I figured out you're here with Harry. I didn't realize he was that desperate, but nothing with him surprises me anymore."

Okay now, what the fuck?

"Excuse me?" I said, the muscles in my back tightening up.

The shadowy stranger laughed. Despite the clear sarcasm, it was a rich and rolling sound. I was pissed that I even noticed. A pleasant laugh was wasted on this douchebag.

"You're in *my* house and acting like I'm the one bothering you? That's fucking rich." He moved closer, stopping at the base of the stairs, and I got a better eyeful of him.

His size, so evident from across the room, was even more notable as he towered over me. His height easily surpassed my five feet, five inches by at least a foot.

I pressed my back to the wall as he leaned in, closing in on my face. What the hell was he doing?

He reached past me and flicked on the light switch next to my head.

Once I recovered from being blinded, I really saw him. White skin with a faded tan, like he spent time outside, even in the cold of winter. He wasn't pretty like Harrison, but his face was arresting. A powerful jaw, high cheekbones. Chestnut-brown hair just a touch too long at the nape. His nose looked like it had been broken at some point. Strong, broad shoulders filled out a blue flannel and a medium-length, neat beard completed the lumberjack style.

"Done staring?"

My eyes flashed up to his. They were an unfair shade of hazel.

The man stepped up to the base of the stairs before opening his mouth. "Harry!" I jolted from his sudden bellowing. "Wake your miserable ass up!"

"Look." I took the opportunity to gather the contents of my purse off the floor, crouching and backing up at the same time. "I didn't realize he was in a relationship. I'm sorry, and I'll just—"

"You think Harry and I are a *couple*? Fuck no." His face showed visceral disgust.

"Well, excuse me for assuming something that so offends you, you homophobe."

Why the hell was I arguing with this guy? I needed to leave.

"Thanks for the lecture, sweetheart, but Harry is my fucking cousin."

Beyond their height and the fact that they were both white men with dark hair, there wasn't a crazy-strong resemblance. He couldn't hold it against me for not figuring it out.

Harrison's cousin directed his scathing attention back to the stairwell. "Harrison Alfred Klein!"

"Hey, hi, what's up?" Harrison rushed out of his room, scrambling to a stop at the top of the landing, clutching a black baseball cap in front of his unmentionables. "Ems, I see you met James!"

"What the fuck, man? Could you put on some fucking pants?"

My head was spinning as Harrison's cousin—James—continued his rant while the nude man stumbled back into his bedroom to hunt down some clothes. "Didn't I ask you to give me one fucking weekend without one of your hookups invading my space? I have important shit to do on Monday, and I do not need strange women creeping around my house. You're lucky I let you live here at all after the last one stole my wallet."

Harrison, now fortunately clothed, made his way to the foyer, where I stood awkwardly next to James.

I did my best not to flinch when Harrison slung his arm over my shoulder and pulled me into his side in a tight squeeze. He turned gleaming eyes toward his cousin.

"Well, you see, Jay, Emma here isn't just a hookup. She's my girlfriend."

Getting murdered would have been a better outcome.

CHAPTER THREE

James

IT WAS SILENT. JUST the way I liked it. I slammed the refrigerator door shut and savored the way it echoed through the house. Harry was already on his way to work, but I hadn't been able to fall back asleep, despite his "date" leaving two hours ago.

My plan for a quiet month was already blown to shit.

I didn't buy Harry's bullshit for a second. No way was that woman his girlfriend. Hell, she'd thought Harry and I were married at first. If they were really dating, wouldn't she know the marital status of her supposed boyfriend? Or maybe she didn't care, which didn't work in her favor either.

After a night like the last, it was clear to me it was time to ask Harry to find his own place. I made a promise to my mother that I would take care of my younger cousin right before she passed away. We had little family left, what with Harry's mom, my Aunt Vicki, living across the country. Neither of our dads had ever been in the picture. My sister was still local, but she lived in a studio apartment, worked an insane number of jobs, and bristled against any apparent threats to her privacy. Harry living with her wasn't an option.

Naturally, all the responsibility fell to me. It was a thankless job, taking care of my younger family members, but I was damn good at it.

Though I was beginning to ask myself daily why my nearly thirty-year-old cousin, gainfully employed and with no apparent impairments, needed looking after. I suspected it was more a case of Harry not wanting to grow up than needing the help.

After sipping from my coffee mug, I settled in to prepare breakfast. I pulled a carton of eggs from the fridge and grabbed a few seasonings from the walk-in pantry. I looked down at my slim pickings—not enough protein to make it through my morning gym routine, let alone the rest of the workday. Scrounging through the bottom drawer of the fridge, I managed to find an almost-expired half-pack of bacon. I barely had time for grocery shopping these days, what with how busy I'd been with new custom furniture and wood-working jobs.

The fast pace was worth it. Even twelve years into owning my business, Klein Custom, I still had to fight off the occasional financial worry. Come Monday, I had a big meeting with one of the regional restaurant groups, McGuire, to discuss supplying the furniture for their three local establishments in the Greyport area. Sketches and proposals had my head swimming, but I welcomed the challenge and the extra influx of money.

The Monday meeting was the reason I had asked Harry to cool it with the overnight guests for a bit. He had seemed fine with the idea when I'd first proposed it a few weeks ago, but his impulse control was notoriously subpar. It was no surprise he hadn't been able to follow through.

What was surprising was my cousin's choice of partner for the evening. The woman—Emma—wasn't Harry's usual type. Sure, she was beautiful, with those dark waves of hair tumbling out of her hairband and the smattering of freckles dotted across her pale skin.

But there were plenty of beautiful women out there. This one wasn't anything special.

I wasn't naïve. I knew my cousin picked up women at Maven's, our local bar. But I also knew for a fact Harry hadn't been at Maven's last night, because I'd been there myself, meeting my friend Ben Till for a night of beer and pool. I rarely got a reprieve from work to blow off steam. Ben owned an in-demand local landscape company and was hammering out contracts for the upcoming season. He was one of the few who related to my crazy, self-employed lifestyle.

As I shoveled salty eggs and bacon into my mouth, my mind wandered again to Harry's supposed girlfriend. She had been annoying and downright rude—yelling at me in my own damn house. I bet she didn't much like being around other people. And I would bet even more money other people couldn't tolerate her either.

I'd never seen her before last night. The area didn't get many tourists, and I hadn't heard about any new residents. If she lived in Greyport, I would have met her, unless she was a total recluse.

So why the hell was Harry, Mr. Social Butterfly himself, claiming her as his girlfriend? Was Emma taking advantage of Harry, manipulating him to say they were dating?

Harry needed to get his shit together—and soon—if he ever expected to make it on his own. And if I ever wanted to get some peace and quiet, I had to get to the bottom of things with him and Emma.

And in the meantime, I didn't want her darkening my doorway again. She didn't belong with Harry, and she didn't belong in Greyport.

Once I discovered what the two of them were up to, I could move on to what was really important: securing the deal with McGuire and taking care of my family.

Chapter Four

Emma

I USUALLY AVOIDED CAFFEINE after lunchtime, but halfway through the Monday shift at Greyport Public Library, I was running ragged. I savored the heat of the metal tumbler in my hand even as the coffee was a touch too hot going down. The library shared half of a large, turn-of-the-century building with the Greyport Town Hall. As the community outreach coordinator, I had been manning a table in the building's main lobby most of the morning, advertising some of the new programs I was developing. I was most excited about a new computer crash course for older adults. A few people had expressed interest when reading the calendar, so I hoped it would be a hit.

God knew I needed something to go my way.

My parents—in particular, my mother—didn't understand my need to move across the state to Greyport. I had worked part time at the library in my hometown, doing similar work, but the main outreach worker hadn't been on track to retire, and I needed a full-time gig with benefits. Still, the work had been enjoyable. I didn't owe rent to my parents, and I even got to see friends from time to time.

But then the accident happened. Riding my bike to work one afternoon, an older man driving a large blue sedan had come out of nowhere. It had led to months of surgeries, casts, and crutches, and hard work with physical and occupational therapies.

But that blue car hadn't just broken my body. It had broken my mind too.

After emerging from that dark period, as I was just finding the strength to poke my head out from the weight of the pain, I found the job posting in Greyport. It had seemed like a sign, and I applied on impulse, not telling a soul.

Not even a month after applying, I was all moved in to my small apartment located a stairwell above the local coffee shop, Greyport Grinds. It wasn't much to write home about, but it was something.

I was sure my colossal fuck-up from Friday night would not ingratiate me to the village residents. I sensed James and Harrison were popular in town. Forward progress on my *How to Make Friends* list seemed less and less likely by the minute.

Harrison had seemed to like me just fine—he had gotten some unremarkable yet satisfying sex out of the interaction, after all—but his strange declaration that we were dating had come out of left field. I had wasted no time leaving after he had announced our new couple status. I figured he was probably out of it after being woken up by his insane cousin. So long as I pretended it never happened and allowed enough time to pass, he would forget about it entirely.

Now, I had to hope he never told another person in town about it. Ever.

I took another sip of coffee and wished it were a shot of something stronger to help me overcome my remembered embarrassment. So much for a dismal first time *Saying Yes*. The other tasks on my list looked far less appealing, considering the experience.

With another bracing gulp of caffeine, I resolved to stop blaming myself. A certain flannel-clad grouch had played a large role in the fiasco. James hadn't inherited whatever friendly gene his cousin had. Maybe I hadn't been at my most graceful, but it had been the middle of the night. His big, burly body and growly voice had appeared out of nowhere. I could hardly be faulted for being caught off-guard by an angry lunatic.

If I ran into him ever again—something I planned to avoid at all costs—I promised I would be well-equipped with only the wittiest of one liners and classic verbal zings.

"Hey, Emma, how are things going?"

The voice popped me out of my daydreaming.

My boss, Tracy Watson, stood to the left of my small table. Tracy was a tall, thin, white woman who I clocked to be in her late forties. Her blonde hair was long with a few hints of gray that served as attractive, sparkling highlights. She also had on a pair of kick-ass chunky, heeled boots that I envied. Despite the rigorous PT I'd put myself through, my legs would never again be up for that challenge.

"Hi, Tracy," I said, summoning up my most chipper voice. "It's been going well so far. Got some early interest in the computer class we're kicking off next month."

Tracy grinned. The older woman's passion for her job was evident. She had shared enough of her background for me to covet her stability and success. My boss grew up in Greyport and moved away for a few years to earn her Master of Library Science degree before coming home to what she viewed as her dream job. So far, she had proved to be a good boss, checking in often to make sure I wasn't left high and dry.

Now, if only I could bolster myself to request a different chair, or at least a cushion, to sit on while working. The current one wasn't cutting it with my hip issues, but the thought of rocking the boat filled my throat with acid.

"I'm so pleased to hear that, Emma. Now that you're feeling more settled, I do hope you'll join the staff at one of our happy hours. We go every Monday night to the local bar and grill, Maven's, if you haven't been there yet. The food is your typical bar fare, but the drinks are good, and the company is better."

The invitation sent a flutter bubbling up through my belly. Was I about to conquer the *Befriend Your Coworkers* task on my to-do list? So soon after disaster?

My colleagues often left work together, but inviting myself along was too cringe-inducing to consider. The small group of library employees seemed close-knit. I wanted to be part of that, but it was as foreign as this town. I kept my circle small, even before I moved to Greyport. Large groups were intimidating, even when I wanted to join in.

I passed Maven's, a green-and-tan building, every day on my way to work. Despite the delicious smells that emanated from the grill, I hadn't gone in, not once in three months. Something about walking into a bar alone felt like punching a membership card to the Lonely Losers Club.

But now I had an invitation and a group. Just when I was feeling well and truly alone, like I had messed up here in Greyport, another opportunity fell in my lap.

Hot, grumpy men aside, maybe I was meant to be here after all.

CHAPTER FIVE

Emma

AFTER MY SHIFT OFFICIALLY ended, I stopped by Fair Street Park, around the corner from the library. I didn't have much time before I had to meet Tracy and my other coworkers, but I needed to sit and breathe. Nobody was in the small park. It wasn't the most popular destination in the dead of winter on a Monday night.

My favorite bench, with its rusted screws and shaky legs, was the perfect thinking spot. I tried to stop at least once or twice a week. If the park was empty, the way it was tonight, I could even talk through my problems out loud. I wasn't so far gone as to name the bench, but I was pretty damn close.

Maybe I am a Lonely Losers Club member after all.

I allowed myself five minutes to catastrophize, to think of all the ways the night could go wrong as I zoned out on the bench, surrounded by a curving path, frozen-over duck pond, and crumbling tennis court. And then I let those thoughts go. If I'd had a little more time, and the air was a little warmer, I would have stuck around longer. But tonight, I had plans.

By the time I made it back to my one-bedroom apartment, I was already late. I made a cursory attempt at applying a fancy cat-eye liner to my upper lids—makeup tutorial pulled up on my phone—before abandoning the effort in favor of a simple coat of mascara. Mental note: glam makeup was not for me.

A layer of glossing serum on my dark hair, a pair of black jeans, and a royal-blue top completed the look.

As I headed out the door, a message rolled in from my mom.

Mom: How was work today?

Emma: Good and busy. I'm meeting some coworkers for drinks!

Mom: Be careful. Have fun.

Mom: Oh, before I forget to mention it, Janet told me that Mei is thinking of retiring. You might have a job here again!

I groaned. I loved my mother, but she was relentless.

Emma: Mom, I already have a job.

Mom: No pressure, I just wanted to mention it.

Oh, there was absolutely pressure.

Emma: Okay. Thank you.

I put the phone away before I went insane. There was no sense continuing the conversation when Mom was on a streak like this. Healthy boundaries were a work in progress.

As I pulled into the back lot, I was shocked by how busy Maven's was for a Monday night. Once I clocked the large number of football jerseys, it all made sense. The season was in full swing, and playoff games were fast approaching. I wasn't a big sports fan, but Dad was. Little bits here and there tended to rub off.

It was especially hard to avoid that sort of thing when you lived with your parents from the tender age of birth to twenty-six.

In the past, I might have sat with that line of thought, beaten myself up with it. Emma of the *Say YES to Everything* era was letting it go and walking into a bar. Alone.

Tracy spotted me a few seconds after I walked in and waved me over to a large high-top. The table laid to the right of a large mahogany bar that took up most of the back wall.

"Emma! I'm *so* happy you came tonight. Here," she said as she poured a glass of beer from a large pitcher.

"Oh, uh, thank you." I took the proffered glass as I hopped up onto the last remaining stool. The table was packed tight. I hoped my coworkers didn't mind us knocking knees. I recognized four library staff members and two other men I hadn't seen before.

"Let me take your jacket, Emma. There's a coat room in the back. Otherwise, it's such a pain to hang onto it all night and deal with the crowd at the same time." This from Jill, one of the part-time staff members who assisted with the children's programming a few days a week. Jill was off in a flurry, her petite frame moving toward the back of the bar, the tip of her blonde braid flying up behind her.

I guess they wanted to make sure I didn't run away. In the past, I would have held that jacket like a shield and left as soon as an appropriate number of minutes had elapsed.

Instead, I settled in for the long haul.

Rubbing my now bare arms, I looked around. Despite the crowd, there was a chill in the air as more football watchers piled in, bringing a cool draft with them. The place had a relaxed atmosphere, its wood-paneled walls covered in photos of local youth sports teams and old issues of *Sports Illustrated*.

"Let me introduce you," Tracy said, diverting my attention back to my tablemates. "There are a few of us you haven't met yet."

Tracy first introduced me to her husband, Scott. I liked the way the middle-aged Black man smiled at his wife. The other man was Varun, the boyfriend of Glenn, a friendly library clerk. They both sent me open smiles. I liked them immediately.

Jill returned from the coat room, sliding back onto the stool next to Kristi Margarucci, the assistant librarian. I had seen the two women chatting during shifts. Both were around my age and pinged my potential-friend radar.

"So, is this your first time at Maven's?" Kristi asked.

I turned toward the olive-skinned woman. Her near-black hair was dyed a deep-purple color that shimmered in the low light. A stack of gold bracelets jingled on her left wrist.

"It is. Thank you for letting me crash your night out."

"Oh, don't even worry about that," said Jill. "You've been here, what, a few months now? We should have rolled out the welcome wagon ages ago. I said something to Tracy this morning when we realized no one had told you about our weekly Maven's nights. Not all of us come every week, but we do our best to make it a regular thing."

"Well, I appreciate it either way." I took a sip of beer, swallowing past the uncomfortable lump in my throat. "I haven't met too many people yet, and making friends as an adult is an unfamiliar experience for me."

"Tell me about it!" Kristi said. "I've lived here going on seven years, and let me tell you, small towns like this are great once you find your group, but *damn* are they insular. This one," she said, gesturing toward Jill, "grew up here and can't relate."

Jill rolled her eyes good-naturedly. "I promise I'm not that bad, Emma. I went away to college, where I was the new girl once too."

"Did you always plan to come back?"

Jill sighed with no real hint of annoyance. Had I struck a nerve?

"To be honest, I had no plan, and if you ask my brother, he would tell you I *still* have no plan. Meddling, over-achieving siblings, am I right?"

"Sounds rough," I said with an awkward grin.

"Only child?" Kristi guessed—accurately.

"How'd you know?"

The other two women laughed.

"Kristi here is *intuitive.* Or that's what she would tell you. I just say she's psychic."

"*Or* I can just read a basic facial expression." Kristi gave Jill a friendly bump with a gauzy-sleeved elbow. "But now I'm super tired of being subtle. Tell us your life story, Emma. You've been the mysterious new girl for long enough, and we want the details."

I downed the last of my now room temperature beer. I wasn't one to divulge so many details so soon, but Jill and Kristi seemed open and nonjudgmental. If I didn't *Befriend Coworkers* right now, when would I get another chance?

"Uh, sorry," I said when I realized they were waiting for me to respond. "There isn't much to tell, to be quite honest. I'm from a little farther downstate, but I always liked the vibe of this area from road trips and pictures. I was doing similar work at the local library in my hometown. Just part-time. Then some shit went down with my health, and I needed a change of pace. Plus, I wanted something full-time so I could get off my parents' health insurance. I saw the posting for the job opening the same night I decided I was going to look for something new."

Small crinkles appeared at the edges of Kristi's dark eyes. "Fate," the purple-haired woman stated. Like a fact.

"Cheers to that," Jill said with a grin.

The three of us clinked our now empty glasses together. The beer pitcher in the center of the high-top was also empty.

"I can get the next round," I said, slipping down from my stool. The last thing I wanted was to come across like a mooch while fighting to make a good first impression.

"Here, let me come with you. We can grab two pitchers and split the bill," Kristi said.

The bar was busy as we approached. I was glad the other woman had offered to join. Waiting alone in a long line would have been boring. And having someone to chat with would keep me from browsing social media in public and looking like an antisocial weirdo.

"There's an opening down here at the end," Kristi said, dashing off to the right side of the bar.

I moved to follow but soon collided—with no small amount of force—against a flannel-clad chest and a flattened takeout container.

"Oh my God, I'm so sorry," I said as the white plastic box fell to the floor, landing upside down with what appeared to be a burger and fries spilling out the sides.

"Fucking hell. Again?"

Of course, *of course,* it was Harrison's cousin, *James,* or whatever he was called. Some boring, white-bread name. Not that I had much room to talk as far as boring names were concerned. I managed three whole months in Greyport without a hint of this asshole, and now here I was, forced to interact with him twice in that number of days.

"It was an accident," I said.

So much for my commitment to clever comebacks.

"Sure it was." He rolled his eyes, like a fucking middle school girl.

"I didn't see you." Why was I even bothering to defend myself with this guy? He was determined to see me a certain way.

"Not sure how—I'm the tallest person in this room." He crossed his arms over his wide chest.

His stupidly attractive chest and stupidly attractive forearms. It wasn't fair that his outsides weren't as ugly as his insides.

"Hey, James!" I heard Kristi greet him—because of course they knew each other. Which meant Kristi, and eventually Jill too, would soon learn of my lousy attempt at a one-night stand.

"Oh, shit. That blows, dude," Kristi said as she noticed the burger and fries on the floor.

"It's fine."

"Did you meet Emma? She works with me and Jill at the library as the new community outreach coordinator."

If it were possible, James looked even angrier at Kristi's pronouncement. Had the man been personally victimized by library employees?

"We've met." He scooped up his crushed meal and stalked off into the thick of the crowd.

"Okay, then."

I twisted my hands in the strap of my purse as Kristi guided us toward the bar. "I feel so bad. His dinner is ruined," I said.

"Honestly, I don't know what the hell his deal is tonight. He's usually pretty laidback. Maybe he's just hangry," Kristi said with a shrug.

"H—how do you know each other?"

Please don't be dating. Please don't be dating. Their interaction hadn't struck me as particularly romantic, and they made a rather odd couple, what with Kristi's cool, witchy aesthetic and James' burly mountain-man look. But anything was possible. I doubted I would remain a fit candidate for friendship with Kristi if the woman's boyfriend hated me.

The pit of my stomach roiled at the thought of James being in a relationship.

Not because of him. Only because I so pitied whomever his partner might be.

Kristi gave a dismissive wave of her hand. "Oh, he's Jill's older brother. He comes around every so often, but he drives Jill a little crazy. He means well, but she likes to do her own thing most of the time."

I was simultaneously relieved—for Kristi not having to put up with James—and worried about what the man might tell his sister. Because if they were siblings, then that meant Harrison was her cousin too. And this checking-off-my-list project was getting more and more complicated by the minute.

Small-town living was getting incestuous—and fast.

"Anyway," Kristi said, "sorry he was such a jerk to you. Jill mentioned he's been crazy-busy at work, but that's no excuse."

I mustered up a smile. The last thing I wanted was for Kristi to think there was more to James' dislike of me than splattered dinner. "It's fine. He had every right to be upset. I'll buy him a replacement meal as an apology." I didn't like the guy, but it was the right thing to do.

Kristi shrugged. "Can't hurt. I think he's over there talking to Jill, so you can give him the food when we sit back down."

Sure enough, he was seated in *my* chair, chatting it up with all *my* coworkers. It appeared he could at least be pleasant *sometimes.*

I knew I hadn't made the greatest first—or second—impression, but he wasn't blameless. First, he had startled me in the middle of the night. And now, we'd both done the colliding. Although he may have been right about being noticeable, the new place and crowd made it hard for me to focus. I hadn't knocked into him on purpose.

Kristi finally managed to find space at the crowded bar. She called over one of the two bartenders—a woman with long white hair, wearing an oversized blue, white, and red football jersey.

Kristi made brief introductions before we placed an order for two fresh pitchers.

"Anything else I can get for either of ya?" the bartender, who Kristi called Eleanor, asked.

"A burger and fries to-go, please."

I waited for the order while Kristi took the two pitchers back to the high-top. There was no need to fight through the crowd again.

It had nothing to do with delaying my next interaction with Mr. Grumpy.

"Emma!"

I didn't turn at first, figuring it was someone calling for another Emma, until I felt a tap on my shoulder.

It was Harrison, dressed in a fitted black t-shirt and dark-wash jeans. Casual attire, but he made it look elevated.

Unlike his cousin, who made no effort whatsoever in a worn flannel, faded jeans, and dirty work boots.

"Uh, hi, Harrison. It's good to see you again."

Before I knew it, he pulled me into a hug. Like the sex a few nights before, it wasn't a bad hug, but that was about it. I mentally prepped myself to issue a kind, but firm, rejection. He was nice enough, but there just wasn't anything there.

"Food is ready," Eleanor said, a flick of her wrist sending a white takeout container sailing my way.

Harrison flung his arm across my shoulders as I dug through my purse for my wallet.

"Looks like you've met my girlfriend, huh, Ellie?" He nudged my wallet away and presented his own card for payment.

I couldn't control my full-body jerk. Was he on this again? Was he delusional?

Eleanor didn't seem to care one way or the other and returned to work once the food was paid for. Maybe she didn't care, but I did. Given that Harry had now brought up the girlfriend thing yet again, I couldn't just ignore it, especially if I worked with his cousin.

Besides, I didn't need a boyfriend right now. I could hardly keep my head above water with only myself to worry about.

"Could I talk to you, Harrison? Somewhere a little quieter maybe?"

He smiled. "I thought you would never ask."

He led us to a hallway near the back restrooms, and we stopped in a small alcove near an old payphone—practically a relic. Harrison's chest rose and fell as he took a deep breath.

"Okay, I'm sure you have a bunch of questions, and I should have reached out to you after Friday and not waited until I saw you in person again, but I need your help."

I waited for him to slow down. Maybe I had entered some weird small-town twilight zone because what could Harrison need *my* help with? Or maybe he *was* a serial killer after all, but one who couldn't bring himself to kill on the first date, so instead, he lured women into fictitious relationships before going in for the kill.

"Continue," I said, unable to disguise my skepticism.

"I'm fucking this up," he said, running a hand through his thick head of hair. "Alright, I know I sound insane right now."

"I won't argue with that."

That earned me a small laugh. *Good, Emma*, I thought. *Humanize yourself to the killer. If he thinks you're funny, he might allow you to live.*

"I do actually know we're not dating, okay? Just wanted to put that out there."

"So, can you tell me why you've now told two different people I'm your girlfriend? I don't do the casual-sex thing often, but I was under the impression you were pretty experienced with it and wouldn't jump to the assumption we were in a relationship. And not to be rude, but I'm not interested in sleeping with you again."

I gave myself an internal pat on the back for my assertiveness.

"No, no, no. I do know that. And trust me, I'm not interested in another hookup either. See, the thing is, I am really, really tired of my cousins thinking I need them to baby me all the time. I figured if I had a serious girlfriend, then they would leave me alone for a bit. But I now realize I roped you in to my issue and should have asked first."

"You think?"

His puppy-dog look was seriously unattractive. He was getting further away from hot-yet-unhinged murderer and closer to presumptuous himbo.

"I am sorry."

The apology was a good start. With a raised eyebrow, I waited to see if he could find a way out of this dilemma. Whatever he had to say, it wouldn't be boring.

"I'd like to propose an idea. I recognize I don't deserve any favors from you, but I am hoping you would agree to be my fake girlfriend."

I scoffed. "Do people even do that outside of books?"

His head tilted to the side as he considered. His likeness to a dog was really becoming strange.

"I'm not sure. I don't read books."

Good thing this man didn't want to be my actual boyfriend, because that was a turn-off.

"What would be in it for me?" I asked.

"The pleasure of my divine company?"

Now I knew why we hadn't talked much the other night. With a comment like that, all he needed was a fedora and a single-stem rose. "Absolutely not."

I turned to walk back to my table when he tugged me back in his direction.

"Okay, let me start over. You're new here, right?"

Now he had my full attention.

"I'm a pretty social guy, if you couldn't already tell. How about I introduce you around town, help you fit in and meet some more people? Then we can amicably break up, say...after Christmas?"

That...could work. The timeframe would be long enough for me to get to know more people but short enough that it would be plausible for us to have a civil breakup and move on.

If I agreed to this fake-dating scheme, I could feasibly check off most of my list too.

"Alright, I'll do it. But you agree to my terms."

"As long as we appear to be a couple and you spend some time with me where my cousins can see how responsible and mature I am, I'll agree to anything. Just don't go falling in love with me, okay?"

I hoped my gag wasn't visible. How had I slept with this man and had an orgasm to boot?

"I think I'll be good," I said. "We will go on no more than three dates a week, in front of your cousins and around town. One of those dates will include other people in a social setting where you will introduce and include me. Light PDA but nothing over-the-top sexual. Think hugs and pecks on the cheek versus make-out sessions. Got it?"

He practically panted. "Don't be mad, but that was hot as fuck."

"Oh my God, no. You can hold my hand while we walk to the table. That's it."

CHAPTER SIX

James

I DID MY BEST to ignore the growling in my stomach as I watched my cousin wrap his hand around Emma's from across the room.

"You good, man?" Scott Watson asked. I'd known him for a few years as Klein Custom had sponsored the youth softball team that Scott and Tracy's daughter played on.

Scott also had some local business connections and knew I was hammering out a deal with McGuire.

"Uh, yeah, just need to get home to get something to eat."

"Alright, well it sounded like you were the one doing the growling, not your stomach there."

I tried to conjure up a laugh that didn't make it out of my chest as I watched Harry and Emma—the reason for my current hungry state—cozy up on the other side of the bar.

"How'd your meeting with McGuire pan out?"

The inevitable question. I didn't have an answer. The buyer and interior designer, both of whom had seemed so enthused about working with local craftsmen and artists, had been hard to read, almost cold today. It was like my sketches and ideas weren't hitting the mark.

I was off my game.

I gave a shrug to Scott. We weren't close enough for me to divulge all the nitty-gritty details.

"Not sure, to be honest. They want an updated proposal and new sketches in a few weeks. I'll be busy."

The pressing need to get back in the workshop was the reason I hadn't wanted to cook tonight. The burgers at Maven's were nothing spectacular, but it beat going home to an empty fridge.

Dragging my gaze along the wall of flat-screens, I landed back on Emma and Harry. They were at last leaving their snug little alcove—and still holding hands.

Emma didn't look at all like a woman in love should. Shouldn't she be smiling, or blushing and giggling, or something? Instead, her shoulders were up near her ears. If I had to guess, the circulation in Harry's hand was nearly gone.

It wasn't just nerves, which would have been understandable when meeting a partner's friends for the first time. For one, she hadn't seemed at all nervous when she'd slammed into me over near the bar and demolished my dinner plans.

I was about to get up and leave when the happy couple pulled up to the table.

"Hey, Jay." Harry released Emma's hand long enough to give me a friendly slap on the back.

I took a brief glance at my sister, trying to gauge her reaction.

Jill was *smiling*. Was she buying this bullshit Harry and Emma were pulling?

Or perhaps Emma had dragged Jill into this somehow. They worked together now. I couldn't wait to grill Harry on what the fuck he was doing, but he hadn't been around much these days. We were both busy with work, but I was willing to bet he was avoiding me.

And I suspected the reason for that avoidance had something to do with a short brunette.

"Harry," I said with a sharp nod.

"What is your problem?" Jill hissed from the chair beside me as the happy couple moved on to the rest of the gang huddled around the table.

"I don't have a problem."

"He definitely has a problem," Jill's friend Kristi Margarucci chimed in.

Jill claimed her best friend was psychic, but if you asked me, that was a bunch of nonsense.

Case in point, right now. Because I was decidedly problem free.

"Really, though," Kristi said. God, it was almost like I had two younger sisters sometimes. "He's butthurt because Emma bumped into him, and his food fell on the floor. I won't even mention the totally weird vibes either."

I took a deep inhale before shoving my breath out through my nose. *Modulate your tone, James.* The therapist I saw a few years ago after my mom's death had given me some deep-breathing exercises I still used when needed.

I needed them now as Harry laughed it up with his arm slung around his supposed girlfriend. My cousin appeared...happy.

It hit me then that if this was real, Harry might get hurt. Because the woman by his side was not smitten.

I watched as Emma smiled at something Tracy said, and my palms grew slick with sweat. She wasn't just interfering with Jill and Harry. Now it was the whole town.

When Emma laughed, I admitted I could see why Harry might be interested. Her hair fell in a shiny wave down her back, and I had the inexplicable urge to run my fingers through it.

If I happened to imagine tracing that wave of hair down to the curve of her waist and to her ass in those dark jeans...

Nope. Not going there.

Thinking about my cousin's supposed girlfriend like this was the last thing I needed when I should be focused on work and getting Harry in a good place.

Jill darted me a questioning look when I pushed back from the table.

"Busy night for me," I said with a grunt.

She rolled her eyes. "Whatever."

God, I kept fucking up these days with my sister. Every little thing I said pissed her off.

Just like I was fucking up with Harry and the McGuire deal too.

I tucked my hands in the thick pockets of my Carhart jacket and made one last attempt at civility toward Jill. "Do you work tomorrow?"

"Am I ever not working?"

I bit down on my tongue. "I meant, are you working from home tomorrow?"

"Why isn't that what you asked in the first place, then?"

Jesus Christ.

"If you insist on checking up on me, brother dear, you are welcome to stop by."

With cursory nods at the rest of the group, I walked out of Maven's, my feet heavy in my boots from the weight of the day.

CHAPTER SEVEN

James

M Y EYES GLAZED OVER as I focused on the pattern forming under the scraper. The table leg rotated hypnotically on the lathe. The vibration and scent of fresh wood chips soothed my frayed nerves as I worked. It was second nature at this point. Having the workshop in the back barn behind my house meant I never had to go far to work.

Tonight, I was being stupid. I wasn't working on something for McGuire or any other orders, just some random table leg in an unorthodox shape that wouldn't fit in any traditional style. But I needed something beyond breathing exercises to turn my mind off. This had been acceptable enough.

I glanced over the rim of my safety glasses to the small digital clock on the opposite wall.

Almost midnight. The game should be close to finishing now.

The muscles in my back ached as I straightened up to full height. I pressed pause on the lathe cycle and slipped my phone out of my pocket as an alert from the NFL app displayed the final score. Maybe I could catch Harry getting home so I could finally talk with him.

Unless he planned to spend the night with his new girlfriend.

I hunkered back down to turn my pointless table leg and listened for the sound of Harry's car pulling in.

I didn't have to wait long, and shockingly, Harry came to me, rushing in on a burst of excitement like a goddamn golden retriever.

He drew to a stop in front of me, just out of range of the wood dust flying off the lathe.

I made him wait as I finished one last turn before powering the machine down. The man could wait another minute, considering he'd been the one ignoring me the last few days.

"That's cool," he said, tilting his head toward the table leg.

I shrugged. "Won't sell, but thanks."

"Sooo..." He was practically shaking with energy. "What did you think?"

"What did I think about what, Harry?"

"Oh, come on, Jay! About Emma. My girlfriend."

"Do you want my honest opinion?"

"I asked, didn't I?"

I removed my safety glasses and looked him straight in the eye. "I don't like her."

Harry scoffed. "You've met her, what, two times? How would you know if you like her or not?"

"Yeah, and how well do you know her, Harry? I don't have to like a person just because you're fucking them."

I gave him my back and started tidying up my worktable.

"You know, Jay, for a thirty-five-year-old man, you're a fucking baby sometimes."

So that was how it was going to be. Did Harry want to get his own house, then? Start paying rent?

I bit my tongue around the angry words. The moving-out conversation was long overdue, but we needed cooler heads for that.

"Was there something else you needed?" I glanced over my shoulder at my cousin. Somehow, I had gone from wanting to give Harry the third degree about Emma to wanting him to leave me alone so I could go inside and go to bed.

"I don't *need* anything from you, James. I wanted you to be happy that I'm happy."

"Well, I can't help it if I don't get a good feeling about this girl. There's something about her I don't trust."

"That's because you don't trust anyone you haven't known practically your whole life. You're so overprotective it drives me nuts. I want to live my life, and this pseudo-dad act of yours isn't helping. It gets fucking old, man."

I gritted my teeth. Deep-breathing exercises weren't taking the edge off anything right now. I didn't need this shit tonight. Or ever.

"I've got to get to bed. Try not to bring your little girlfriend around when I'm here. I don't want to deal with her." *Or you.*

"You might want to take this," Harry said as I shouldered past him. He shoved a white plastic container with a Maven's logo embossed on top toward my chest.

What the hell was this?

Harry smirked at my look of confusion. "My *little girlfriend,* the one you hate so much, replaced your meal out of the kindness of her own heart. And she *will* be around, so you'd better get used to it."

I've had enough, I thought as I stormed into the house, leaving Harry to follow at his own pace.

For about a second, I considered warming the food in the microwave, but I tossed it toward the back of the fridge instead.

Yeah, I was hungry, but I didn't have the mental fortitude to deal with the implications of that burger and fries tonight.

CHAPTER EIGHT

James

I TUGGED MY HAT farther over my ears the next morning, guarding against the chill in the air. A shit-ton of snow had dumped overnight. I tramped up the slick stairs leading up to Jill's upper-level studio apartment, clearing a path with my boots. Her landlord never iced or shoveled the steps. It looked like the bucket of rock salt I had bought for Jill last week was still unopened next to her door. I'd have to remind her to use it again. Someone was going to fall and get hurt. I didn't want that on my conscience.

I didn't bother knocking, using my spare key to get inside. Jill's voice came from the other side of her door, on a call for one of her many jobs. She had told me I could come by, so it wasn't like I was surprising her.

The dirty look she sent me when I entered her line of sight might have killed a lesser man.

I was used to it—especially lately.

Jill, on her headset, was bobbing her head up and down in response to the person on the other line.

I posted up against the move-able kitchen island on wheels that I had built for Jill's small space. The wood grain was smooth under my fingertips as I ran my hand across the surface.

The island was one of my earlier creations, crafted just for Jill when she moved into this place. It was still one of my favorites.

"So, my recommendation, ma'am, would be one of our customizable creature products. We have a variety of creatures to meet your desires, whether it be alien-, dragon-, or tentacle-shaped. Plus, if you spend over seventy-five dollars, you get a free, full-size bottle of our newest flavored lube."

What. The fuck.

I took the four steps needed to get to Jill and silenced her next words with my hand. I did not want to listen to this.

Jill turned her head and swatted me away. "Ma'am, my connection seems to be suffering. Let me transfer you over to one of our other sales reps real quick." Jill swiftly pressed a few buttons on her laptop and ripped her headset off.

"I get paid on commission, dude! If you fucked me over on that one, I will murder you."

"What the hell kind of job are you working now?" I said, pacing in front of Jill's narrow coffee table. Another one of my projects.

Back when I used to have time to create things just for fun.

"I don't see how that is any of your business, Jimbo." She crossed her arms from her perch on her daybed.

"Are you selling…" I said, choking on the words, "*alien sex toys*?"

Jill shot me a smarmy grin. "I sell a large variety of different creatures in addition to aliens. In fact, I will happily show you our online collect—"

"Stop. I do not want to hear this from my sister."

"Well, then you should have knocked first."

I didn't bother bringing up the fact that she gave me permission to swing by when we had talked last night. I would not win this battle.

And if anything, having to hear my sister talk about monster dicks only proved her right.

"So, this is a new job?"

She nodded.

"And, uh...what inspired you to work there?"

"Is this your roundabout way of asking me if I have a personal interest in what I'm selling?"

I mimed a gag.

My sister laughed—a sound I didn't get from her often these days.

"Alright, I'll stop fucking with you. And because I know you were *really* asking whether or not I need money, the answer is no. I'm doing fine. I took the job because it sounded fun, and I get to work from home. Truthfully, I'm enjoying it a lot more than I expected."

"I'm glad...I guess?"

Jill hopped up from her spot on the daybed, giving me a sarcastic pat on the cheek as she made her way over to the fridge. "You'll get over it, Jimbo."

I followed my sister the two steps into the kitchen as she poured a glass of ice water for herself. She raised her brows at me in silent question, and I nodded back.

She pulled down a World's Best Uncle mug—one she'd likely thrifted—from her cupboard and handed it over after filling it to the brim with coffee.

"Even though you have problematic timing, I did want to talk about something career-adjacent with you."

This wasn't where I had expected this morning to go. Whenever I tried to bring up the job topic, Jill usually got her back up. Maybe she was finally coming around to the idea of some stability. This chaotic version of adulthood my sister had going would only lead to disaster, and I had told her that time and again.

"Go on," I said as I stirred a spoonful of sugar into my coffee.

Jill settled her back against the counter. "Okay, so since I've been working selling the...creature appendages...I got to thinking that Greyport could use a place where adults can come and buy things like that."

I tempered my initial reaction. I really, really, did not want to talk about this with my sister. But Jill seemed happy. And she was talking to me for a change.

Plus, I could only handle one of Jill or Harry being mad at me at once. Not both.

"You want to sell monster dicks in Greyport?"

She threw her hands up. "Ugh, I knew you would be weird about this!"

I guess I hadn't controlled my facial expression as well as I thought.

"I'm trying to understand."

She waved her hand dismissively. "It wouldn't solely be creature-related products but more general sex toys. Or even lingerie. Or I could offer classes on safe BDSM practice. Maybe even a bar area. Things like that. It would have to be something more than just toys in order to compete with online stores."

She had put some thought into this. "I'm not saying it's a bad idea. Talking with my sister about opening a sex toy store is not something I want to be doing in my spare time. Which is non-existent, by the way. My spare time, that is."

Jill's face fell. "What if we kept the details vague. Because I get it, and you're right. There is a definite *ick* factor there. But the entrepreneurial side of things is confusing for me, and that's what you're good at."

Jill's confidence in me was something I couldn't find in myself lately.

"As much as I want to help, I'm swamped at work. If you can give me a couple weeks, we will figure something out. But there is someone else who may be willing to help."

"Who?"

"Would you be open to talking with Ben about it?"

I would get past the whole sex topic if Jill needed me, but I worried her interest might be fleeting if I wasn't available right away.

However, my friend ran a successful business himself. He and Jill were familiar with one another, and Ben was in the midst of his slow season. It could be the ideal arrangement.

"He would really want to help me?" Jill said brightly.

"He will if I ask. I'll give you his number before I go."

Jill gave a delighted squeal and leaped into my arms. It had been a long time since she'd interacted with me this way.

I patted her back with a stiff hand. Physical affection always felt strange. I was so much bigger than most people, and I worried I might break someone someday.

She pulled away and hopped back over to her daybed, where she sat cross-legged atop her flowered duvet.

She patted the space beside her. I rolled my eyes but sat down in the indicated spot anyway.

"We can talk about what you're really here to talk about now."

I flopped back on the bed, unable to stop the grumbling sigh from creeping up out of my chest.

"Oof." A breath shot out of me when I got nailed in the stomach with a beaded throw pillow.

"What the fuck, Jill?"

"You need to grow up. You're acting like a child right now about Harry and Emma."

"*I* need to grow up? You just hit me with a pillow!"

"Get over yourself, Jimbo."

"Did you have any idea Harry was dating someone? Before last night, I mean. You didn't look shocked." I wondered if Emma had mentioned something to Jill at work.

"Nope. Harry doesn't talk to me about that sort of thing. And Emma is new around here. We only just started talking. I wouldn't expect her to disclose things to a coworker she doesn't know that well. It seems pretty early days for them anyway."

"I find it a little strange how Harry goes from random hookups to a serious girlfriend in the blink of an eye. There is something I don't trust."

Jill mimed a choking motion with her hands. "Jimbo, what the hell is your issue here? Get over it, and let them live their lives. You can't control everyone."

"I can't help it if I don't like her. She's not right for Harry." I crossed my arms protectively over my front, bracing for another hit from the beaded nightmare pillow.

It never came.

"What don't you like about her?"

I struggled to find an answer before settling on, "It's more a general vibe."

"You're going to need to be more specific than that. Harry likes Emma, and it would be a dick move if you ruined that because of a non-existent *vibe.*" Jill threw air-quotes on the last word.

"Look, I don't want to go airing out dirty laundry, but the first time I met Emma, she was sneaking out of Harry's room at three in the morning. She didn't even know someone else lived in the house. And then she had the audacity to be mad when I asked who she was—in my own home."

"Who cares if that's how things started? It's a brand-new relationship! You need to give them space to figure their shit out. Even if you disagree with it."

God, I hated when my little sister was right. "Do you actually think Harry is into Emma? She isn't his type."

Jill shrugged. "You would know better than me, living with Harry and all. What do you mean?"

"Harry is always bringing home loud, outgoing women. Emma seems more...understated." When she wasn't yelling at me, that was.

"First, Harry's type is attractive women in his general age group. Emma seems to fit that bill pretty well, wouldn't you say?"

"She's...pretty. I guess."

"Don't sound so enthusiastic. It's like you're looking for problems. And you're a dumbass if you can't see that Emma is beautiful. Her table today in the lobby was pretty popular, and you can't tell me it was only because people wanted to learn about computer classes."

Jill stood up and walked our empty mugs over to the sink. "Anyway, what I'm hearing you say is that Emma is different from other people Harry has hooked up with. But there's a reason Harry hasn't gotten serious with anyone before. Different might be a good thing."

"When did you get so smart?"

Jill snickered. "I have a really great older brother who taught me well."

"I already agreed to give you Ben's number. No need to suck up."

"Oh, I'm definitely sucking up to you, but it's not about the business proposal thing at all."

Blood rushed to my head as I sat up. "What is it now?" She couldn't expect me to survive too many shocks to the heart.

"We're going ice skating on Thursday night. With Emma and Harry. Better find those old skates!"

CHAPTER NINE

Emma

H ARRISON'S KNOCK SOUNDED AT my door as I smoothed my hands down my fleece-lined leggings.

He gave me a soft smile when I opened the door. "Hey."

This wasn't even a proper date, but I still had jitters. "Let me just grab my coat, and we can go." I grabbed my light jacket off the hook before we stepped out into the night.

There were two ice rinks in Greyport: one at the local community college and another at Greyport State, across town on a hill overlooking the canal and Main Street. The locals tended to stick to the one at the community college, leaving the student-set to skate at G-State.

I hadn't been ice skating since I was a child, so this was the opposite of my ideal date, no matter what rink we went to. But Harrison had been insistent. Skating at the rink was apparently a town staple and would be the perfect opportunity for me to get out and meet more members of the town.

By the time Harrison parked and we were making our way across the icy parking lot, I was a mess of nerves. A gust of wind cut through the thin wool of my fawn-colored coat. Not for the first time, I made a mental note that I needed to overhaul my winter wardrobe. I was living in the heart of the snowbelt now.

"You good?" My date glanced over as I shivered.

We reached the lobby and hopped in line at a kiosk for Harrison to purchase tickets.

"Yes, only a bit chilly." He was already looking away, scanning the crowd for arrivals.

I knew he was waiting for Jill and James. He'd dropped the bomb that both of his cousins were joining our date on the ride to the ice rink. I had been tied up in knots ever since.

Would my hip act up? Would I fall on the ice like an idiot in front of everyone? With my luck, I would take James out at the knees, giving him more ammo to use against me. I wished I had insisted that my first public date with Harrison be something less physically taxing.

Harrison snapped his fingers and turned back, as if he suddenly remembered I was standing right next to him. "Oh shit, I forgot to mention this to you in the car, but I'm the tow guy on call at the garage tonight. I doubt any calls will come in, but if they do, I may have to cut out early. Please don't be mad?" His sad-puppy eyes came out to play again.

If this were a real dating situation, I would voice how his lack of communication left me disregarded. But it wasn't real, and all I could do now was hope he wouldn't abandon me in the middle of an ice-skating rink with his cranky cousin and seventy plus strangers.

I pulled my white beanie snugly over the crown of my head. "Hopefully you won't get called out, then. And I should warn you, I have an old injury that might—"

"Over here!" Harrison's voice was loud as he shouted over the noise of the packed lobby—and my words—to his cousins, who were walking through the double doors.

I saw James first. He stood a head above most of the other patrons, carrying a large black hockey bag slung over one shoulder.

Well, fuck. If he had a hockey bag, he probably *played* hockey and knew how to skate. I was going to look like even more of a bumbling fool. I would just have to stick close to Harrison or blend in with the rest of the skaters.

A young kid ran past with a walker-like contraption, and I silently weighed the pros and cons of finding one for myself.

I continued my covert perusal of Mr. Grumpy as he and Jill drew closer. Same scuffed work boots but with a different, newer-looking pair of jeans. They fit tightly around his thick thighs and...

Nope. I was not going there.

I forced my focus back up. Like me, he had on a thick beanie hat that covered most of his hair, a few dark curls visible just above his ears. He had opted against a flannel shirt—what I was coming to think of as his uniform—for a black hooded sweatshirt. It pissed me off that he'd probably taken less than five minutes to throw his outfit together yet somehow looked like the epitome of a sexy mountain man.

I pivoted to greet Jill as she and her brother came up alongside me and Harrison. Jill bounced in her shoes, cute as a button with twin blonde braids.

"I'm so excited. I barely got to skate at all last winter, and I'm itching to go." She had been talking about the open skate night for the last few days at work.

"Harry."

"Yeah?" Harrison looked over at James, who had just said his name.

"I got the tickets already. Ordered ahead online to avoid the line. Let's go."

A muffled snicker came from Jill's direction at the look on Harrison's face.

I was beginning to see why Harrison was chafing at James' attitude. It reminded me a little too much of how my own parents acted with me since my accident.

As the four of us laced up our skates, I resolved to be the most convincing fake girlfriend Harrison could ask for.

If the added benefit was in making James angry, then it would be well worth it.

CHAPTER TEN

Emma

NOT EVEN TWENTY MINUTES into skating, I decided that Harrison—or Harry, as he'd given me permission to call him—could go fuck himself and his stupid fake-girlfriend plan right in the ass.

My rental skates were a half size too small, and I knew there would be uncomfortable blisters on my pinkie toes for the next week.

But the blisters would pale in comparison to how achy I would surely be in the morning. My joints already screamed from overexertion. The muscles required for ice skating weren't ones I routinely used, even when I diligently practiced the home exercise plan my PT had given me.

And the falling. My God, the falling. I hadn't factored in how much landing on my bad hip would hurt. Harry had allowed me to lean on him at first, but now he was having a skating race around the rink with a group of teens from the high school hockey team.

Even sweet Jill had grown tired of going at my glacial pace and had disappeared somewhere along the way.

I trailed my gloved hand along the boards surrounding the rink as I struggled to get to the short door leading off the ice. Jill had mentioned a hot chocolate stand, and I figured now was as good a time as any to find it.

Any excuse to sit down for a few minutes.

I held back a snarl when three kids whipped past, tripping me up. Pain made me irritable. On any given day, I enjoyed kids—I did work in a library, after all—but tonight I felt akin to an old man ordering everyone off his lawn.

"You doing okay?"

"Excuse me?" I said, lashing out in building irritation. My target was, fittingly, James, who had slid up without me noticing. Where had he come from, and why was he acting like he cared? He had skated off pretty much the instant his skates hit the ice, and I hadn't seen much of him since.

Which was good. Great, really. He could go be annoyingly attractive as he skated forward, and backward, and sideways, somewhere far away from me where I didn't need to see him.

His eyes widened, and his nostrils flared. "I asked if you're okay. You're limping."

"Is it considered limping if I'm technically gliding?"

He huffed out a laugh.

I tempered my corresponding smile. He wasn't supposed to find me funny. And I wasn't supposed to like his laugh. Liking the current bane of my existence was not acceptable.

"I am serious, though. Do you need help? I don't know where Harry fucked off to, but I can go find him for you." He gestured with a thumb in the general direction the other man had gone.

"I just want to find somewhere to sit down. I'll be fine." I gritted my teeth and continued my labored shuffle.

"If you're hurt and favoring a leg, you are not fine. At least let me help you off the ice." He reached for the sleeve of my wool coat.

Without thinking, I jerked my arm away.

And proceeded to fall right on my ass.

"Shit!" I hissed in pain. My bitch of a hip was going to hate me in the morning.

I wiggled my right leg, hoping to intercept the inevitable muscle spasms. A hot bath and a muscle relaxer were in my near future.

"Relax, I've got you." One of James' large hands circled my thigh, heat spreading through the thin fabric of my leggings. As he focused on my leg, I found myself irresistibly drawn to his face, like a moth to flame.

This was the first time I had seen him in full light up close. Not in a dim bar or a moonlit hallway at three in the morning. His dark lashes were unfairly long. The perfect frame for hazel eyes that looked almost green in the fluorescent brightness of the ice rink.

While James' movements were clinical, I was far from detached. His long fingers gave a firm squeeze to my upper leg, pulsing rhythmically as my muscles loosened up, little by little.

I felt an answering, shameful pulse in my pussy, and the fabric of my thong underwear grew slick. I let out an involuntary sigh, and James' eyes shot up to mine, his pupils large.

Oh no. This was not okay. There were actual children mere feet away.

I scooted back on my butt, putting distance between us. Shoving up from the ice, I hugged the sideboard in an effort to steady my shaky legs. I wasn't sure if the wobbling was from exhaustion or the proximity to my fake boyfriend's cousin.

I slowed my breathing and forced myself to make eye contact with James.

He was looking at me like I was an alien from some other planet. *Fucking great.* I was going to have to play it cool, pretend an impersonal muscle rub hadn't completely turned me on.

I didn't even have the excuse that it had been a long time since my last round of sex. Not when I had slept with this man's cousin less than a week ago.

James cleared his throat. "Is it okay if I take your arm? Sorry, I should have asked you that before grabbing you."

God, why couldn't he go back to being a jerk? He was seriously not helping with my unhealthy attraction to him by suddenly being so *nice*.

The last thing I needed was for it to be obvious to everyone that I was more attracted to James than the man I was supposed to be in a relationship with.

I nodded my assent and clasped my hand around his forearm in a strange pantomime of a bridal escort.

I bit my lip as we glided forward, my hip twinging in protest.

"You should get that checked out tomorrow. If it's bothering you that much, you may have hurt yourself." The words were gruff, like he didn't want to say them at all.

Because he still didn't like me. He was only being polite, probably because he felt obligated now that I was more than just a hookup to Harry.

I swallowed. "It's an old injury. Trust me, I know what a break feels like. I'll take it easy when I get home."

James' brow furrowed at my words. "Why did—"

There was a rush of air and ice shavings as Harry executed a hockey stop right next to us.

"Jay and Ems!" I really needed to have to talk with him about that terrible nickname. "So, I've got some bad news." He skated backward as James and I went forward. "I got a call for a tow outside of town, so I've got to run. You'll give Ems a ride back to her place, right, Jay?"

Harry spun around, racing toward the exit before I could even respond.

Chapter Eleven

Emma

I RUSHED TO ANSWER the video call request, stubbing my toe on the end table between my cramped kitchen and couch. A stack of vinyl records on the table nearly tumbled, but I managed to save them in time. Taking a breath, I schooled my facial expression, hoping to project calm, unfrazzled serenity.

I was surprised my parents had taken this long to call. I'd been dodging their messages and calls—in particular, my mother's—for days. Linda and Mike Hartwell's patience only lasted so long. I'd hoped they'd adapt the longer I was gone, but it seemed the opposite happened. My dad was a bit more understanding, but neither he nor my mother truly understood why I had decided to move.

"Hey," I said, settling into the deep couch. The sofa had come from my parents' finished basement back home. Despite having a loose spring or two, it smelled like home.

"We haven't heard from you in a week!" Mom was starting strong today. She and my dad sat side by side at their dining table, faces scrunched in close together.

"I'm sorry, Mom. Things have been busy here getting ready for the holiday festival. I have a booth that I'm manning," I said.

It wasn't an outright lie. But work wasn't the *only* thing keeping me occupied. A week had passed since the disaster of the ice-skating date, and Harry and I had already squeezed in three more dates. First, a Sunday morning coffee just down the stairs at Greyport Grinds. I appreciated only needing to roll out of bed for that one. We'd next gone for a lunch date with Jill at The Sticky Pig, a local barbecue joint that had left me in a food-coma for the second half of the day. Then, there was trivia night at Maven's, where Harry's team had taken dead last. I'd tried to get into it, especially since it was a prime chance to meet more new people, but by that point in the week, I could hardly move. Harry was affable, but his energy never lagged. It was almost annoying how chipper he was. All. The. Time.

The one blessing was I hadn't seen James at all. Harry had tried to arrange something with him, but evidently James was dodging him. Every time Harry expressed his frustration about James sending his calls to voicemail, I breathed a sigh of relief. I was being a shitty fake girlfriend—convincing James that Harry was a big boy now was the whole point of the plan, after all—but being around James was the last thing I wanted. Because I had a full-blown, capital-C Crush on the grumpy asshole, and it did nothing but piss me off.

"Emma, you need to take better care of yourself. I knew a new job and a big move like this would be too much."

I called my attention back to my parents. Apparently, using the work excuse only gave my mother something else to harp on about.

I angled the phone screen down a bit, hiding the crazed facial expression I made in response to her words.

"I am fine, Mom." I re-centered myself back on the screen.

"Well, I only fret because I care."

Oh boy, now she had her arms crossed. Never a good sign.

"What your mother means to say," Dad said, earning himself a dirty look from his wife of twenty-nine years. "Is that we know you're doing a great job in Greyport. We just miss you, and you being so far away has been a lot to get used to."

My body relaxed a fraction, muscles loosening up as I sank further into the couch. Dad was trying.

"I miss you both too. And I'm not ignoring you on purpose. I really do have a lot going on."

"Tell me more about this festival and your booth."

I settled in to tell them about the Festival of Lights. The main street in the village shut down around Christmas for a short parade, and local businesses set up booths with their holiday products on display. I would run a booth focused on advertising some of the library's newer programs as well as raffling off prizes from local businesses. Proceeds from the raffle all went back to support library programs.

Mom's face softened the tiniest bit by the time I finished talking. Despite the recent tension in our relationship, deep down, I knew she loved me and was proud. Maybe we could get there eventually, if I could just get some breathing room.

"Are you making sure your whole life isn't work, my sweet girl?" Mom asked.

Well, at least I had positive news to report on that front. "I have, actually. I've made some new friends recently and also started seeing someone." It hadn't been my plan to tell them about Harry, but I figured keeping it vague would be enough to get them off my back. It wasn't like they would ever meet Harry, after all.

"Oh, that is...exciting news." Dad's facial expression belied his words, and Mom's was worse. I could practically see the thoughts broadcast across their foreheads. They did *not* like the idea of me settling down hours away from them.

If only they knew the reality here. I was definitely not settling down with Harry. I wasn't settling down *at all* anytime soon.

"It's really new. Nothing serious at all. But he's very nice."

If you like hyperactive golden retrievers.

"Well, I can't say I'm not a little worried about so many changes in your life all at once…"

"*Mom.*"

I needed to cut the call before I got more of an earful and the rest of the night was ruined.

"Can we talk about the Christmas topic, instead?" Dad was stepping out of one minefield to another.

"Mom, Dad, I am still standing firm that I'm not traveling back to your house for Christmas. It's too much so soon after the move. Plus, driving that long distance isn't good on my joints." I knew how to lay a guilt trip too.

"Should we tell her, Lin?" My dad looked excitedly at his wife.

Oh, fuck.

"We are coming to Greyport for Christmas!"

Chapter Twelve

Emma

I ALMOST LET MY phone go to voicemail when it rang an hour later. The video chat with my parents had me in a funk. Nothing could deter them from coming to Greyport for Christmas. Not only would they be staying an entire week, getting all up in my business, but they expected to meet Harry too.

It had been idiotic to mention him in the first place. Had I known Mom and Dad were cooking up a surprise visit, I would have never brought it up.

I tossed my empty soup bowl—my sad, boring dinner—into the sink and swiped to answer the call. I didn't recognize the number, but it was a Greyport area code. Maybe it was a vendor calling about the booth for the Festival of Lights.

"Hello?" I did my best to sound professional, just to be safe.

"Emma! It's Kristi! What are you up to tonight?"

An hour and a half later, I squeezed into a rideshare with Jill and Kristi, venturing out into the night. Joining them for a spur-of-the-moment night out was a welcome distraction.

We were going to a night club a few towns over, in Merlin Heights, intending to let loose and dance. I dressed in a dark-blue top, the jewel tone contrasting nicely with my dark hair and eyes, and showing far more skin than my norm.

I hadn't had a night out like this since college. Hadn't had friends who were up for this sort of thing in nearly as long.

The rideshare pulled up to a busy curb, and the driver waited for the three of us to hop out before speeding off to pick up more Friday-night party-goers. I shivered against the biting wind, my light coat no match for the winter weather.

"You look fucking *amazing*!" Jill said over the music filling the room as we entered.

I gave a playful shoulder shimmy as I removed my jacket. "You too! Thank you so much for the invite. I haven't done something like this in ages, and let's just say it was perfect timing."

"Everything okay with you?" Kristi raised a dark brow as we moved farther into the bustling club. It was chock-full of Merlin Heights residents and students. Along with Greyport's community and state colleges, Merlin Heights has a well-regarded community college, so the area tended to attract a young and boisterous crowd.

Jill offered to grab the first round at the bar while Kristi and I found a group of chairs where the music was a touch less loud.

"Just stressed, I guess. I'm loving my job so far, but getting every-thing planned for the Christmas festival has been a trial by fire. On top of that, my parents just told me they're coming into town for Christmas, so now I have to get my shit together for that. Thank God they're booking a hotel, because I am *not* up to hosting in my tiny-ass apartment."

Kristi's gaze turned sympathetic. "That's rough. For what it's worth, you're doing a kickass job in the community outreach role. Tracy was trying to manage it all before, but it was just too much for one person. You'll get the hang of it in time. Besides"—her inquisitive brow wiggled suggestively—"you've got Harry Klein to help you relieve *any* stress on your body. All. Night. Long."

"Gag me." Jill appeared with three tall glasses of something pink and fruity. "That's my cousin you're talking about."

"Sorry, girl, but your cousin is hot as fuck. Your brother too. Don't you think, Emma?"

"Huh?" My cheeks heated—and not from the sudden influx of alcohol to my system.

"Harry and James. They're both fucking gorgeous. Runs in the family."

"I, uh...only pay attention to Harry, I guess." I figured some loyalty to my fake boyfriend was warranted.

Kristi laughed. "You may be dating Harry, but I don't expect you to be blind. James Klein and the whole hot-lumberjack thing he has going on? Sexy as hell."

"Alright, Kris, that's enough. Don't embarrass Emma."

Kristi glanced sheepishly at her friend, but it didn't stop her from giggling. I suspected the two women had been pre-gaming for a while already.

"Speaking of attractive men." Kristi now aimed her knowing gaze toward Jill. "I heard around town you and Ben Till were seen getting lunch the other day."

Jill's expression turned hard, closed off. "It was work related."

"Are you starting a fourth career as a landscaping professional now?"

"Nope. Something else that's none of your business. You know I hate the gossip shit."

My neck was on a swivel as I watched the volley back and forth. Sure, Kristi had been pushy, but there was no disguising her hurt at Jill's defensive reaction. The bubbly blonde was keeping secrets, and her best friend didn't like it.

I spoke loudly over the tension. "I love this song! How about we go dance?"

CHAPTER THIRTEEN

Emma

I LIFTED MY SWEAT-DAMP hair off the back of my neck as we made our way off the dance floor.

Ridiculous dance moves to remixed eighties songs proved to be the mood lifter we all needed. I hadn't spared a thought about the mess with my parents, and Kristi and Jill seemed back to their usual selves.

"Let me check how long the wait is for a car." Jill pulled her phone from her back pocket. "Fuck. Seriously?"

"What's wrong?"

"There's a crazy-long wait time. Hang on, I'll check another service." She navigated to another phone application. "Nope, this one is even worse. Looks like there's some convention going on tonight. Ugh."

Kristi looked over at me, pursing her lips. "What if Emma calls her *boyfriend*?" She said the word in a sing-song voice.

I gulped. "I can give him a try." Harry and I hadn't planned a date night this weekend, but if you couldn't count on a fake boyfriend to pick you up after a night out, who could you count on?

I placed the phone to my ear and listened to the outgoing ring. Once, twice, and straight to voicemail. "Huh, maybe the call isn't going through?" I tried again with the same result.

Swallowing, I looked up at Kristi and Jill. "Sorry, he isn't answering."

I was still getting to know my new friends, but I could have sworn the look in their eyes was pity.

Great.

"Definitely might just be your phone service in here. I'll see if I can get him," Jill said.

A moment later, it was apparent Harry wasn't answering Jill's calls either. I could tell from the hard-pressed line of her jaw that Jill was fuming.

The blonde shoved her phone back into her bag.

"I won't say anything too negative about Harry since your relationship is brand new, and I like you, Emma, but he is on my shit list right now."

It seemed Harry had puppy-dog-eyed his way into being my fake boyfriend, only to sabotage his own efforts early in the game.

The night, meant to be a stress reliever, was going downhill fast. Harry was supposed to be a solution to my loneliness problem, not an additional source of angst.

"We do need to figure something out, though, Jill," Kristi said, cutting in.

"I am well aware, Captain Obvious." So, the dancing hadn't completely eliminated the tension between Jill and Kristi. "I'm calling my brother. God knows he has no life other than work, anyway."

And there it was. James Klein showing up on my fun night out, acting as a savior, was my worst nightmare.

"I'm going to go pee," I said.

"Want one of us to go with you?" Jill asked.

"No, I should be good." It was a clear shot across the club to the restroom.

I selfishly hoped James would be busy and we would be forced to deal with the inconvenient wait time for a car. Better that than another night spent in close quarters with him, now with two observers. The last thing I needed was for Jill or Kristi to notice my weird crush on him. Especially Kristi with her supposed psychic abilities.

The bathroom line took longer than expected, and almost fifteen minutes had passed by the time I finished. A woman had been crying with a friend in one of the stalls. Something about a shitty ex-girlfriend and shared custody of a miniature schnauzer.

My phone vibrated, and I slid it from my purse. It was from Jill. She and Kristi were already outside, anticipating James' imminent arrival.

The night was coming to a close, and the club was clearing out. As I beelined for the exit, a slick hand grabbed my arm, jerking me to a stop.

"Where are you off to, beautiful?" A man in a silky-looking bright-green shirt lurked too close. His skin was pale and shiny. I could smell the beer on his breath.

I rolled my shoulder in an attempt to dislodge his hand, but his fingers were like claws. "Just going home."

It was too much to hope my blunt answer would deter him. "You should be going home with me." I imagined he thought his smile was charming, but it was just smarmy.

"No, thank you." I stepped back quickly, causing his hand to fall away. But somehow, even in his drunk state, he was faster. He roped his arm back around my waist and dragged me into his beer-breath bubble.

"Don't be like that, beautiful."

"I have a boyfriend," I said, twisting and turning my upper body as far from him as possible. Some men respected a woman belonging to a man more than they did a simple no.

"Yeah, she has a fucking boyfriend."

In an instant, the pushy man's arm was gone, and a wall of flannel stood between Green Shirt and me.

James.

"Sorry, man, I didn't know she was your girl." Gone was the slippery pickup-artist voice, replaced by a tittering tone.

"He's not—" I snapped my mouth shut at the thunderous look James shot at me.

"It doesn't fucking matter if she's my girl—or anyone's girl, for that matter. If she says no, then you don't fucking touch her."

The green-shirted man attempted a laugh. "Whatever. Not worth my time," he said as he scampered off.

I caught the tail end of a head nod from James to one of the bouncers. Some man-code to keep an eye on the creep. James watched until the other man disappeared from view.

His head whipped back toward me. "Why weren't you with Kristi and Jill?"

"I had to use the bathroom. Is that not allowed now?"

James closed his eyes for a beat before directing his hazel gaze back at me. "Just get out to the truck, Emma."

He sure was growly tonight. It made parts of my body tingle—parts I was supposed to be ignoring.

CHAPTER FOURTEEN

James

I DRUMMED MY FINGERS along the steering wheel of my truck as Emma and I watched Jill climb the stairs into her apartment and head inside.

I had wanted to drop Emma off first, but Jill had insisted her apartment was more on the way.

Now, we were alone in the dark heat of the truck cab. The windshield kept gathering a layer of frost, so the defroster was on full blast. It was cozy. Intimate.

Intimate was the last thing I wanted around Emma, especially after that weird moment at the skating rink. What the fuck had I been thinking, touching her leg like that? She had clearly been uncomfortable. I would have to be careful not to repeat what had been my instinctual reaction to seeing her in pain.

Which was why I needed to stay as far from her as possible. I still didn't trust her or her motives. My plan was to drop her off and be done with it.

I reversed out of Jill's small private lot and signaled to turn back onto the road. The snow was coming down with a vengeance. If I wasn't so pissed off at my cousin, I might sympathize with him being out towing a car in this weather.

I stole a peek at the woman in the passenger seat. A streetlamp lit up the right side of her face. "You said you're off Market Street?"

She nodded. A few dark strands of hair had escaped her beanie, glancing across her cheek.

My fingers twitched with the urge to smooth them back.

What the hell was wrong with me?

A few beats of silence followed before I broke. "How is your hip feeling?"

I felt her gaze on me but kept my eyes glued to the road.

"Pretty shitty, if I'm being honest."

"Why'd you let Harry take you on an ice-skating date if you have an old injury? Seems kind of silly to me." The question had been bouncing around my head since Emma had mentioned the injury back at the rink. Harry finally found a woman he liked well enough to date, and he chose to torture her with activities that caused her pain. It made no sense.

"What the hell is that supposed to mean?"

That statement had sounded better in my head. "I meant my cousin was being silly, not you." I hoped that would be enough to turn the mood around.

Although, if we went back to sniping at each other, maybe we could get rid of the weirdness that had been building since I touched her at the rink.

"It didn't sound like you were talking about Harry. It sounded like you were implying that it was silly of me to participate in a physical activity because I've gotten hurt before. First off, I wasn't forced to do anything. And second, I know the risks, and I'm not a child. I'm not made of glass just because my hip got fractured."

"You feel better now that you got that out?" I looked over, only to catch the tail end of an eye roll. *Brat.*

"Yes, as a matter of fact, I do."

"Alright, then. I am sorry."

I almost laughed out loud at her answering *hmph,* but I wisely contained it.

"Hip fracture, huh? That sounds intense." As much as I wanted to contain my curiosity, I had to ask.

"Yup." All I got was the back of her head as she faced out the window.

Damn, I had pissed her off. "Sore subject, I take it?"

"*Traumatic* subject, actually. And no, I do not want to talk about it."

If I didn't have both hands gripped on the steering wheel, I would have held them up in an 'I surrender' gesture. I *had* been trying to needle her, but the last thing I wanted was to make light of something serious. Something real.

I coughed past the hard lump in my throat that tasted strangely like guilt.

We drove for a few minutes in quiet, the only sound that of the defroster working overtime. I turned, at long last, onto the side street where Emma lived.

"How far down are you?"

"Right above Greyport Grinds. You can drop me off right here." She pointed to an open space along the sidewalk.

Yeah, right. "Not gonna do that."

Emma looked at me again, half confusion, half heated anger.

"I'll walk you inside. It's slick, and you're already hurting." I didn't care about poking the bear. Not when it came to her safety.

It meant nothing. I would do it for anyone.

Before she could protest, I hopped out of the truck and hurried to the passenger door. Emma had already opened it and was about to jump down.

"Would you stop? The last thing you need right now is to end up on the ground again."

"You can quit acting like you care. I know you don't like me. Let me go inside so we can get this done and over with."

"I do care if I end up breaking my back trying to peel you off the ground. Now, let me help you out of the damn truck before we both freeze our asses off."

She uncrossed her arms and took my waiting hand.

I wanted to pull away. The touch of her skin on mine was so right it was wrong.

I was the biggest piece of shit known to man. Emma was still, presumably, my cousin's girl.

I pulled her close to guide her down from the tall truck, jaw aching as I clenched my teeth. Her tan jacket was thin—too thin for the weather—and I could feel every inch of her. The shape of her soft hips under my hands. Her firm breasts pressed into my chest. The sharp intake of her breath as she inhaled.

The delicate curve of her ear was *right there.* I wanted nothing more than to take the smooth lobe between my teeth and bite down. I wanted to know how she would react, what little noise she might make if I did.

I had never felt like more of a motherfucking asshole in my entire life.

Once Emma's feet were on the ground, I felt an answering wobble from her direction. Her injuries were bothering her more than she let on.

"Lean against me while we walk." I cringed inwardly at the rough sound of my voice. "Do you have to go up one flight or two?"

I had delivered a set of bedroom furniture to one of the units above Greyport Grinds a few years ago, so I was familiar with the setup. The couple who owned the coffee shop were great, but I'd heard the company who rented out the upper apartments was unreliable. I didn't like the idea of anyone, Emma included, living there.

"Just one flight. Thank God."

I heard the pain in her voice. It set me again to wondering just how she had fractured her hip. I was far from an expert, but whatever happened must have been pretty severe to cause that level of injury in a younger person. The healing must have been grueling.

We muddled our way across the slick sidewalk, pausing at an outer door for Emma to grab her keys. I reluctantly agreed she could maneuver up the stairs with the railing for support while I followed behind.

Truthfully, I welcomed more distance between us. I shouldn't have been having any sort of thoughts about Emma. She was dating Harry. Even if I had doubts about her being the right person for my cousin, the man was into her, as much as I hadn't believed it at first. His grinning like a fool back at the rink had sold me, as much as I hadn't wanted to buy it.

When we hit the narrow landing at the top of the stairs, pausing at the door to Emma's apartment, the distance had once again eroded.

"This is me. And, uh, thanks." Emma shifted from left to right.

"You're welcome."

Emma paused at her door before I stopped her. She turned back, looking annoyed. I didn't blame her. It had been a long night.

"We didn't get the best start," I said.

"Right. We did not. Where is this going, James? I need to lie down."

"I just wanted to formally apologize for the way I've talked to you. And propose a truce. You're going to be around whether I like it or not. We may as well be civil."

Civil. Not close, not friendly. I didn't think I could handle friendly. Not with the underlying attraction I felt for her thrumming through me. In time, it would go away, like exposure therapy.

Emma sucked in her lips, considering my offer. A moment passed. She nodded once, firmly. "I accept your truce. Goodnight, James."

I made my way down the stairwell, leaving her in the hall.

The quiet no longer offered me comfort.

CHAPTER FIFTEEN

Emma

I couldn't find my keys.

"Are you *sure* they aren't in your truck?" I asked James.

He had already trudged out to and from his truck to find the missing item once. So far, no luck, but I was desperate.

I patted down my coat again. Maybe the apartment key had fallen into the lining of the jacket—it had happened before.

"Call your landlord."

"I'm not calling my landlord at almost one in the morning, James."

"That's what a landlord is for. There should be an after-hours line for tenants for shit like this."

"Unfortunately, that number is written on a piece of paper *inside the apartment.* The one I currently cannot enter. Because I don't have my key!"

"Why is that number not programmed into your cell phone?"

Why did he look so angry about it? What I did with my life wasn't any of his business.

I crossed my arms against the draft coming up the stairwell. "I haven't lived here all that long, and I've been busy with a new job. Forgive me for not being the picture of responsibility here."

"Yeah, well, maybe a little more responsibility is warranted if you're planning to make it on your own, hours away from any friends and family."

What the fuck. My stomach dropped. I wanted to scream in his face, tell him he was dead wrong. But that was the problem. He wasn't wrong, was he?

"You don't know me, James," I said in a whisper.

He stared at me for a beat before turning away. "Let's just go."

"Go where?"

"I'll take you back to my place for now. Your *boyfriend* will show up eventually. Then he can deal with you."

Like I was some...burden he couldn't stand to carry.

"I don't want to go anywhere with you right now."

"And I don't think you have much of a choice."

He stomped down the stairs. A moment later, I followed.

He was right. I had no choice.

CHAPTER SIXTEEN

James

S HE WAS IN MY house, and I didn't like it. I was restless and cagey, my skin two sizes too small. All I wanted was to get in my workshop and throw some wood around. But it was too damn late and too damn cold for that.

Not to mention, Harry was still nowhere to be found, and I had to make sure Emma didn't burn my house down.

Not that I wouldn't deserve it. I'd been a fucking asshole to her tonight. No sleep and another unproductive day had me in a piss-poor mood. And while I would never leave my sister stranded, driving out of my way in city traffic to a damn nightclub wasn't at the top of my list of favorite activities.

That motherfucker who'd put his hands all over Emma only reinforced why I avoided places like that altogether.

I swore Emma had no instinct for self-preservation. And now, for the second time tonight, I was rescuing my cousin's girlfriend.

She was all up in my space, walking around my living room. Her tight blue shirt had some sort of contraption with straps and ties all down her back. I kept catching glimpses of bare skin that had me wanting to shove her back into that stupid tan jacket that definitely didn't keep her warm enough.

She sat down, stiff, on the brown leather sofa, perched on the edge like she couldn't wait to run away.

I told myself to stop staring at her like some creep and act like a good host.

"You want water or something?"

"Sure, that would be good."

She gave me a close-lipped smile, rubbing her bare arms as I walked a glass of water to her. I hadn't bothered starting a fire in the living room fireplace tonight. After spending the evening in the workshop, I had planned to go straight to bed. No sense heating a room that wouldn't get used.

I regretted it now, watching Emma shiver.

I crossed to the hallway closet and snatched down one of my old sweatshirts, a faded-royal-blue one from my college days, and tossed it over.

Emma shot me a questioning look as she grabbed it off the arm of the couch.

I shrugged. "You looked cold."

"Thanks." Her voice was muffled under the blue cotton.

The fabric dwarfed her. I should have given her one of Harry's sweatshirts. There had been one hanging right next to mine in the closet. But I had given in to some instinctual caveman urge to see her wearing something of mine. There had been no turning back once I'd pulled that sweatshirt off the hanger.

Harry could have Emma in his bed, but I had her in my clothes. It would never go further than that. I might be an asshole on a good day, but betraying my cousin wasn't in my makeup.

I shifted my weight from foot to foot.

"So, are you okay?"

Emma paused from smoothing down her hair that had gotten rumpled by the sweatshirt. "I'd rather be home in my bed, but I'm fine. Thanks for letting me hang out here for a while. I should have paid more attention to where my keys were tonight. I'm not sure what I would have done otherwise. Sleep curled up in the fetal position in front of my door, most likely."

I coughed. "I shouldn't have yelled at you about the keys. I'm sorry. But I meant after what happened at the club. You know, that guy?"

Emma scoffed. "Not the first time I've had to deal with an overly persistent dickhead."

God, I fucking hated that. If I had anything to say about it, it would be the last time she put up with some creep. I would have to talk to Harry, make sure he looked out for her.

"Can you sit down? It's making me feel weird with you looming over me like that."

I sat. I knew enough from dealing with Jill to recognize Emma was trying to redirect the conversation.

The brunette looked down at the peeling white letters emblazoned across her chest. "Is this where you went to school?"

I nodded. "For a few years. Didn't graduate, though. My mom got sick, so I moved back home to help her until she passed away." I didn't love talking about Mom's last few years, but therapy had taught me not to bottle it up.

Her eyes softened. "That's admirable, James. And it must have been a tough decision. Do you think you'll ever go back to finish your degree?"

I shook my head. "Nah. I was getting a general business degree, and the woodworking thing was always my ultimate plan. I got what I needed out of my apprenticeship easily enough."

"You make custom furniture, right? Harry mentioned it. I wasn't stalking you or anything."

"No need to get defensive. I'm not that hard to figure out." My lips tipped up just a little. "But yeah, that's what I do. Lots of smaller orders, but I have a few larger clients too."

"That has to be fun, getting to be creative like that." She tilted her head down to a pile of paperwork I had left strewn across the coffee table. "Are those some of your sketches?"

My poor attempts at coming up with ideas for the McGuire job. "Uh, yeah, but those are shit. Don't look at them."

But Emma was already sliding them over to herself with one long, graceful finger. I heard a quiet gasp.

"Are you kidding me? These are gorgeous, James." She pointed to a sketch of a chair I'd been experimenting with and angled it toward me. Somewhere along the way, she had scooted closer on the couch. I could smell whatever shit she put in her hair. It smelled good enough to eat, like coconuts.

I shifted, ill at ease with the praise. "They're alright. A little too out there for the client, I think."

"If I had unlimited money and enough space in my tiny-ass apartment I would buy ten of these chairs immediately. They're amazing." She grinned up at me.

I was struck by the idea that Emma's entire apartment, her entire living space, should only be filled with items that I personally crafted, meticulously and reverently built just for her.

Harry would just buy her some prefabricated shit from Home Depot and call it a day.

I sipped my water, willing away the unfair thought. But was it really unfair when I was the one here, right now, saving Emma's ass—not once, but twice tonight—while he was nowhere to be found?

As if the thought had conjured him out of thin air, Harry blew through the front door, his wet boots thudding against the wall of the foyer as he kicked them off his feet.

"Ems!" He barreled across the hardwood floor of the living room, shaking out his snow-damp hair like a dog after a bath. He grabbed Emma by both cheeks and laid a brief, smacking kiss across her lips.

I looked away.

Harry flopped on the couch, laying his legs across Emma's lap. His socked feet landed on my thighs.

"Get your nasty feet off me." I stood up, shoving the offending appendages away. Harry cackled.

"Where have you been?" I asked.

"Bowling with Mark and Landon. Why?"

"You might want to check your phone for a couple missed calls. I picked Emma, Jill, and Kristi up in Merlin Heights a few hours ago when they couldn't get a hold of you."

"Oh, yeah, I lost my cell phone today. I'm pretty sure it fell out of my pocket in one of the cars I was working on, and it's on some old man's floorboard now. Sorry." Harry wriggled his feet, impervious to my death glare. "So, what're you doing here so late, Ems?"

"If you hadn't lost your phone again, like a dumbass, you would already know the answer." I backed away, using a refill on my water glass as cover to leave the room.

Emma murmured to Harry. Stupid drafty rooms and their lack of real privacy. I was trying not to see or hear them.

"I'm going to bed," I said, slamming my glass down into the sink. Somehow, it didn't shatter.

"Sounds good, sunshine. Ems and I are gonna get some sleep too. We'll call around in the morning to find those keys."

I watched as Emma and Harry walked hand in hand up the stairs toward Harry's bedroom.

I slammed out the back door to my freezing-cold workshop.

CHAPTER SEVENTEEN

Emma

I JUMPED OUT OF my skin at the sound of the bedroom door slamming shut behind me and Harry. The noise echoed throughout the house, reverberating off the wood floors.

"Don't!" I said to Harry, aiming my best dagger eyes at him. "James said he was going to sleep. It's rude to be so loud."

Harry lounged back on his bed with his head propped up on a stack of pillows. "Aw, relax, Ems. There's no way he's already in bed yet. You sound just like him—so worried about getting me to behave all the time."

He crunched up to sit at attention. "Although...if forcing me to be a good little boy is your thing, I am more than happy to oblige."

I didn't bother curtailing my expression of disgust at the enthusiastic eyebrow waggle that accompanied his words.

"I am trying to help you gain credibility in the eyes of your family. I highly doubt slamming doors in the middle of the night is going to help your case. Did you forget that, Harry?"

"But it's so *boring,* Ems. Here, let me show you some pictures of the crazy parkour moves Landon and I were doing when we got done bowling." Harry scooted one butt cheek up and pulled his phone from the rear pocket of his jeans.

Wait. *His phone?*

"I thought you lost your phone, Harry." I crossed my arms.

His mouth formed an *O* of surprise.

"You didn't think I would remember the conversation we *just* had? What the hell, Harry? Why would you make up some crazy story about losing your phone at work in an old man's car if it wasn't true?"

Worse, what excuse did he have for ignoring calls from Jill and me from the club? He could have at least answered and said he was busy with friends.

He buried his head in his hands with a groan. "Look, Ems, I'm really sorry. I walked in and saw you and James looking all serious, and I freaked out. I got worried you told him about our fake-dating deal now that you and him are getting along."

He moved his hands and looked up at me where I still stood just inside the threshold of the room. His head tilted in question. "Hold up. *Are* you two...getting along now?"

I couldn't tell if he sounded happy about that development or not.

"We declared a truce. It's not important," I said with a hand wave. "But don't change the subject. Harry, if you actually want your family to think you're not a fuck-up, well...you need to stop fucking up. Don't ignore your phone for hours if you can help it. And don't make up absurd stories to cover things up." Ironic, considering the fact that I was an active participant in one of those absurd stories. Not exactly the picture of honesty myself.

"Don't give up on me, please, Ems." He pressed his palms together in a pantomime of prayer.

I rolled my eyes. "I seriously considered being done with this whole fake-dating thing tonight, Harry. It was embarrassing. My friends looked at me like they felt sorry for me, all because my boyfriend wouldn't answer the phone when I needed help."

"I'll be better, I promise. I have a shitty habit of self-sabotage, and I'm working on it. Sometimes I get wrapped up in things, and James and Jill just don't get it. Especially James."

"For what it's worth, I bet if you explained it to him, he would at least try to understand where you're coming from. As much as it pains me to admit, he seems like a legitimately good person." And I was the worst sort of person for lying to him and Jill and Kristi. The whole rest of the town too.

Harry blew a raspberry with his lips as he star-fished back down on his checkered quilt. "James is the *best* person, and that's what makes it even harder to admit to him when I screw up."

"Harry, what are you going to do? Because this pretend relationship isn't sustainable, and I don't think it's actually helping."

"Can you give me another chance? Please, please, please? Just until Christmas, at least. I am begging you."

A lock of wavy hair fell over his right eye as I looked at him, considering. It wouldn't be so bad. Only a few more weeks. And I needed him through my parents' visit anyway.

Once they went home, Harry and I would be done for good. No more guilt, no more lies, and no more weird interactions with James Klein.

"Fine. But you're meeting my parents when they're here in town, whether you like it or not. And you're sleeping on the floor tonight."

I sent the fluffy pillows scattering across the floor as I hip-checked him off the bed.

CHAPTER EIGHTEEN

Emma

T HE HALLWAY WAS COOL as I tiptoed out of Harry's room on soft feet the next morning. The sun was beginning to rise. Harry was still sleeping peacefully on his blanket fort next to the bed, snoring away, but my bladder had woken me earlier than I would have liked after my late night. I needed a bathroom and a hit of caffeine. I rarely indulged in alcohol, and though I had only been a little tipsy, those few drinks had left me with a nagging headache.

After I finished washing up, I took a few minutes to snoop in the bathroom, located down the hall from Harry's room. There was a large clawfoot tub I envied, thinking of my own minuscule bathroom with its boring, free-standing shower stall. Besides the plumbing, everything else in the bathroom looked custom made. James' work, I figured.

I trailed my fingers along the smooth wood of the cupboard that sat between the tub and wall. I popped open the front-facing door to find a stack of fluffy navy towels. The medicine cabinet above the sink was stunning with its detailed carving along the trim, but there was nothing of interest in it aside from a jar of high-quality hand balm I imagined both James and Harry made use of, given their jobs.

I gave myself a final onceover in the mirror, smoothing down my wild hair and rubbing a finger over an errant mascara smudge I had missed last night, before exiting.

I was focused on the screen of my phone, swiping away messages from my mom and searching for the nightclub's phone number to call about my missing keys, as I came around the corner into the kitchen.

"Morning," James' gruff voice said.

I nearly lost my grip on my phone. James was standing at the stovetop, cooking up something that smelled delicious, his bare back facing me. He wore only a thin pair of gray sweatpants on his bottom half.

The gray sweatpants were an evil choice on his part. I was convinced men knew what they were doing to people when they dressed in gray sweatpants.

"Good morning." I put an extra dose of pep into the words. "Did you sleep well?"

"No."

So, James Klein wasn't a morning person. Good to know.

"Do you have any coffee? If not, point me in the right direction, and I can get a pot started."

"I got it." Without a word, he took a clay mug down from an open shelf. I watched as the muscles of his back stretched and bunched with each movement, like some sort of sexy visual symphony.

"Here you go." He placed the now full mug in front of where I sat on a stool pulled up to the kitchen island. From the way his upper lip quirked as he turned back to the stove, I knew he'd caught me ogling him.

I couldn't help it. He was strong and well-muscled, but not in a showy way. A thin layer of hair covered his chest and trailed down his abdomen toward his waistband. He looked...capable. Like he could field dress a deer, cook a delicious venison stew, then make a woman come in ten seconds flat.

"Do you ever go hunting?" The words fell out of my mouth.

"What?" He looked over his shoulder, brow furrowed in confusion.

My cheeks heated. "I was, uh...just wondering."

He shook his head and turned back to whatever was sizzling on the stovetop. "I haven't been hunting in years. I don't have time."

So much for my venison-stew theory.

I valiantly moved to another subject. "So, that smells good." I wouldn't turn down a plate of whatever James was making, whether he hunted down the food or not. I needed fuel for the day, and who knew when I would get back to my place? I might be searching for my keys all morning.

His strong shoulders rose and fell. "A veggie omelet and hash browns. Want some?"

I breathed a sigh of relief at the offer as I went boneless. "Fuck yes."

He gave me a full laugh, and I nearly fell off my stool in a puddle of aroused goo. The man was unfairly hot, and when he laughed, his hot factor increased tenfold.

This crush was not only pointless, it was stupid. He thought I was dating his cousin slash roommate slash best friend. Not to mention, he barely seemed to tolerate me half the time—the guy ran hot and cold like a marathon champ. There was a less than zero chance my feelings for James would ever go anywhere, and I needed to rein it in—and fast. Cozy nights and mornings with him were not helping.

His laughter was contagious in the still of the morning, and I couldn't help but to smile. I rocked the feet of my barstool back and forth, enjoying the sound of its light thumping on the hardwood.

He shot me an irritated look at the noise. We were back at odds. I thought about keeping the thumping going, but decided to spare him the annoyance. He was making me breakfast, after all.

"Did you make these stools too?" I asked, deflecting.

"What do you think?" He smirked before giving the omelet a flip.

I remembered the way Harry smirked at the garage the first day we met. James had the same smirk, but somehow it was even more potent.

The silence built as he continued cooking, but the quiet was comfortable and oddly domestic.

James handed me a full plate—the food looked even better than it had smelled—and slid into the seat next to me.

I struggled to ignore the way his knee brushed against mine every so often while we ate.

"Did your mom teach you how to cook?" I asked around a bite of eggs.

He chuckled. "My mom was a terrible cook, actually. I learned out of necessity. It was that or boxed macaroni and cheese every night. So, I guess you could say she was responsible for my cooking skills in a way. Not that I do anything complicated in the kitchen, anyway."

"I love to cook. But so does my dad, and until I moved here, I lived with my parents. If I ever cooked, I had to deal with his unsolicited opinions the entire time, so I'm a little rusty. The kitchen in my apartment is awful. Half the burners on the stove don't even work. That's what I get for cheaping out, I guess."

James' facial expression was downright dark. He speared a hash brown and shoved it into his mouth. I couldn't help but notice the tick in his throat as he swallowed.

"How long is your lease for?" he asked.

"Six months. I'm hoping by then I can find someplace better to rent—once I know the town a little better and can save up for a deposit."

"I can help you." He coughed. "Er, Harry can help you. He knows a lot of people around here."

"I'm getting that impression. He's social and active. I think the only time I've seen him sitting still is when he's in bed."

I froze as James pushed back, grabbing our empty plates and tossing them in the sink.

"Is everything alright?" I braved asking the question. He was moving on to the icy part of his hot-and-cold thing.

"Fine. Just gotta get to work."

After that, I was left sitting in the kitchen—alone.

It wasn't until several hours later, when I was back home after collecting the keys I'd dropped at the club, that I realized I was still wearing James' hoodie.

Chapter Nineteen

James

I CALLED BEN LATER that morning, after spending a few miserable hours in the workshop. I spent most of the time working on the chair Emma had seen the plans for—the one she'd said was gorgeous. Wasting time I didn't have. Next on my agenda was to call the cell phone provider to request a replacement phone for Harry.

I shouldn't have gone cold on Emma again. But her mention of my cousin tucked warm in his bed had been a punch to the gut. If I were a masochist, I'd spend more time going down that rabbit hole, picturing Emma in Harry's bed, Emma curled up next to Harry, Emma getting fucked by Harry... I needed a change of pace.

Thank God my friend had been free to meet me at Greyport Family Diner. The run-down restaurant was a town staple. I doubted the building had been updated in the last two decades, but the food was greasy and delicious.

Ben was already there, flagging me down from a booth. I slid in across the ripped vinyl seat. The booths were big enough to accommodate our tall frames—my friend was a few inches shorter than my six foot five but almost as broad in the chest and shoulders—so I didn't mind its state of disrepair.

Other than our size, my best friend and I couldn't have looked more different. I was way too lazy to keep up with the clean-cut look, keeping my beard as neat as I could. If I went a little too long without trimming it, it didn't bother me. Same for my dark hair, the ends curling around my ears.

Ben, on the other hand, kept his dirty-blond hair buzzed close to his scalp without a whisker in sight. The effect, combined with blue eyes so light they were almost silver, made him an intimidating presence. We always got a few startled looks when we were out together.

We put our orders in with the waiter, a local high school student with a curly mop of hair.

"How's it going, man?" Ben asked. We hadn't talked since I had asked him to meet with Jill about her business plans.

"Not too bad. My old router shit the bed, so I had to order a new one. Pretty fucking annoying."

"You think you have it bad? The new guy I hired quit already—before his first day."

"That's rough. You gotta post the job listing all over again?" I'd never been so happy to run a one-man show.

"Yep. How's the McGuire job going?"

"It's been better. I can't put a finger on it. I'm not feeling creative, and they were pretty unenthusiastic when I last met with them."

"Do you think they were actually unenthusiastic, or were they just non-committal? Sometimes my landscape clients are so unsure what they want for their designs I end up making the decisions for them. I am the expert for a reason, and nine times out of ten, they love the end result."

"That one time out of ten is what I'm freaking out about. Nothing I'm sketching up lands right either."

"You'll find it. You always do. There's a reason they wanted you."

We chatted for a few minutes about work until our lunch arrived. A burger and fries for Ben and a fish fry for me. I'd been eating like garbage lately with the stress of everything and was planning to hit the gym after we finished at the diner.

Throwing heavy shit around might also work off some of my irrational jealousy about Emma. Because even while she had been eating my food and wearing my sweatshirt, I had to remember that she slept in my cousin's bed.

I hadn't been intrigued by a woman in a while. I wasn't a virgin, but I hardly had time to tie my shoes, let alone meet someone.

Now, the first woman to make me look twice was dating the man I considered a brother.

Frustrating didn't begin to describe it. If I had a second to spare, I might find someone to help me take the edge off my horniness.

Another night of fucking my own hand would have to suffice. At least Harry and Emma, if they'd done the deed the night before, had been quiet enough to spare me from hearing.

"So..." I dabbed my beard with a napkin, removing a smear of tartar sauce.

"So?"

"Did you talk with my sister yet?" Jill hadn't told me anything. Acting as chauffeur to three tipsy women had offered little opportunity for serious discussion.

Ben took a bite of his burger and chewed—for a while. "Um. Yes," he said after swallowing.

"And how did that go?" My bullshit receptors were firing on all cylinders. Why was everyone acting so goddamn evasive lately? I wished I could pull a reset and go back a month to when things had been normal.

"Not bad...at first. But, dude. I think your sister might hate me."

"Are you kidding me? What the fuck happened?"

"I have no idea! One minute, things seemed fine. I was asking her questions about her jobs and her business plan. Then, the next minute, it was like she was quizzing me, and I couldn't get a single answer right. Even though she's your sister, I don't know her all that well."

It was true. I tended to keep my connections compartmentalized. Ben and Jill had a shallow familiarity, mainly because they lived in the same town, but their personal relationship was minimal.

I scrubbed my palms down my beard, releasing a groan. "My sister is a mystery. Are you willing to give mentoring her with the business thing one more shot? If the answer is no, I won't be mad. I need to know if I should step in. I'll find the time if I have to."

Ben shook his buzzed head. "No, it's cool. I'll try one more meeting with her. Maybe it was a bad day for her. Anyway, I sent her a message this morning, asking to meet up, so don't go thinking I'm only saying it now because you made me feel guilty. I'm doing this for you as much as I am for Jill. Let your family fuck up on their own. Especially your asshole of a cousin."

There was little love lost between my friend and Harry. While Ben didn't know Jill well, he and Harry were on the same beer league hockey team. I used to be on the team until work got too hectic, but Harry and Ben still played.

I groaned at the mention. "That idiot lost his phone last night. *Again.* I had to drive all the way into the city to pick up Jill, Kristi, and Harry's girlfriend from a club in Merlin Heights when they couldn't get a ride."

"Seriously? Don't tell me you're replacing it for him. He can call the service provider himself to deal with that."

I said nothing.

Ben pointed a long French fry at me. "You were totally gonna call for him. Don't do it, man. When are you going to cut the cord with him?"

"I'm trying. But I'm all he has."

"You need to let him sink or swim on his own. Harry is an adult. Start today with the phone thing."

Ben was right. "Maybe his girlfriend can help him instead of me. If she wants to rely on him, she'll need a way to keep him on a short leash."

"What's up with Harry having a girlfriend all of a sudden, anyway? Jill mentioned it. Said she's nice."

I paused. I wasn't certain how to explain Emma.

Saying nothing would only draw more attention to my strange state of mind about the situation. "Her name is Emma. She works with Jill at the library. I have no idea how she got together with Harry of all people. They don't have much in common. I was hoping she might be a positive influence on him, but I've noticed that he kind of treats her like shit too, always leaving her on her own, and she has no one in town to help her. Take last night, for example. Emma was locked out of her place, and she lives in one of those crappy rentals above Greyport Grinds. You know the ones? Since we couldn't reach Harry, I ended up bringing Emma home to chill with me while we waited for Harry to show up. And then he didn't even seem to care."

"What?" I said at the look on Ben's face.

"Dude, I'm sorry if I make things weird here, but...do you have a thing for your cousin's girlfriend?"

"No!" the word shot out. I tried again. "Definitely not. I just met her. And she's annoying half the time."

Ben still looked skeptical. "Alright, I won't push any more, but most people don't talk half as much about someone they don't like. You may want to get that under wraps."

"I would never do that to Harry."

Ben threw his hands up, open palms toward me. "I am well aware. You wouldn't do that do anyone, let alone to your cousin. I'm just saying. Sometimes we can't help who we're attracted to."

"So, say I did feel some kind of connection to Emma, what would you advise I even do about it?"

"Well, since you can't exactly fuck her to get it out of your system, I suggest you stay as far away from her as possible until it passes."

Chapter Twenty

James

My phone buzzed as I finished a set of squats at the gym. I ignored it, toweling off the sweat dripping down the back of my neck, planning to hit up one of the open treadmills.

I felt it go off a second time. It was a good thing the fitness center was blasting some annoying synth-pop song with enough intensity to drown out my audible grumble. I hated when my workouts were interrupted, throwing off my rhythm.

The number wasn't familiar, and I didn't recognize the area code.

Unknown: This is Harry from Emma's phone lol.

Unknown: We need u and the truck ASAP.

What the hell?

I tapped the call icon under the new number and brought my cell phone up to my ear.

"Hello?" Emma answered, a question in her tone.

"Emma."

"James?"

I gritted my teeth. Fuck if her voice didn't sound good saying my name. I wasn't supposed to notice that.

"Put Harry on the line."

She gave an annoyed huff. There was a shuffle before my cousin came on the phone.

"Hey, hey, Jay."

"Dude, did you not tell Emma you used her phone to message me?"

"Oh, yeah. I told her I needed to look up a map and then forgot. Sorry, Ems! I'll make it up to you later. Now you've got James' number in case you're ever in a pinch. Oh, don't forget, we should get some—"

"Harry," I said, loud enough to draw his attention back to me. This had happened before—Harry forgetting he was on a call, leaving me to listen in on countless side conversations. I'd once listened to him ordering fifty-two pizzas for one of his coworkers as a prank. Best to head it off before he got rolling. "What do you need me and my truck for?"

He took a gulping inhale. "After I helped Emma get her keys from the club and brought her back to her place, I went home and took a nap. And during my nap, I had this crazy dream about that super sad Christmas tree from Charlie Brown. Do you remember that movie? Mrs. Epps made us watch it in first grade, I think. Mrs. Epps was cool. So, when I woke up, I realized there must be a lot of lonely Christmas trees out there that people haven't picked out yet. So, I called up Ems and explained about these sad trees, and she felt bad for them too. Now, Ems and I are at Meyer's Christmas Village, and I want to get a tree, but I don't have an ax or a way to bring it home. That's where you come in."

I pressed a hand to my forehead, hard, pushing against the building pressure.

"I'll be there in twenty minutes. Don't do anything stupid."

CHAPTER TWENTY-ONE

Emma

I KEPT MY HANDS wrapped around a piping-hot paper cup of hot chocolate Harry had bought for me. I had been about ready to curl up in a blanket on the couch when he called, asking if I wanted to get Christmas trees—one for my apartment and another for his and James' house. I almost said no, but he sounded so excited to visit Meyer's Christmas Village. It was hard to stay annoyed with him when he was a good person—a failure as a boyfriend, but a good person.

I stomped my feet on the hard-packed gravel in an attempt to ward off the cold. I wore thick wool socks under my thin rain boots, but they weren't enough to fight the chill.

A family rolled past—a mom, dad, and two kids in a little red wagon. They had the right idea, all bundled up with hats, gloves, and blankets. I followed their trajectory as they headed toward the children's activities. There appeared to be a petting zoo of goats and reindeer, a realistic-looking elf toy factory, and a chance to meet Santa.

Gravel crunched as a large, black truck pulled up next to Harry and me in the parking lot.

"There he is," my fake boyfriend said as he moved toward the pickup.

James.

My stomach was still flipping from when I'd heard his voice earlier. For several minutes after we hung up, I debated if I should save his number or erase the message thread Harry had started.

I saved the number, telling myself that, like Harry said, I would only use it in case of an emergency.

The two men chatted on the other side of the vehicle before coming around to the truck bed where James popped the door open. He handed his cousin a roll of twine before reaching in for a red canvas bag he slung over his shoulder. The two men approached me where I stood waiting near the entrance to the Christmas Village.

"Hi," I said around a burst of nerves.

He was wearing one of those ridiculous-looking fur-lined hats with earflaps. Those hats were supposed to be silly, but somehow, he made it work. Despite the thick jacket and pants he wore, all I could think about was the way his bare back had looked this morning. How his naked arm felt brushing against mine...

If he pulled out an ax at any point today, I might spontaneously combust.

"Emma," he said with a sexy head nod and a dirty look at my clothing. It was becoming a pattern with him, having a problem with my clothes.

Harry clapped his gloved hands together in a muffled sound to draw our attention. "Alright, my two favorite people—"

That was an alarming statement. I hoped he was faking it for James' benefit, because a designation as one of Harry's favorite people seemed way out of touch.

"We are on a mission today to find and secure two Christmas trees. These will, ideally, be of fine quality yet also lonely in some way. Perhaps they will be trees standing alone in their rows. Perhaps they will have some minor defect that deters other Christmas tree cutters. We will not rest until we secure two such trees. Are we ready?"

That was...intense. Who would have thought the guy cared so much about anything, let alone sad evergreens?

James and I followed Harry's lead, and the three of us walked through the busy, arched entry to the farm.

Meyer's Christmas Village offered a wide variety of fir trees, I soon learned. It was overwhelming. I recalled getting actual trees as a child but always purchased from the local big box hardware store. The last few years, my parents had opted for an artificial one instead.

Harry was insistent that a Fraser fir would be the best species. Something about having the strongest branches to hold the heaviest ornaments. I didn't ruin the fun by telling him I owned no ornaments.

After getting into a tractor and trailer filled with several seats of Christmas Village patrons, we journeyed past rows upon rows of the other, inferior, Christmas tree varieties. Families hopped off the trailer every so often until it was our turn.

Close to an hour later, I was cold to the bone and arguing with Harry.

"For the last time, Harry, I do not need a gigantic tree. I live in a tiny apartment."

"Emma, this *cannot* be your ideal tree. You could have found this in the parking lot of any old grocery store. There is nothing special about it. Christmas trees are supposed to be special."

I had long ago crushed my paper hot chocolate cup. Harry was like a dog with a bone.

A deep voice cut in. "Harry. Let it go. It's not your decision to make."

"Really, James, now you want to get involved?" I turned on the tall, bearded man, launching the scrap of cup at him. It landed just short of his boots.

I knew it was unfair. Poor James had been lugging around the large tree Harry picked for their house for the last forty-five minutes. Of course Harry had found *his* ideal tree within minutes of getting off the trailer.

But I couldn't forgive James for only stepping in now, when I was practically a popsicle. I had cast *at least* six to seven beseeching looks his way while Harry droned on. He ignored all of them.

I was lucky he had made eye contact with me at all this afternoon. James was strangely quiet, not even snarking at his cousin.

The look he fired at me now had me regretting inviting his notice.

"Did you just throw garbage at me?" Warm hazel eyes turned into black storm clouds. "The two of you are acting like fucking children right now. Harry, Emma decides on her own tree. Emma, grow up. Just pick the damn thing so I can cut it, and let's go. Now."

"Whoa," Harry said.

A shiver traveled down my body. Not from the cold and not from fear of James' outburst.

No, he had scolded me like an errant underling, but instead of anger, his growled order had me trembling from another kind of feeling. One that led to kisses pressed against walls, hands shackled around wrists, and red handprints on my ass that would linger for days.

If he asked me right now to drop to my knees in the snow, take his cock out of his thick pants, and suck him, I half thought I would do it. Fake boyfriend, chilled ground, and the public be damned.

Another beat of silence. A cloud of condensation gathered in the cool air as James exhaled, hard, waiting for my retort.

"This one is fine." I motioned to the tree Harry and I had been arguing about. My pseudo-boyfriend wisely stayed quiet.

I didn't speak the whole time James sawed the thin tree trunk and carted both trees back to the trailer.

CHAPTER TWENTY-TWO

Emma

I SAT IN BED later that evening, feet tucked under me, typing and deleting the message on my phone, cursor blinking back and forth, back and forth. I had to apologize to James for snapping at him at Meyer's, but I was too much of a chicken shit to do it face to face. After loading the Fraser firs in the bed of his pickup, he'd taken off in a flash.

I couldn't blame him for that. He had taken time out of his day to do me and Harry a favor. And I had returned that favor by acting like a complete bitch. James had borne the brunt of my annoyance at Harry's antics.

Fuck it, I decided, tapping SEND and settling back into my mound of propped-up pillows. I lifted the book I'd checked out from the library earlier in the week to eye level, determined not to pay attention to incoming messages.

Emma: I'm sorry.

Keeping it simple.

The phone buzzed precisely three minutes later. Not that I was counting. I fumbled to open the message.

James: What for?

Well. At least he wasn't pretending not to know it was me messaging him. I'd half prepared for that.

Emma: Throwing things at you. And snapping at you for something that wasn't your fault.

James: Is that all?

I huffed, wracking my brain for the appropriate response.

James: You better come up with some way to make it up to me.

Um, wow, okay. I sat up straight in bed. He was a man full of surprises. A double-texter. And had that last message been...suggestive?

Emma: What is that supposed to mean?

I gave him a moment to explain. Surely, he wasn't trying to imply I owed him some sexual favor, especially when he thought I was dating his cousin.

My phone vibrated in my hand again, this time in continual pulses, indicating an incoming call.

This should be good. "Hello?"

"Did that message come across creepy as fuck? Because if it did, I'm sorry. I was trying to make a joke about how you needed to repay me, like how you bought me a new burger after we bumped into each other at Maven's. Clearly, I suck at both jokes and text messaging."

I laughed, and the anxiety lifted off my chest and flew away. "How are those two scenarios related here? Would I have to un-throw garbage at you in this case?"

"I don't know! That's why it was a shit joke. It made no sense."

I relaxed back into my pillow pile and smiled at the sound of his rich chuckle.

"What are you up to right now?" I heard movement and clanking coming from his side of the line.

"Doing some stuff out in my workshop. It's late, but I got hit with a little inspiration. Figured I would roll with it."

"Yeah?" I tried to tamp down some of my excitement, but the small snapshot of his work I'd seen the night before had me giddy. I knew next to nothing about woodworking, but I had always been a sponge when it came to learning about new topics. "Will you tell me about it?"

"Hold on. I'll do you one better." A request came through to switch from voice call to video.

Oh, fuck. I had on his sweatshirt. He would have thoughts about that, even if I only wore it to keep warm in this drafty apartment. Not at all because it smelled amazing.

"Um, hang on one second." I tossed my phone onto the pink duvet and tugged the sweatshirt over my head. I had on a black tank underneath but no bra. It would be fine—the camera wouldn't display anything lower than my clavicle area unless I angled it that way. I couldn't do much about the wild bun on the top of my head, otherwise delaying the video further would become suspicious.

"Okay, I'm here," I said as I accepted the request.

"Hey," he said, his face appearing in the center of the screen.

"Hi."

We were talking like we hadn't already been on a call for several minutes.

"Want to see what I've done so far?" He had a smile on his face, eyes crinkling at the corners. He liked his work.

"I would love to."

The view flipped from James to a tabletop covered in various cuts of wood. "So, this is for one of my bigger clients, a restaurant group. They haven't given me much direction, which has been a struggle. But after talking with my friend Ben this morning, and then that debacle with the Christmas tree, I decided to just stop with the indecisiveness and decide for them."

"I'm glad our awful experience shopping for Christmas trees for *hours* was good for something, then."

That earned me another laugh. "We did not suffer in vain."

James went into greater detail about what he was building, a prototype version of a table and chairs that struck me as both unique and timeless. He hoped to nail one idea down and then plan the rest of his designs around it. He would ultimately make several different sized tables, a full bar, and a stand for the host. I didn't understand a lot of it, but it was impressive.

I felt similarly about my work at the library.

"Could I watch you make something?"

He flipped the camera back around to his face. The man looked surprised, though I wasn't sure why he would be. What he did was fascinating, and surely my interest wasn't out of the ordinary.

"You would really want to see that?"

"I'd love it, actually." I gave him a small, reassuring smile.

I could have sworn he blushed.

"It's a little hard to show you on a video call. I need both my hands." He gave a wiggle of his fingers to demonstrate.

"That's a solid point that I probably should have considered. Maybe it's a sign I need to get to sleep." I was loathe to end the call, but the long day of trekking through the tree farm after being locked out the night before was catching up to me. My eyelids felt heavy, and my brain was mush.

"You're still planning to come over tomorrow to decorate the tree with Harry, right?"

Harry and I had made the plan earlier in the day, before the spat with James. Jill and Kristi were joining us too.

"I am, yes."

"I can show you a little something in the workshop then—if you still want to, that is. I wouldn't want to intrude on your time with your boyfriend. Probably should have thought of that before I even asked." He rubbed his palm over his beard. The motion tugged down the tan skin under his eyes a fraction.

"James, your cousin had me running all over the biggest Christmas tree farm I have ever seen, looking for what he kept calling *The Ideal Tree*. I think he'll survive giving me a few minutes to look at your workspace."

"He really is something else, huh? Did he tell you where he came up with the Christmas tree idea? Because, believe me, what you saw today was not a long-standing family tradition."

"Oh my God, yes, the Charlie Brown dream! Absolutely ridiculous," I said with a laugh.

James paused, clearly caught up in a thought. Did he suspect there was something off about my relationship with his cousin?

"You can ask what you want to ask, James."

Did I want him to suspect, want him to ask if it was real?

"Is he...good to you?"

Oh God, I couldn't do this. The lying was getting harder and harder by the minute. But I had a deal with Harry, and I needed to honor that. I should never have messaged James an apology, should never have accepted his call, and should definitely *not* be setting up a private tour of his workshop. But it was too late now. If I canceled at this point, he would want to know why. I had no good explanation other than that I was inappropriately and inexplicably drawn to him.

After the workshop tour, I would stay away. No more one-on-one time. I owed that much to Harry, who, despite his quirks, was a good guy.

Not to mention, James was scary. Not in a way that I thought he would ever hurt me. His grumpy nature had been off-putting at first, but I was starting to see more sides to him. And that was the dangerous thing.

Because even if James knew I wasn't really with his cousin, even if he thought I was single and free as a bird, I wouldn't be good enough for him.

James Klein was a *man,* and I was a mess.

"Harry is a great person, and he is always, without a doubt, kind to me."

That, at least, was not a lie.

James nodded once. "Goodnight, Emma. See you tomorrow."

He ended the video call, and I was left cold, lying in my bed.

I padded over to where that royal-blue sweatshirt sat in a puddle on the floor and slipped it back on over my head.

CHAPTER TWENTY-THREE

Emma

"I KNOW IT'S A jerk move to bring up work on our day off, but did you ever hear from that last vendor about a donation for the Festival of Lights? I want to enter to win, but I need to know all my options first."

Holiday tunes were blaring through surround sound as Jill, Kristi, and I took a break from tree decorating.

We'd annoyed Harry by pausing before he was ready, so he was pouting upstairs in his bedroom.

I turned to answer Kristi's question, taking a sip of mulled wine—wine that James had generously poured for all of us. I had to give it to him. He made an excellent host despite his antisocial nature and lack of enthusiasm for the holiday cheer invading his space. Even now, he was crouched down, stoking the embers of the fire. If his ass and thighs looked incredible while doing it, I wasn't looking. I was above noticing things like that—being the greatest fake girlfriend ever.

"Not yet. The guy I talked to seemed excited to supply a prize when we first spoke, but he's been impossible to reach. I hope he's okay, but I've got to come up with a back-up plan. There are less than two weeks to go before the parade." I was doing my best to avoid asking any national chain businesses for prizes, trying to stick to local shops only. But I was running out of options.

"Who was doing the last prize?" James, still on the floor, twisted from his hips to direct his attention toward where I sat with Kristi and Jill.

I forced my attention to him. There was no way I could continue ignoring him without appearing rude.

His hazel eyes sparked in the firelight.

I looked away again. "Art Wilson, from the craft supply store. He said he was going to put together a gift basket of knitting supplies and instructions on how to make an ugly Christmas sweater."

"Art gets big ideas but struggles to follow through. I'll throw something together for you." He rose from his position at the fireside in one smooth motion and stowed away the fireplace poker.

I blinked in surprise. At Jill's insistence, he had already donated a generous gift card to be used toward a piece of custom furniture. Anything more was above and beyond.

"Jimbo, you are the best, most kick-ass big brother ever."

He rolled his eyes. "I'm your only big brother. You wouldn't know the difference, even if I wasn't the best, which I am."

Jill snorted as her brother sauntered away toward the kitchen. I followed his path with my eyes.

"That was really nice of him to offer," I said after he disappeared from view.

"He has his moments, for sure. He's been way more chill with me lately, which is good. I guess he's more focused on Harry. Would you mind working out the arrangements with him? I would, but I'm slammed at my other jobs and won't be in the library much."

"I'll take care of it, Jilly Bean," Kristi said. "No need to force Emma to deal with your brother's grumpy ass more than necessary.

Although, I will say he is being a lot nicer to you tonight, Emma. What's up with that?"

I was seeing why Jill thought Kristi was psychic.

"Oh, nothing major. We agreed to a truce the other night is all." With any luck, my nonchalant tone would deter the woman from probing further.

Harry slid into the room on socked feet. "Alright, party people, it's time we started decking out this tree again. Chop chop!" Harry clapped his hands together and cranked the sound system up several more ticks.

Break time was over.

CHAPTER TWENTY-FOUR

James

I HID IN THE kitchen while Christmas chaos reigned in my living room. The holiday was tough without Mom, even a few years after her death. I preferred to lie low. I figured Harry was doing the opposite, leaning hard into the happy traditions as a distraction. As for Jill, I couldn't even speculate. She never talked about Mom.

I faced the stove, heating another pot of mulled wine, when Emma entered the room. I didn't hear or smell her, but I knew it was her all the same, as if some thread inside me was now tied to one in her.

It was damn inconvenient being shackled with the sensation.

She had been strangely avoidant the entire night, so her seeking me out was a surprise. I was waiting for her to come up with some reason not to come out to the workshop.

"That smells great," she said as I glanced at her over my shoulder.

I went back to stirring in the mulling spices. If I looked at her too long, I'd start noticing things like how pretty she looked, and how her white sweater hugged her breasts, and...

I whipped the whisk around the pot of sloshing alcohol. "Want another glass?"

"Just one more. I've got to drive home after this."

I waited. She clearly had something to say.

Emma cleared her throat. "I wanted to tell you how much I appreciate you offering to donate a second prize to the Christmas booth. You didn't have to do that."

The wooden spoon I had been using to stir the wine clattered as I slammed it in the spoon rest, betraying my attempt at acting casual.

"I didn't agree to do it because I felt obligated, so stop with that line of thinking."

"Even so, you don't need to do anything over the top. A second gift card is fine. You're busy, and the last thing I want to do is add to that."

"I'm not doing another gift card. Art promised a basket, and I'll think of something similar. I'm not too busy."

I sure as hell *was* too busy, but I would never admit it.

"Okay. Well, I better get back out there before Harry yells at me again. You should come back out too, grab a glass and make it fun."

"We'll see. But no wine for me. I fucking hate this mulled shit." The idea of hot wine made me gag.

Emma tilted her head in silent question. "Why'd you make it, then?"

Because you made one off-hand comment to Harry at the tree farm about liking it. Because I'm pathetic and obsessed.

"No reason."

CHAPTER TWENTY-FIVE

Emma

"THIS LOOKS GREAT, HARRY." I had to give the man credit. His neuroses about the tree and the decorations had paid off because the house looked amazing—like the set of a Hallmark movie. Jill and Kristi had taken off a few minutes before, and James had disappeared again, leaving Harry and me alone to survey our finished product. The cozy winter wonderland made the thought of going back to my stark, drafty apartment less and less appealing.

Harry sketched an elaborate bow. "Thank you, madam. I'll grab a few presents to put under the tree now that it's set up." He skipped into the dining room, carrying back two large, wrapped boxes, along with a few gift bags, the handles twisted in his fingers.

"Starting early this year, huh? I haven't even started my Christmas shopping."

Picking out presents made the idea of my parents' visit seem real.

"Oh, most of those are ones James bought. He's Mr. Prepared every year. Me and Jill are last-minute shoppers too." He arranged the gifts, stepped back, and rearranged them again.

"Perfect," he said as he completed the arrangement and tossed himself backward onto the leather couch.

"You did a wonderful job with this," I repeated. "Sorry I've been a bit of a Grinch. Between the booth for the parade and my parents coming to town, I've been stressed out."

He reached a hand over and gave me a friendly pat on the leg. "No worries, Ems. I sprung this on you at the last minute, but you were a good sport overall. Don't be too concerned about your mom and dad visiting either. We can pull this off, I promise. Makes me wish my mom could come this year, but she said the flights were ridiculous."

"How long has she lived out of state?"

"Right around twelve or thirteen years now. She moved just before my Aunt Callie died."

"That must have been hard, losing your aunt and your mom moving away around the same time." And here I was, complaining about my mom and dad wanting to visit for a week. They drove me crazy, but at least I still had them.

"It would have been a lot worse if it weren't for James. He let me move in here with him after he inherited the place, helped me get a stable job and everything. I was bouncing around from job to job a lot, but the mechanic thing has been awesome. James is more like a brother since our moms were so close. It's why I hate when he's disappointed in me."

I smiled, a pit of unease in my gut. The weight of our fake-dating lie was growing more and more intolerable. But how could I back out after hearing Harry say *that*?

A heavy clock clanged the time, and he shot up, shaking the couch.

"Oh shit, is it already seven?"

"Looks like it. Why?" He hadn't mentioned other plans.

"I've gotta go. I'm so sorry, Ems. At least you have your car this time. Lock the door behind you on your way out." Harry skidded over to the hallway closet, pulled on a thick jacket, and hopped into his boots. In an instant, he disappeared with a slam of the heavy front door.

The house was quiet. Still no sign of James. I wondered if he, too, had left.

So much for the plan for me to see his workshop.

I busied myself, picking up scattered wine glasses and taking them to the sink.

A noise came from out in the backyard as I finished rinsing. Out the back window, I saw a barn with light shining from under its door. A trail of boot prints was visible on the snow-covered paving stones that led from the kitchen door to the barn.

I found James.

A minute of silent debate followed, then I slipped into my coat and shadowed the footprints on the paving stones.

CHAPTER TWENTY-SIX

James

EMMA CAME IN THROUGH the sliding barn door as I ran a long board along my jointer, flattening the wood into a smooth, straight edge. Nothing fancy but satisfying as fuck when done right.

I pulled down the respirator mask that protected my lungs from wood dust.

"Hey," I greeted her. Eloquent. Just call me William Shakespeare.

"Hi. I was wondering where you had disappeared to."

"Surprised you didn't take off already."

Her brow furrowed just the tiniest bit. My fingers itched to smooth away those thin lines of worry.

"Why would you think that?" she asked. "We agreed to it last night, didn't we?"

I cut in before she could run off. "Stay. I'm not kicking you out."

"Sure seemed like it." Her accompanying foot stomp was cute, but I wisely kept my mouth shut.

"You're welcome here. You just seemed a little...uninterested earlier. I won't make you do anything you don't want to do. If you changed your mind, it's fine."

"I'm here now, aren't I?"

I nodded. "Guess you are."

"Can I come in further? Or do I need, like, equipment and stuff?"

"You can come in. I'll let you know if you need a mask or eye protection. I'm not doing anything too crazy tonight. There's a space heater over near my toolbox if you get chilly." I pointed over to the corner.

I watched from a distance as she strolled over. She had to be freezing in that thin jacket and canvas sneakers. The woman never dressed for the damn weather, always shivering and shaking in threadbare clothing.

I watched, rapt, as she ran one gold-painted fingernail along the matte metal of my toolbox. I could almost feel that fingertip running along my skin, a straight line to my cock.

What the fuck was wrong with me? I was getting hard watching this woman touch a fucking toolbox, for God's sake.

"This might be the biggest toolbox I've ever seen."

"It's huge." Fuck. I coughed. I had to stop thinking about my dick. "But, uh, yeah, it's nothing out of the ordinary in my line of work. Expensive as hell, though. You haven't been in many workshops, I take it?" I could name a million people with similar setups. Unique, I was not.

"James, I work in a library. What do you think?"

I shot out a laugh through my nose. The dangerous ease, so present in our late-night phone call, was back. "Plenty of librarians have hobbies. I'm pretty sure Tracy has been taking a flying trapeze class on Thursday nights."

"No shit? I'd love to try that sometime, but I'm afraid of heights. I'm not a librarian, so I can only aspire to be that cool."

"What are you if not a librarian, then? And yes, I am aware that not everyone who works in a library is one. Jill reamed me out a couple years ago for even suggesting that."

"My undergrad degree is in social work, but I wasn't sold on any of the available jobs in that field. I helped with community outreach at the local library at home, as a part-time thing, and realized I liked it. I got my Master's degree online in business administration, concentrated on marketing. I finished that about two years ago, and now, here I am."

"Smart girl. I can see why Tracy hired you."

Emma grinned at me. I felt like I got hit with a tractor beam of pure sunshine, straight to the heart.

"Thanks. It's my first *big girl job*. I want to live up to her expectations. Greyport Public Library has a great reputation in the community. I'm lucky I ended up here."

"They're lucky to have you too." I busied my hands, lining up a stack of wood panels. "And uh...you'd never have met Harry if you hadn't come here either."

There. I was trying not to be a complete piece of shit.

"Yes...that is true." She drummed her fingers along the metal toolbox, producing a hollow tinny sound. "Speaking of Harry, did he mention to you he had other plans for tonight?"

That was strange. "Nope. He's not still here? I just assumed he was being a baby about coming out here while it was cold."

"No, he rushed off right at seven. Acted like he had somewhere important to be. I was hoping you might know."

Harry had been busier lately, but I had attributed it to Emma's appearance in his life. If he wasn't with her, what was he doing?

"Not a clue. I can ask him when he gets home."

Emma shook her head, the brightness of the hanging lamps shining off her dark hair. "That's okay. This is new, me and him. I don't want to crowd him. He'll tell me when he's ready."

"If you're sure."

She tipped her chin down once. "Positive. Now why don't you show me some of your secret woodworking magic?"

Chapter Twenty-Seven

Emma

WHEN HE WORKED, GRUMPY grump James Klein lit up like the very Christmas tree we spent hours decorating. I refrained from telling him that—I was starting to realize that he was self-conscious. But it was the truth, and seeing his passion in person was even better than hearing it through the phone. He was setting up wood for me to sand while he did other, more complicated tasks, chattering away about what made his process work.

The safety glasses and mask should have dimmed his impact, but honestly, the man was wearing a leather apron over the top of a dark Henley shirt, sleeves shoved up to his elbows. It was lethal.

I never thought I had a type before now. My dating history was brief. One relationship lasted around a year and a half, and a few others a couple of months. The men I dated varied in race, body type, and style. But it was like someone had crafted James Klein in a lab just for me, piecing together everything I liked about the men of my past into one crazy-hot package.

Too bad he would never, ever go for me, because he was a good person, and I was dating his cousin.

And after tonight, after my talk with Harry, I wouldn't dream of giving away the plan he had hatched up. Not when I now knew why it was so important to him.

James was completely out of my league. He was a proper adult, as made abundantly clear by the professional setup he had going on.

"You ready?"

I jumped. Last I'd looked, he was on the other side of the shop. A safe, comfortable distance away. Now he was right alongside my elbow, holding up a handheld sander.

I smiled gamely. "Ready."

It wasn't long before I realized I was not ready—not at all. The sander flew wildly across the wood cut James had given me. The neon-green tool fell to the floor with an explosive clatter.

"Shit! I am so sorry. I'm really, really bad at this."

With an affectionate smile, James shook his head before refocusing on his project. At least he wasn't getting upset with me for ruining whatever I was sanding.

I bent down to grab the sander again, placing it back on the wood piece. Concentrating, I restarted, using the method James had shown me. He'd made it appear so stupidly simple I hadn't thought I would need much direction.

I had been very, very wrong. I couldn't seem to get into the groove like he did, with his smooth, effortless motion. Meanwhile, he was at the opposite end of the shop, cutting on an enormous machine. He referred to it as some sort of saw, though I didn't remember the exact name.

My focus fell from the rough cut of wood and toward the man. His shoulders flexed beneath the fabric of his tight shirt as he lifted and pushed around heavy stacks of material.

The large saw rested on a table that met him at hip height. I bit my lip as my favorite part of his routine was about to happen. At any moment, he would use the strength in his hard thighs to press the wood firmly against the guide where he was cutting.

Thrusting. Hard. Rhythmically.

Who knew building custom furniture could be so hot?

"You're a great teacher, you know that?"

He was. His patience with my struggle spoke volumes.

He paused his work. "You think so? I've been thinking of taking on an apprentice, but...I don't know. Not sure I'd be any good at that."

"You should. If I—ow, fuck!" My hand slipped off the sander, and a sharp poke jabbed the skin of my palm, right at the base of my thumb. The sander stopped spinning.

I lifted my hand to find a large splinter stuck in my skin. Despite the lack of visible blood, my head spun, like it was still running along with the sandpaper.

"What the fuck happened? Are you okay?" James rushed over, cradling my elbow and raising my injured hand to his eye level.

I offered him a shaky smile. "I suck at woodworking."

"Here, sit down." He used his firm grip on my arm to guide us to a stool. The chill of the metal seat seeped through my jeans, and I gasped.

James knelt down, one knee on the hard concrete, looking up at me with worry in his hazel eyes. "You dizzy at all?"

"At first, but it's getting better. I just can't look at the splinter, or I'll get wobbly again." I focused on my breathing, willing down my panic.

Once upon a time, I had been tough with blood-and-guts type stuff. Riding bikes and climbing trees as a kid, followed by a short stint with field hockey in middle school, had meant exposure to the odd skinned knee, sprained wrist, and yes, even a few splinters from time to time. But ever since the accident, even the smallest of injuries had the power to send me reeling.

"Can you feel my hand holding yours?" James asked. I kept my eyes locked on his as I nodded. "How about your feet flat on the floor? Can you feel those too?"

"Yes," I whispered.

"Good girl, Emma. This happens all the time. I know it hurts, but you're doing such a good job." His voice was a deep rasp.

He tugged a clean, white cloth from his apron pocket and pressed it to the side of the splinter, applying slight pressure. I twitched from the pinching sensation, but the shard of wood didn't budge.

"Sorry. I have some numbing spray across the room, but I don't want to risk you passing out and falling off this stool. The last thing we need is for you to crack your head open."

Somehow that made me laugh, though my belly was still flip-flopping.

James gave me that eye-crinkling smile. "I have an idea. Hold still for me, okay?"

"Okay."

His head bent to where he held onto my fingers. The dark waves of his hair were made up of a whirl of colors—brown, and black, and iridescent blue. I wanted to sink my hands into it, into the slight curl at the nape of his neck, twisting it around my fingers and tugging. Not enough to hurt, but enough to sting while I guided him closer and closer and closer, directing him to the spot where I was wet and needy.

The heat of his mouth was on me then, warm on the cool skin of my palm, sending a trail of goosebumps up my arm. In one smooth, precise motion, he grabbed the small wood fragment between his teeth and pulled it free. I tried to pull back, to close my palm, but he held fast.

His gaze held mine as he spit the splinter onto the floor.

The sound of our breathing echoed through the barn. I was light-headed once more—but for an entirely different reason.

James broke our stare first, as if only now recalling where we were, who I was, what we were doing. His throat bobbed.

"Don't look down. There's a little blood."

He brought the white cloth up to my hand again, first dabbing and then applying pressure with his thumb.

A gust of wind whistled outside, bringing me out of my James-induced trance. I shivered once, cold everywhere except for where our fingers still touched.

"Um. I think I'm okay now." I pulled out of his grasp to cradle my wounded palm against my stomach.

"Yeah. Sure," he said, sounding dazed as he pushed to standing.

He towered over me for a moment before backing up one, then two steps, and turning.

I was powerless to look away from the hard lines of his back as I sat curled in on myself on that hard stool.

Whatever had passed between us, I knew James felt it too.

I could barely make out his profile in the dimming light. It was a long time before he spoke.

"I'll put some antiseptic and a bandage on the kitchen counter for you. Go home, Emma."

He didn't have to tell me not to come back again. I heard it all the same.

CHAPTER TWENTY-EIGHT

Emma

I RUSHED INTO THE library's small conference room on Monday morning. All the focus was on the impending Festival of Lights parade and associated fundraising activities, my booth being one of the major efforts.

I had been up late the night before after getting home from James and Harry's house. My kitchen sink was leaking, a steady drip from under the cupboard onto the warped linoleum. My landlord's emergency call line—the number now saved in my phone contacts—went unanswered. I had made an impromptu trip to the local hardware store and purchased a bucket. It wouldn't stop the leak, but it would protect the floor until the landlord called me back.

There was one upside to dealing with a leaky sink. Worrying about that meant I wasn't thinking about the James situation, not until I was tossing and turning in bed long past midnight.

My palm was still tender, but worst of all, my hip was flaring up with soreness. Too many nights with too little sleep were doing me in. I couldn't keep up these hours. Between late nights with new friends, ruminating over my complicated feelings, and now trying to piece back together my falling-apart apartment, the crash and burn seemed inevitable.

I scooted my squeaky chair up to the long conference table and cast my undivided attention to what had brought me here in the first place—Greyport Public Library.

"Good morning, Emma," Tracy said, all bright-eyed and bushy-tailed. "Grab a bagel while we get started. I got a box from Brett Brothers Bagel House this morning. They're hot and fresh."

Glorious carbs. It was the little things in life.

I shifted around in my chair, trying—and failing—to find a position that would take the pressure off my aching hip. I still needed to talk with Tracy about getting approval for something with more support, but for some reason, I kept putting it off. Mom would yell at me for waiting this long to bring it up, but she wasn't the one who had to deal with it day in and day out.

I stretched my leg out under the table, finding a little relief. I made apologetic eye contact with Glenn when my foot brushed his, and he smiled back.

The meeting concluded, and we all parted ways, moving to our separate areas of the building. I was gathering up my things when Kristi stopped me outside her office door.

"Hey, Em. I'm glad I caught you. James messaged me early this morning to tell me he's got the second prize ready to go for the booth. He said he'll hang on to it until the day before, just in case it needs last-minute changes. Want to see a picture?"

Kristi gave her phone a wiggle. I clamped down the urge to snatch the device before she handed it over.

On the screen was a beautiful and ornate drawer insert with cut-outs for silverware. A set of gorgeous wooden spoons laid to the side, wrapped in a sparkling red ribbon.

I grazed the photo with my fingertips, wishing I could touch the wood grain through the display. "Wow. I didn't realize he made things like this."

"I'm fairly sure that man could make anything, including my babies if he wanted."

"Oh." My face fell.

"Okay, what just happened?" The purple-haired woman eased the phone from my claw-like clutches.

"N-nothing, I'm super out of it, and tired, and in pain, and—"

Kristi took me by the shoulders and ushered us into my cramped office. "Emma. Girl. Sit down for a minute."

Crowded in a small room with a psychic was the last place I wanted to be. I looked for an escape route, tried to come up with an excuse to leave, but Kristi was already shutting the door.

"So, are cutlery trays, like, especially triggering for you, or did my comment about making babies with James freak you the fuck out?"

"Oh my God," I said with a groan, burying my head in my hands.

"Before you spiral even more, I will mention that I was joking. James is sexy, talented, responsible, and somehow also a nice person, but there is zero romantic chemistry between him and me. It might even be hovering in the negatives at this point. The chemistry between *you* and James, however, is off the charts."

I made an indecipherable, involuntary sound. I had no way to explain the situation to Kristi, not without totally and completely blowing my cover story. But the alternative was to seem like the most uncaring and disloyal girlfriend ever.

"You may as well come out from under there so we can talk like adults. You can't hide forever."

"I know," I said, dragging out the word. I peeked out from behind my fingers to see the other woman sitting on a wooden crate, smiling serenely, one leg crossed over the other as her lacy black skirt brushed her ankles.

"Hi there." She gave a jaunty wave.

"Stop being funny. I have a serious problem here."

"I would love to help with your problem, but you're mumbling. Speak up and tell Madame Kristi all about how you're torn between the strong, handsome wood man and the hot, charming car guy."

I tossed my hands on my cluttered desk in a loud slap. "It sounds horrible when you put it that way."

"Well, what way is it, then? Because objectively, it does sound a little horrible to have a thing for a guy while you're dating his cousin. Just saying."

"It's...complicated."

"So un-complicate it," she said, popping a handful of tiny breath mints into her mouth.

"That's the problem. I don't know how to get out of this mess. I have no idea what I'm doing."

"Some people say I'm a fount of good advice."

"Do they now?" The tension in my body loosened in the face of Kristi's non-judgmental stance.

But would she understand once she had the full story? Once she found out I had been lying to her and Jill since the night our friendship began?

I would have to take that chance.

"I'll start with the disclaimer that Harry and I are not a real couple."

"What. No way. I never would have guessed that in a million years," she deadpanned.

I gave her a flat look.

She had the audacity to laugh. "It's not my fault it's so obvious. You appeared in town, and suddenly, Harry was dating you. We barely knew you as coworkers at that point, but somehow, he had established an entire relationship? Plus, you give more sibling vibes than anything. I suspected when I first saw you with him. Now, when you and James interact? Phew." Kristi fanned her face.

My cheeks warmed. "I mean, I did have sex with Harry. That would be pretty gross if we were siblings." I had to at least try defending my poor performance.

"And was it good sex? Did you go back for more?"

"It was fine. Orgasms happened. And no."

"My point exactly. A mediocre one-night stand doesn't always transition to a meaningful connection once you get to know a person. I have great orgasms with my vibrator on the regular, but I'm not in a relationship with a piece of purple silicone, you know? The real question is, why are you pretending to be a couple?"

"Before I get into it, can you tell me if Jill suspects too? I'm not sure how much more humiliation I can take, so I'd like to prepare myself for that inevitable confrontation."

"Jill has no idea. I haven't said anything to her about my suspicions. From the day I met you, I had a gut feeling that you're a good person. I figured the lie was for good reason, and you would come clean eventually. As for Jill, from what she's told me, she believes you and her cousin are dating for real. Although, she did tell me she thinks you're too good for him and will ultimately dump him for being a man-child. She doesn't see your smoking sexual tension with her brother either, which, for her sake, is for the best."

"It's going to sound pathetic on my part."

"Do you know how many pathetic things I've done in my life? You don't get to the age of thirty without at least a few of those moments. Now, stop delaying and spill."

I launched into the story, starting with my hookup with Harry and the initial standoff with James, before moving on to Harry's plan to impress his cousins. I did my best to give only vague details about Harry's reason for the deception. After our talk around the Christmas tree, I could tell he hid a lot under his cheerful, friendly facade. I wouldn't divulge his insecurities.

Kristi listened with steepled fingers, interjecting every so often. I could envision her sitting at a round table with a swirling crystal ball before her.

When the time came to reveal my personal motivation for the girlfriend plan, I clammed up.

"Emma. Jill and I were talking about inviting you to hang out for weeks. Before we even thought you were dating Harry. You're awesome. You don't need a boyfriend, fake or otherwise, to find people to befriend you."

"Yeah, but have you ever just felt...alone? I know it's silly, and you have all been so welcoming. But moving here, all alone, after living in a home where my parents were practically on top of me all the time? It was scary. It still is scary."

"I did the same thing years ago, so yes. I can't say I would have pretended to date someone in order to overcome that, but who knows? The opportunity never presented itself. But now that you have established friends, why not jump to the breakup and focus on getting to know the guy you actually like?"

"For one thing, my parents are expecting to meet Harry. And for another, nothing is going to happen between me and James, so there's no point in rushing to split up."

Kristi snickered. "You keep telling yourself that. If I had that kind of chemistry with another person, I would be all over it. That doesn't happen every day. What if you never feel it again?"

"How do I even know James would want me?"

"I think it's pretty damn evident."

"Not to me! He's so...put together and successful. You said it yourself when you listed all his amazing qualities. I'm...a mess. And that's putting it lightly."

"I think you're selling yourself short, but that's something you have to address within. Keep an open mind."

I inhaled, a well of panic rising in my throat. "I just don't think I'm ready to be the person James deserves. Besides, I'm not looking for anything serious, and I'm sure he is."

"Well, if you don't intend to be honest with him about the situation with his cousin, then I hate to say it, but I think your only option is to spend as little time with James as possible. Because one of these days, all that combustive energy is bound to explode. And a lot of people are going to get caught in the blast."

CHAPTER TWENTY-NINE

James

I BRUSHED A LAYER of sawdust off a freshly smoothed tabletop, relishing the texture of the wood grain under my callused palms. The McGuire team had given me solid feedback on my newest plans, and the prototypes were nearly finished.

It wasn't hard to pinpoint the source of my creative burst. It had been several days since Emma's visit to the workshop, and the energy she left behind still lingered.

I couldn't see the rusted old stool she'd been sitting on without wondering how she would have tasted if I had just taken things one step further. Just crossed that line, taken one of her graceful fingers between my lips and sucked. I imagined the sounds she would make, all the breathy, moaning exhales in my ear.

Fuck, I couldn't even look at my sander without thinking of straight-up porn-worthy scenarios.

Thank God, Klein Custom was a company of one. Explaining to someone else why I was getting turned on by power tools would have been embarrassing as hell—not to mention an HR nightmare.

Maybe it was simply old-fashioned lust with a helping of guilt and jealousy to go with it. I wouldn't examine it too closely. As long as I kept my distance and didn't say a word to Harry, I could ride it out until the feeling subsided.

I glared at the cutlery tray and spoon set sitting on one of my work benches. I'd stayed up late into the night after Emma had left on Sunday, crafting the pieces for her booth. If anyone asked, I'd done it for my sister. But it was impossible to lie to myself.

The heavy barn door slid on its tracks, and Harry poked in his thick head of hair. My cousin still wore his coveralls from the garage along with a smear of grease across his cheek.

"What's up?" I hadn't expected to see him home so early in the day.

"Hey, man. I finished up my jobs early. You want to go do something? We could hit up the gym since it's been a while."

"You sure you don't want to hang out with your *girlfriend* on the one day you get out early?" The word was bitter on my tongue.

Harry hooked his thumbs in the pockets of his coveralls. "Nope. You and I haven't spent much time together lately."

"Not my fault. You're the one with all the big-boy obligations now." God, when had I gotten so damn bitchy? I took a gulp of air and shot it out in a forceful exhale. "But you did organize the day at Meyer's Christmas Village and the tree decorating party last weekend, so I won't give you a hard time. Let's go."

The whole ride to the gym, I held onto the memory of the infectious grin on Harry's face when I agreed to go with him. We even had a pleasant conversation without the tension and frustration that seemed ever present the last few weeks. Now that I'd gotten to know Emma, I could see she wasn't the cause of the rift. But something *was* going on with my cousin.

The gym was close to empty as we changed, only more of that obnoxious synth-pop filtering through the open space.

"You plan on talking my ear off the whole time?" I asked as I lowered my body onto a weight bench. The man had a habit of chattering his way through most of my sets. He was a good spotter, though.

Harry grinned, pushing a stray curl off his brow. "You know it."

I shook my head. He didn't do anything silently.

"So, have you come around at all on Emma? She was kinda...you know...at the tree farm, but overall, she's cool as hell."

I wiped a drip of sweat off my forehead before switching places with Harry. "And how was she at the tree farm?" I wasn't sure I liked the implication behind his tone.

"She bit your head off, dude! You don't need to worry that you'll offend me by being honest. She was acting like a you-know-what."

I was tempted to leave him alone with the weight of the barbell, but that was a step too far. "If you won't even say the word, you shouldn't be implying it either. She was irritated because you put her in a shit position, and she was freezing cold. Anyone would have snapped at a time like that."

"Okay, *Dad*. And yeah, you're right. I already apologized to her when we were decorating the tree, and we're all good now."

Harry set off for another machine as we finished our sets. I stopped him with a glance, a non-verbal reminder to help me re-rack the weighted plates at each end of the bar.

"You don't really think I act like your dad, do you?" Neither of us had the most involved fathers growing up—part of why our moms were so close as we were growing up.

"A little."

"Are you serious right now?"

"You do realize you just scolded me for not cleaning up these weights, right? Besides, don't get mad at me for answering a question you asked. You may be six years older than me, but you don't have to act like I'm a child you can't stand half the time."

I stopped moving.

"You think I can't stand you?"

My chest was tight. Was my approach doing more harm than good?

I watched as he rubbed his hands over his curls in a frantic motion. "That was too harsh. But you're annoyed with me all the time. I know some of it's my fault. I do fuck up a lot." He pasted on a smile. "But hey, it's a good thing my girl is so patient, right?"

He stared at me, waiting for me to laugh.

I couldn't conjure one. "Speaking of *your girl*, why does it seem like you're running away from her or flat out ignoring her sometimes?"

He sighed, collapsing, loose-limbed, onto the seat of a rowing machine. "I'm not ready to tell you yet, but I am disappearing for a good reason, okay?"

"And you won't just tell me what that reason is?"

"No, because then you will feel the need to give me advice, and I won't be able to say I did it on my own. I need to do this on my own, Jay."

I bit down on the urge to argue. No way I was *that* bad about giving unsolicited advice. I just didn't want to see Harry struggle. Wasn't it clear to him that it stemmed from care and love?

At least Jill still needed me.

"Ugh, I can see it all over your face that you're upset. Don't take it personal, okay? This is about me and only me for a change. You've done so much to help me over the years, and I want to pay you back. I mean it."

I had to admit, that was admirable—and strangely grown up.

"What inspired this? Because a few months ago, when I dared mention you moving out, you got all weird."

Don't say Emma. Don't say Emma.

"To be honest, it's Emma. She makes me feel like I can do and be more."

And there it was. For my cousin, this was more than a casual fling.

"Here she is, moving so far from her family and making her way in a brand-new town. And can you believe she's only twenty-six? Three years younger than I am, but way more accomplished. She's so amazing, and she picked me."

I swiped off another bead of sweat, hiding my face behind a thin gym towel. I understood in that moment that I had carried a bizarre hope that Harry didn't like Emma. That the disappearing act he kept pulling was a sign he wasn't invested. As if that would absolve me of my guilt for wanting Emma for my own.

Fuck, my first shameful thought when Harry had mentioned her age was that she was nine years younger than me, wondering if she would ever go for a thirty-five-year-old.

I had to bury every fleeting thought I had about this woman six feet under.

"I'm happy for you," I said with a gulp, clapping Harry on the shoulder with feigned enthusiasm.

We finished our workout not long after, too exhausted to continue. When we got home, I stopped Harry as he was hopping down from the truck. "Hey. Don't think for a second that I forgot about this mysterious plan you've got going." He shot me a snappish look, and I threw my hands up in defense. "I won't force it. You're right that I need to back off a bit. Come tell me when you're ready."

"Jay, why don't you spend less time worrying about me and a little more time focusing on yourself. Have some fun, get a hobby. Get laid. Things you haven't done in the last century." He flicked me off with a grin before turning and heading into the house.

I dropped my head down on the steering wheel. If only he knew *who* I wanted to get laid up in bed with.

Chapter Thirty

Emma

I WAS HIDING.

The last few days, I had thrown myself into prep for the Christmas parade with gusto, finishing up last-minute trimmings for the booth and printing off activity calendars to display.

And avoiding all unnecessary human interaction.

Each night after work, I scoured local thrift stores for anything to spruce up my apartment before my parents' arrival. A tiny bistro table and set of chairs was my favorite purchase so far. A cheap fabric tablecloth in an over-the-top reindeer print concealed the large gouge on the table's surface.

My mind wandered to James' workshop and the furniture he could create for this space. Jill had told me all about the custom pieces he had built for her studio apartment. It sounded like a dream. Far better than my hodge-podge of alternatives.

I surveyed the apartment from my sunken-in position on the plaid couch, pleased with my work so far. I'd even managed to decorate my own Christmas tree, though the cheap plastic bulbs I'd bought from the discount store left much to be desired.

It was nothing like the picturesque holiday movie-worthy scene at James and Harry's house.

I was spent, burdened with the weight of fatigue from the weekend prior and a demanding work week. But the most troubling part was that I was being a coward—pointedly ignoring messages from Jill, Harry, and Kristi. At least I had the excuse of needing a hefty dose of well-deserved rest. Lugging the thrift store table up the steep flight of stairs had kicked my ass. Even the short walk down to Greyport Grinds, just under my living room floor, was too daunting to consider.

I shifted on the sofa, struck by another twinge of pain in my hip. With a sigh, I rolled off the couch, started up my favorite folk-rock playlist, and settled into my mobility routine. It was long overdue. My former PT would be furious knowing how long I'd been neglecting the exercises.

In a burst of vibration, my phone rattled off the beat-up coffee table and onto the bare wood floor. I didn't bother reaching for it and continued with hip openers, trailing my legs through the movement.

It was most likely my fake boyfriend. He had reached out the day before, wanting to plan a public outing. I took one look at his message and shuttered my phone. Harry might be upset with me for phoning it in, but my energy levels were too sapped to handle his dog-like enthusiasm.

I moved into a set of sumo squats, dropping to the point my hip objected. My legs seemed to weigh a thousand pounds, pulling me down, down, down toward the floor with each motion.

I did a few more and then sat, flopping my head and torso down onto the couch. I had no strength left to even pull my legs up. This had been a humbling experience. Ten squats were my new pathetic limit.

Maybe if I closed my eyes for a minute...

In sleep, I could forget all about my messy relationships, my fear of appearing incompetent at my job, and worst of all, the dark thought that my parents were right. I couldn't hack it on my own.

I was too broken.

Furious pounding on the door and still-thrumming acoustic guitar from my playlist pulled me out of that hazy half-sleep. I lifted my head off the couch cushion, cocking my head to listen.

The sun was low in the sky, casting deep shadows across the room. I had no idea what time it was or how long I had been next to the couch, in and out of sleep.

The pounding noise came again as I blindly felt around for my phone. My eyes burned, like someone had rubbed them raw with James' neon-green sanding tool.

"Emma!" said a voice on the other side of the door, joined by another accompanying thud. "Open up. People have been trying to get a hold of you since last night."

"Wh—" I cleared my throat, shocked at how raspy it now sounded. When had that happened?

"Who is it?" I said, trying again with more volume, before a fit of coughing overcame me. A wave of dizziness hit, and I folded back down to the sofa.

The door creaked open. I opened my heavy eyelids to find an angry, lumbering James Klein peering into my tiny apartment.

This had to be a fever dream. There was no way the man was here, in the flesh. Not after the way he had all but abandoned me in his workshop and ordered me out of his home.

"Why wasn't this damn door locked?" he said under his breath. "Jesus, what's wrong?"

He crossed the room in three gigantic steps and crouched at my side, bringing with him the scent of clean laundry and fresh wood chips. He always smelled like that in my dreams.

His cool fingers brushed my brow. "You're burning up, baby. Let's get you into your bed. Being on the floor like this isn't good for you."

Soft, worn flannel rubbed against my cheek, and then I was floating in the air. A calm, swinging sensation was followed by sweet relief as my back pressed against a soft mattress.

I was drifting away again when James nudged me back into awareness, pressing a glass of cold water to my lips along with two white tablets. I swallowed past my rough throat.

James smoothed a strand of hair off my forehead and coaxed me down into my bed of pillows. "Good girl. Sleep now."

I nuzzled in. Dream James was the *best*.

Chapter Thirty-One

James

MY HANDS SHOOK AS I jabbed the button to end the call with my cousin. Emma was sick as a dog, and Harry didn't seem to fucking care, too busy with his stupid fucking bowling league and their stupid fucking award ceremony.

Before taking a seat on the worn-looking sofa, I checked on Emma through the cracked doorway of her bedroom, making sure my call with Harry hadn't woken her up. I breathed a sigh of relief to find her out cold, her chest rising and falling under the thick duvet.

I'd been hoping my cousin would step it up when he heard Emma was ill, would take a break from a night of fun to help. I couldn't have been more wrong. Despite his insistence he was getting his shit together, despite his supposed feelings for Emma, at the end of the day, Harry was Harry.

But I wasn't going anywhere. Not after finding Emma slumped over on the floor. The shock of pure fear when I'd walked in sent me back to the early days when my mom had first gotten sick.

I still didn't know what compelled me to come to Emma's in the first place, though I was glad I'd done it now. Harry had made an offhand remark about not hearing from her in a few days. I had thought little of it, knowing how busy the lead-up to the holiday parade could get. But when Jill said something similar, all logic left my body. I had been operating on sheer adrenaline the entire drive to Emma's place.

Here and now, though, I was in control. Taking care of people was my bread and butter. I could do it better than anything, even woodworking.

I opened up the notes section on my phone, making a list of supplies for flu recovery.

What she really needed was a new damn couch. The monstrosity in her tiny living room had a loose spring that kept poking me in the ass no matter how I shifted. I doubted I could swing a new sofa as a friendly get-well-soon gesture, though.

Instead, I stuck to sick-day essentials: a thermometer, flu medication, and chicken noodle soup. I had already forced a fever reducer into Emma before she fell asleep, locating a bottle in the bathroom cabinet. I double-checked the timer I'd set to alert me when it was time for her next dose. While she dozed, I set to searching for the other items in Emma's apartment. I could go to the local pharmacy across the street to buy what she didn't have.

In a matter of minutes, I had everything on the list in a pile on the chipped laminate of Emma's kitchen counter. Besides a general cold-and-flu liquid, I also found two other prescriptions—a muscle relaxer and a pretty heavy-duty pain med. Both bottles were mostly full.

It hit me then how little I knew about Emma. Sure, she was beautiful and funny and smart and sarcastic. I knew how she took her coffee, that she liked omelets for breakfast, that she was passionate about her job, and she hated being cold. But her background was still a mystery.

I figured the prescriptions were connected to the hip injury she had mentioned but didn't like to discuss. Her reaction to her splinter had also been strong, a lot like a panic attack. Was everything tied to the same event? I wouldn't pry, not if she was uncomfortable, but I couldn't help wanting to know.

If I had my way, I would be an expert on every nook and cranny of Emma's history, every corner of her mind and curve of her body.

A fit of coughing from the bedroom had me rushing back to her side. Her slight frame shook with the force of each cough. One hand flailed out toward her nightstand as she searched for something.

I crouched near the head of the bed to grab the glass of water I'd placed there earlier.

"Hey, Em. Let me help you." I kept my voice gentle, but inside I was a maelstrom.

"James. You're still here." Her eyes were bright, her forehead shining, as she smiled up at me sleepily.

"I'm not going anywhere." I helped her sit up and offered her a sip of cool water, keeping one hand on the glass. "Let's get you out of this sweatshirt so you aren't so warm."

I should have done that already, damn it. But I had been so focused on helping her get settled in bed I hadn't thought of it.

"Okay," she said docilely, lifting both arms straight up above her head as I tugged and pulled the blue hoodie up and off. Her hair, up in a messy bun, fell in a lopsided fashion.

If I hadn't already known she wasn't feeling well, that would have clued me in right there. Normally, she'd be giving me some sort of snark.

She sagged back down into her nest of pillows. I did my best to ignore the shadow of her dusky nipples through the thin fabric of her pale-yellow tank top. The last thing a sick woman needed was a man who couldn't control his dick.

"I'm never giving that back," Emma said, voice half muffled by her duvet.

"Huh?"

She cuddled her pillow and burrowed in further. "Sweatshirt. Mine now."

I glanced down at the blue cotton I still gripped. It was my old college sweatshirt—the one I let her borrow the night she got locked out.

She kept my sweatshirt—and wore it often enough that she was claiming it for her own. What did that mean? I squeezed the hoodie hard in my fist as I stared down at it, as if I could force answers from a hunk of faded fabric. I couldn't ask Emma. She was back asleep again, and even if she were still awake, I wouldn't interrogate her while she was half delirious.

Needing something—anything—else to do, I checked her temperature with the thermometer I had found earlier. Still higher than I would have liked, but it was coming down a bit.

Walking in a daze back to the living room, I resolved to ask her about it in the morning.

CHAPTER THIRTY-TWO

James

THE SOUND OF A ringing phone startled me out of a fitful sleep. I snatched my cell phone from the end table and quickly swiped to answer the call. If the noise woke Emma, I might murder whoever was on the other line.

"What?" I said.

"Hey, Jay. Where are you? I just got home from the award ceremony. Didn't you want to grill up a couple steaks?"

I rubbed hard at the crease between my brows. "Harry. I'm at your girlfriend's place, where she's sick with the flu. Or do you not remember that?"

"Oh, shit, dude. You're still there? I thought you were going to get Emma to sleep and head home."

"She barely knows anyone in town. I wasn't going to leave her when she needed help."

"Maybe Jill can stop by tomorrow to check on her. She's off work."

"Are you fucking kidding me, Harry? Jill can do it? How about *you* stop by to check on Emma since, I don't know, you're her *fucking boyfriend*?" My jaw muscles screamed as I gritted out the words from between clenched teeth.

"Are you serious, Jay? We just talked about this. I don't need this shit from you. Don't lecture me on how to treat my girlfriend when you haven't dated in years. You wouldn't know what to do with a woman if she fell in your lap at this point. You'd probably ask her to help set up a table saw or something."

I stayed quiet and let Harry rant. "Every time we have a decent day and you start to act like I'm not some joke to you," he continued, "you go and flip it around on me. I'm sick of it, and I'm sick of you. You wonder why I don't like to tell you things about my life. Well, this is why!"

Harry's exhalations were loud on the other end of the call.

"You done?" I asked.

"Fuck you, James."

The call went dead.

I dropped that cursed phone onto the couch, drilled my fingers into my hair, and pulled.

"James?" I looked up to see Emma standing a few feet away, squinting at me. "Is everything okay? I thought I heard yelling."

I was pissed off at the sight of her shivering, dressed only in that thin tank and a loose pair of sleep shorts. I forgot all about Harry and our argument as I walked over to her, grabbing a throw blanket from a basket on the floor as I went.

"What are you doing out of bed? You're freezing." I held both ends of the blanket tight, settling it around each of her smooth shoulders.

"Yelling. Like I said." Her head tipped to the left, like her neck was too tired to bear the weight. Her dark eyes were drifting closed again.

"Everything's okay. It was a thing between Harry and me. Nothing you need to worry about. Come on, back to bed for you."

I guided her back to her bedroom, keeping a steadying hand on the small of her blanket-covered back.

"I don't want to come between you and Harry," Emma said, stopping at her door frame.

Too late for that. I shook my head. "Not your fault."

And it wasn't, not truly.

I continued to herd her back to our destination. A touch more dilly-dallying and Emma would be asleep on her feet.

"Bed. Now," I said with a motion toward the queen-sized mattress.

"Bossy," she said back, some of that signature snark peeking through. But she listened.

"I'm sorry that I'm the one you're stuck with, Emma," I said as I closed her door. "I'm sure you'd rather have your boyfriend here."

Despite that disaster of a phone call and my cousin's insults, I would not bad-mouth him to Emma. My dreams might be riddled with dirty fantasies about Harry's girlfriend, but I still had some loyalty.

"Mmm, that's okay," she said sleepily. "He isn't my real boyfriend anyway."

My head exploded.

CHAPTER THIRTY-THREE

Emma

I T WAS THE GROWLING of my stomach that woke me in the wee hours. I padded to the kitchen on bare feet and shaky legs. My bedside table was a graveyard of messy tissues and half-full cups, but I felt half human again.

The light above the stove illuminated the room just enough for me to find food. A granola bar or a bagel—something low effort but filling enough to satisfy my nagging hunger.

"Damn it," I said under my breath. I forgot to empty the bucket under the sink before getting hit by the flu from hell. No water overflowed onto the linoleum, so maybe something was going right for me.

I used my foot to open the under-sink cupboard, bracing myself for what I was about to find.

"I fixed it last night."

"Holy shit!" I whirled around and stumbled, the small of my back colliding with the lip of the counter.

James Klein was reclining on my couch, a black baseball cap resting over his face. It was unmistakably him. And had he said he fixed my leaky sink? Maybe I *was* still feverish...

He moved the cap off his face and flipped it around so it sat backward on his head.

I was sick, but I wasn't dead. I would have to be dead not to feel a stirring in my ovaries at the sight of a backward baseball hat on this man. But why was he here, in my apartment, sleeping on my furniture?

"Don't remember much, I take it? You were pretty out of it." He kicked up to a sitting position.

My apartment had never seemed so small.

Bits and pieces of the last twenty-four hours filtered through my head. He had gotten me off the floor, given me medicine and kept me hydrated. Made me safe and secure.

"No, I remember. Thank you. I'm just surprised to see you had stayed. It's...Sunday, right?" I had been out of commission since Saturday mid-morning.

"Yep." He stared straight ahead toward my little TV. Sports highlights played on mute.

Did I do or say something to make him think less of me? Other than his general presence at the peak of my illness, the details were fuzzy. Surely, he couldn't hold that against me. So why was he acting this way?

My stomach growled, distracting me from the man and his mood. I reached above the fridge for the box of granola bars I kept there.

"I've got it."

He surrounded me, his arm stretched out alongside my own. The warm, solid heat of his chest pressed against my back.

Too soon, that warmth was gone, and he was handing me a yellow cardboard box.

"That's a shit breakfast," he said, watching me rip open the wrapper of the granola bar and tear off a chunk with my teeth.

"I don't have the energy for anything else right now," I said around a mouthful of chocolate and cashews. My energy level was already creeping lower and lower with each moment I was out of bed.

A fresh wave of coughing hit as I finished the last bite.

"Go sit down." My cranky caretaker handed me a fresh glass of water and pointed to the couch.

I watched, confused, as he pulled a small saucepan from under the stove and popped open a can.

"What," I said, pausing for another cough, "are you doing?"

"Exactly what it looks like. Making you soup."

I glanced around for the thermometer. This was definitely still a fever dream.

"But wh—why?"

"I told you. Your breakfast is shit."

"Soup isn't a breakfast food."

"It's a hell of a lot better than what you just had. Now, would you stop talking? I can't take it. I can't."

Oh, my God. An unwanted pressure rose in the back of my throat. Not a cough this time. Why was he talking like this? What had happened while I was sleeping? Sure, James had been crabby and borderline mean during our first few interactions. We weren't friends now, but I had thought he could at least *tolerate* me.

The weight of everything settled in my chest. The move to Greyport. The loneliness. The failure to make any progress with my list. The last few days running ragged. The flu. Now, James was mad at me, and I had no idea why.

The cold slap of a tear hit my clenched fist. I turned halfway and discreetly attempted to wipe the wetness from my cheeks. I would not cry in front of James Klein. If he was going to act like this when I was barely coherent, he wasn't worth a single drop of my tears.

"I don't want soup." All I wanted was for him to go home so I could cry alone.

"Emma? Are you crying?"

I looked over to see him staring me down. Of course now he was looking when I least wanted him to see me.

I shook my head in denial, but he didn't buy it. He walked closer to stand in front of me.

"Don't lie. Why are you crying right now?"

"I thought I wasn't supposed to be talking."

Ha. *Take that.*

James stuck his hands in his messy locks and groaned. The spikes left behind in his hair would have been cute if I wasn't so mad at him.

"Fuck. No. I'm so sorry. I'm a dumbass. I told you not to talk because it's making you cough."

Well. That was...considerate of him. A bit of the anger and subsequent rush of adrenaline lifted. I brushed away the last of the moisture lingering on my face.

"I get it. But you're a shit communicator." I paused again, sipping water to avoid another spell of hacking.

His full lips tipped up. "You're not wrong about that." He walked back over to the stove. "But you still need to rest your voice. *Please.*"

I curled my feet up under me as I waited. A few minutes later, he carried over a steaming bowl, placing it next to the couch. He propped one hip on the corner of my new bistro table and proceeded to watch me eat, like it was the most fascinating sight he'd ever witnessed.

His eyes were dark and menacing in the low light. I struggled to ignore him and carried on eating. I was too hungry to stop. He was right. My makeshift breakfast had been shit, and I needed the calories to refuel.

I glanced up at the tall man from under my lashes. He hadn't moved. If this version of James was the one Jill and Harry saw regularly, I could see how his attention might chafe. But to me, it was a bracing hug.

And sometimes hotter than a hug. It made me think about him turning all that single-minded attention to me in...other ways. About how he might use that stern voice of his to order me around.

Not that I was in any kind of shape to do something about it. And even if I weren't sick, that fantasy would remain locked in my head forever. Kristi had been right. James and I in close proximity was a recipe for disaster.

So how did I keep finding myself with him, again and again?

I cleared my throat as I dragged my spoon through the last dregs of chicken noodle soup. It tasted like the brand my mom bought. It probably *was* the brand Mom bought if James had found it in my cupboard. She had overloaded me with food from her own pantry when I'd packed for Greyport.

I bet James had a ready supply of soup and other staples he purchased for himself like a responsible adult. I'd put grocery shopping on the back burner the last week while dealing with my crazy schedule.

I set the empty bowl aside and braved another glance at the man. His face was in shadow, his expression offering few hints toward his mood.

"Feeling any better?" His voice came rumbling out.

"A little." The heat of the soup had helped my scratchy throat.

He nodded once, up and then down, like he was deciding on something.

"Good."

"Why do I get the sense you're waiting to pounce?"

I was running low on the bandwidth required to play games.

"Because I need to talk to you, and I'm having trouble figuring out how to say what I need to say."

"I won't break." I wasn't even fully pieced together yet. Things that weren't whole couldn't be broken.

He straightened up from his half-perch and stalked into the kitchen. I watched, stifling a reluctant laugh, as he turned around, walked toward me, and repeated the cycle. He was a pacer.

When he stopped, I gestured for him to sit down. He was too damn tall, and looking up at him strained my neck. He graciously lowered himself down to sit on the surface of the coffee table. If I stretched out my legs, our knees would touch.

"What is happening, James?"

He was so close I only needed to whisper.

"Are you and Harry really dating?"

My jaw dropped. No, no, no. This couldn't be happening. Harry was going to kill me.

"It's a simple yes or no answer, Emma."

I snapped my mouth shut, working frantically to come up with a response—any response—that might explain my hesitation.

"Never mind. You can't even answer the question." He rose to his feet and resumed pacing.

On wobbly limbs, I stood, drawing his attention. I wanted—so badly—to tell him the truth and let go of the burden of the lie, but this wasn't my secret to tell. Not only would it upset Harry but it would hurt James too. He clearly carried a responsibility to his cousin. Learning that Harry lied in order to avoid James' disappointment would kill him.

"Your cousin and I agreed to date, yes."

James laughed, but there was no humor in it. "That was some politician-level bullshit, Emma."

"You should talk to Harry."

"Well, he's not here now, is he?"

"It isn't my story to tell. Please, just talk to Harry about this."

"Harry isn't talking to me right now, Emma, and I feel like I am going insane. Just give me something here."

Too soon, he whirled around, making a noise of frustration. He stood with his back to me, arms stretched out and hands braced against the chipped kitchen counter.

The sound of his heavy breathing echoed through the silent space. He sounded...pained.

I couldn't leave him like this.

"I'm trying to find the words, James," I whispered.

"Find them faster."

He half turned, giving me his profile, that slightly crooked nose on display.

"Harry and I agreed to pose as a couple that first night you saw us at Maven's. I will not tell you Harry's reasons for it, but I can only say that I saw it as a good way to meet people and make friends. It wasn't malicious."

"That's the stupidest thing I've ever heard in my life."

I wrapped my arms over my midsection in an instinctual, protective move. "If you're just going to insult me, I won't say another word. You don't deserve my explanation. You can leave."

Fuck him and his attitude. It didn't matter how good a caretaker James was if he treated me like garbage the moment I was feeling marginally better.

He whipped around, throwing his arms out wide. "I swear, you're determined to misunderstand me. *You* aren't stupid, but it's stupid you thought you needed Harry of all people to make friends."

"I'm pretty sure I did need Harry, James. I made exactly zero friends in the first three months I lived here. Zero. I had to make a fucking list to motivate myself to get out there and socialize. And it didn't even work."

He crossed his arms. "I find it hard to believe that you had no opportunities to make friends until you made this asinine deal with my cousin."

"Believe what you want, James. You've lived here your whole damn life. You have roots and family and friends. I had none of that, and I was desperate. Before the deal with Harry, my preferred activity was sitting on a bench in Fair Street Park. I was having conversations with a slab of wood. I was so lonely it *hurt*. So don't tell me what I did and didn't need."

I looked down at my bare feet. I had told no one about the list, about the bench, and here I was, confessing it all to James in a rush of pained anger.

"Emma." I raised my gaze back up. "Everyone who meets you falls in love with you. Half the town is signing up for classes at the damn library. Jill and Kristi won't shut up about you. Christ, I made an extra prize for the Christmas fundraiser, even though I have no fucking time, for *you*."

The pulse in my ears beat wildly, overwhelming my other senses.

"I think I need to sit back down."

I swayed on my feet. James' powerful arms were there in an instant, carting me back to bed.

"You don't need to do this." I looked up at his hard-set jaw. The muscles below his ear coiled like tightly wound springs.

"Yes, I do. I got carried away. I should have waited until you were in a better state." He set me down on the mattress.

I rolled away. I couldn't look at him anymore. He was too big, too intense, too much for me to handle.

Harry was simple, good-natured, easy to please. At least, that was the side he showed to the world. But Harry was fake.

James was moody and taciturn. I never knew what side of him I was going to get. And I didn't know how much of his mood reflected who he was as a person or how much was the strange situation we were in.

"Do you plan to stay?" I asked as I heard his footsteps moving away.

He stopped. "Do you want me to?"

"Depends. Are you going to yell at me again when I wake up?"

His sigh was so heavy I felt it brush over my skin from several feet away. "I'm not mad at you. I'm mad at Harry for getting you involved in this mess. And I'm mad at myself, too, because I sense Harry's plan has something to do with me."

"How did you figure it out? The fake-dating thing?" It had been nagging at me since he'd first asked.

"You."

"What do you mean?"

"Half Asleep Sick Emma babbles. Kind of blew my mind, actually."

"I'm sorry, James."

"Yeah, me too. I'm not going to tell Harry that I know. For whatever reason, he needs me to believe he's dating you. I'll give him that for now."

"You're a good cousin."

"No, Emma, I'm not. That's the problem. I'll stay and clean up. Then I'll be out of your hair."

He left the room.

I forced myself to stay awake, listening to him rinsing dishes in the sink.

I didn't fall asleep until I heard the door to my apartment shut behind him.

CHAPTER THIRTY-FOUR

Emma

I RETURNED TO WORK early the next week, ready again to face the chaos. Other library staff members fluttered about, working on last-minute preparation for the Festival of Lights.

More holiday events were kicking off too. A *Read with Santa* event, organized by Kristi and Tracy, had a high number of kids signing up. Tracy's husband, Scott, had his Santa suit at the ready.

"Good morning, Emma!" Jill skipped from where she had been laying out boxes of fake presents under a Christmas tree in the children's section.

"Hey. I didn't realize you were working today." She had mentioned at the decorating party that she was swamped with her retail job and taking fewer hours at the library because of it.

"I wasn't supposed to be, but Tracy asked if I could swing a few hours for last-minute holiday prep."

"It's wild around here, huh?"

She smiled. "Sure is. How are you holding up? There's been a lot on your plate the last few weeks."

"I got hit with a nasty bug over the weekend. I don't feel great, but I'm on the mend."

She made a sympathetic noise. "Let me know if you need any help. Although, I'm sure Harry has you covered."

"Uh, yeah." I doubted Harry even realized just how sick I'd been. "Well, I better get to my computer. So much planning left to do before the end of the week."

"I feel you there. Take care of yourself, though. Oh, hey. I almost forgot. There was a package for you outside when I got in earlier. It's still at the front desk, but I'll swing it by your office before I head out for the day—unless you need it sooner?"

That was baffling. I wasn't expecting any deliveries, especially not here. "No, that's okay. I must have ordered something and then forgotten about it. Drop it off when you get a chance. Maybe you, me, and Kristi can eat lunch together?" I wanted to make up for the way I'd ignored them last week.

"Kris is out for an appointment today, but the rest sounds like a plan!" Jill said as she flitted back toward the children's programming area, blonde curls bouncing.

The morning dragged on as I sent emails to local community groups and made edits to the final draft of the library newsletter. When Jill knocked on my door at lunchtime, I breathed a sigh of relief. Some reprieve from the monotony.

"Your package is outside the door," the blonde said, her words muffled around a mouthful of turkey sandwich. "It's pretty heavy. You have no clue what's inside?"

"Not a one." I rose from behind my desk to peek out the door. Sure enough, a large, square-shaped delivery box sat along the hallway wall. I gripped the edges and heaved it up, shocked at the weight. I shot Jill a skeptical glance as I heaved the box onto the desk's surface. "How the hell did you carry that across the building?" My office was the one farthest from the main entrance, and I was out of breath just from lifting the package briefly.

Could be I was simply out of shape. The pretense of dating Harry hadn't gotten me any closer to my *join a gym* goal.

"I stole one of Glenn's carts. I would have kept it to bring the box all the way in, but he yelled at me. Apparently, he needs it to do his job or something."

I snorted a laugh into my salad. Jill was so different from her brother. Light-hearted and jovial in comparison. I had a hard time imagining James bending the rules and laughing it off the way his sister did.

My brain needed to stop coming up with reasons to think about James. He'd made it pretty obvious when he left on Sunday morning that he was done with me.

Jill interrupted my musings by handing me a pair of scissors, a silent urging to open the package.

"You're nosey."

"I know," she said with a grin.

A thick layer of bubble wrap was the first thing I saw. I peeled it back to find a thick canvas jacket in a light-mauve color, a dusty rose.

I lifted it out of the box to get a better look. It was heavy and lined with gray fleece. I recognized the brand as the one James and Harry both wore often.

"That is gorgeous. And super expensive. I had my eye on a similar one, but my budget said no. Who sent you that?"

"I have no idea. Could it have come to the wrong address? Why would someone send me a personal gift to my job?"

Jill reached for the box flap with the shipping label and angled it so she could read it. "Nope. Definitely has your name on it. Quick, see what else is inside."

Stranger and stranger. I ran my hand over the jacket, the canvas zipping along the lines of my palm. I placed it on my lap and reached back into the package. My hand struck the surface of another, smaller box.

"That looks like a boot box," Jill said from over my shoulder.

She was right. The rubber soles were black, and the rest of the boot was a rich, camel-brown suede. Stretchy laces crisscrossed up the center, and the top of the boot ended in a puff of faux fur. They were stunning.

A few minutes later, I stood in the middle of the room, encased in winter gear. Both the coat and boots fit perfectly.

"Girl, I don't know who sent this, but if you could send them my way, I won't complain. All that must have cost close to five hundred dollars. There's no note or anything inside?"

I had looked. There was nothing but a generic gift receipt.

"Maybe it was Harry?" Jill surmised. "But why would he send it to you at work? Not to speak ill of my cousin, but I doubt he even knows the library exists. He wouldn't know the address."

"I'll ask." I shot off a brief message, asking my fake boyfriend if he had sent anything over, before pulling off the boots and coat.

A pang of guilt struck at the sight of our message thread. Harry had reached out a few times, but my side of the chain was barren. I was failing spectacularly as a fake girlfriend.

My phone vibrated with an incoming alert.

Harry: Nope, I didn't send you anything. Want to come out to Maven's tonight? I'll get us a round!

Ugh. I wanted to say no, but I should say yes.

Emma: Sure thing. Meet you there around 7pm?

Harry: Sounds good.

"Well, the package isn't from Harry," I said, placing my phone face down next to my mousepad. "Want to join us at Maven's tonight?"

"Aren't you still recovering from the plague? And no, thanks. I'm supposed to meet up with Ben again for that thing I'm working on."

"How is that going?" I was treading lightly, recalling Jill's reaction toward Kristi at the club.

"I'm not sure. I've been putting off meeting up with him, but I do need some business advice. Tonight is the first time I'm seeing him since our initial disastrous meeting."

"You know, I've got my MBA if you ever feel like picking my brain. I'm not an entrepreneur, but I could always reach out to some contacts from my grad program."

"I appreciate that. And I just might take you up on the offer if this meeting with Ben is another failure. It's just so... I can't even find a word to describe him."

"I haven't met him yet." From all reports from people around town, Ben was a great guy. I'd heard nothing about him that warranted such a powerful reaction from Jill.

"Count yourself lucky. But let's not waste our time talking about him anymore. Who else do you think sent you this gift?"

I could only shrug. "It can't be my parents. They're due to arrive in two days, so they would have just brought this themselves. My dad is too cheap to pay for shipping if he doesn't have to." Not to mention they wouldn't want to miss the opportunity to lecture me in person about my lack of suitable winter garments.

"Well, all I can say is cheers to your secret admirer." Jill tilted her water toward me in a jaunty motion before we tapped our plastic bottles together.

CHAPTER THIRTY-FIVE

Emma

M Y SHOES CRUNCHED IN the snowy gravel of the Maven's parking lot. Despite Jill's giddiness, I couldn't wear my new boots without feeling strange. Until I figured out who sent them, I was sticking with my trusty wool coat and sneakers. Not the most weather-appropriate attire, but at least their origin wasn't a mystery.

An icy wind whipped past, chilling me to the bone. I walked faster toward the double door. I reached to pull it open when it shot out in my direction, pushed from the inside, nearly knocking me to the ground.

"Oh, sorry—Emma?"

It was James. The last person I wanted to see.

"What the hell are you doing out right now? You should be sleeping in bed, resting." He gestured wildly, the white takeout container he carried almost flying away.

I gripped the thick sleeve of his jacket in my fingertips, stilling him.

"I took a nap after work. I'm doing a lot better now."

As if to call me a liar, my body gave a full, visible shiver.

James glared before looking me up and down, taking me in from head to toe.

"What kind of bullshit clothes are you wearing? You *just* got over being sick, and now you're walking around in the flimsiest coat I've seen in my entire fucking life. You know what, I'm leaving. This isn't my business to worry about."

He stalked toward his truck, which I now noted was a few spaces down from where I had parked my car.

I glanced down at my offensive attire, and I knew.

James. The package. He was the one who sent the new boots and coat.

I tore off after him, racing behind to keep up with his long strides.

"James Klein!" I shouted, out of breath from exertion.

He paused by his truck, turned, and waited for me to approach. He tossed his takeout container on the hood of the vehicle.

We were shielded from the wind by a large SUV on one side and the wall of his pickup on the other.

"I know it was you."

"What was me?" He crossed his arms over his broad chest.

"You know exactly what I'm talking about." I jabbed my index finger into the upper part of his chest, the only place not covered by his big biceps.

He smirked down at the finger pressed into him and leaned against the truck door. "I'm afraid you're going to need to be a little more specific."

A rush of doubt hit me. What if it hadn't been him? But no. It had to be.

Fine. If he wouldn't admit to it, I could play the game right back.

"Play dumb all you want, big boy."

He chuckled low in his throat. I ignored him and continued. "I do need your advice about something."

James perked up, lifting his shoulder blades off the vehicle, just a fraction. It was subtle, but he was hooked. He couldn't resist acting the hero.

"I'm planning on going for a hike tomorrow on one of the local trails. Do you think if I wear some thick socks under these shoes, it'll be okay?" I wiggled the toe of my canvas sneaker in the wedge of space between our feet.

"Goddamn it, woman," he said in a growl. He grabbed for the handle of his truck, pulling it open. Then, in one smooth motion, he lifted me by the waist, turned, and placed me on the seat of the pickup. My legs dangled out the side, knees on either side of James' hips where he stood outside.

Our eyes met. The intensity in James' gaze matched the wild pounding in my chest.

"You want me to admit I sent you the jacket and boots, huh?" He spoke quietly, but I heard him clear as day.

"I know you sent them. But why?"

"You shouldn't need to ask, Emma. My question is why aren't you wearing them?"

"I needed to be sure."

"Sure about what?"

"Sure that it meant something. That you wouldn't take it back. That you wouldn't get weird on me. Like before."

Hot and cold.

He wasn't cold right now. I could feel the heat he gave off through the layers of our clothing. I tried to squeeze my legs together but only succeeded in pulling him closer.

"Those other times before, I thought you were my cousin's girl. Now I know better." His fingers came up to grip the top of the open door.

I gulped. James' eyes flicked down, following the movement.

"And what are you going to do now? Now that you know better?"

I barely finished the sentence before his lips were on mine. His hands came down from above, one fisting the back of my head, tangling in my hair, while the other gripped my wool collar.

My own palms dove inside his coat, pulling him closer. Our lips slid together, wet and slow. I tasted the flavor of my lip balm on his mouth. He took my bottom lip between his in a gentle suck, and I couldn't suppress my answering moan.

"Fuck, you feel amazing," he murmured against my mouth before diving in for more. He shifted, his hand sliding down to my ass, pulling me closer to his hips. The hard press of his cock hit me where I needed it most, layers of fabric be damned.

The smooth, warm length of his tongue teased my lips. I welcomed him inside and met the stroke of his tongue with mine, met the beat of his hips with my own in answer.

My heart pulsed in my ribcage and between my thighs. Two minutes of James Klein had me wetter than an entire night with my vibrator.

The big hand in my hair moved as he twisted it around his fist in a crude ponytail. My scalp tingled as pain and pleasure melded. He used his leverage to tilt me back, baring my neck to trail wet kisses down the slender column. He bit down, just so, where my pulse thrummed. My legs jerked.

"I like the sounds you make for me." He dragged his tongue up my neck to my ear. He took the delicate lobe between his teeth before soothing it with his tongue. "I bet I could pull down these pants, right here, right now, in this parking lot, and find you soaked. Are you soaked for me, Emma?"

Oh, fuck. I nodded desperately.

He gave my hair another tug. "Use. Your. Words."

I was in the middle of the most wonderfully depraved sexual experience of my life, and he expected me to *talk?* I couldn't even think.

"Yes," I finally said on a groan.

"Yes, what?" He kept my body close but held firm so I couldn't move, couldn't grind against him.

"Yes, I'm w—wet."

"Mmm, I bet you are. I wanna touch you so bad." He nipped my ear once more before returning to devour my mouth.

He was everywhere at once, engulfing me. His scent, his heat, his taste. Fresh sawdust and clean laundry. The crisp air didn't register even with the pickup door wide open. The only thing that mattered was getting him closer.

I dragged up his flannel shirt, smiling against his lips when he shivered at the touch. He was blessedly hot there, firm and warm. My palms tingled as I worked my way up his spine, tangling in the soft prickles of hair.

James pulled away, ripping his lips from mine. We panted, breath smoking in the frosty night air. He placed one booted foot up onto the step bar of the truck, sending me to my back on the bench seat. His other foot followed as I scrambled to make room for him. He pressed all the way in, rising above me in the dark cab.

He wasn't wasting any time. And I didn't want him to. I held his eyes as he lowered his head down, anticipating, wanting nothing more than the taste of him on my tongue.

I expected ferocity, but what I got was tenderness. He surprised me, placing one large hand on my cheek, stroking the skin with a callused thumb.

"Fucking gorgeous."

My breath hitched, my stomach barreling away on a wave of some unnamed emotion. There was more than just lust here. Something more was brewing beneath the surface, impossible to ignore.

A car door slammed, and the sound of raucous laughter hit my ears. James heard it too, his head turning to listen.

"I haven't seen her yet," someone yelled out.

He pulled away, coming to a seated position in the driver's seat. I tucked my feet up to my chest, feeling small and cold now that the heat of him was gone.

"Let me guess. This was a mistake." I spoke the words flatly, surprised they came out at all.

He cleared his throat. "Just got carried away, that's all."

My laugh was like glass coming up through my throat. "Sure. Yeah. I get it."

Gathering up the last shards of my dignity, I slid out the passenger side. Head held high, I walked to the front entrance of Maven's.

"Emma!" I stopped at James' shout but didn't bother turning. "Wear the fucking jacket and boots."

I whipped around to glare at him. "Go fuck yourself, James Klein."

I strutted into Maven's, hoping he was watching. I had a fake boyfriend to meet.

CHAPTER THIRTY-SIX

James

I STORMED THROUGH THE entry of the Victorian, not caring, for once, where I kicked off my boots. If Harry could make a mess in the house, I could too.

I hadn't seen my cousin since our argument on the phone when Emma was sick. I was itching for a confrontation, and my body vibrated with tension I couldn't relieve.

I knew its source, and no amount of yelling at Harry would appease it. I had been ten seconds from fucking Emma in the Maven's parking lot, truck door wide open for all to see. It was a good thing I came to my senses in the end. But my dick wasn't quite ready to forgive me.

I knew Harry and Emma weren't a couple. But the rest of the town did not. How would it have looked if someone had seen me dry humping my cousin's girlfriend in public?

Not great for me, to say the least.

And not great for Emma either.

It was impossible to ignore the fact that, while their relationship was fake, Harry's feelings for Emma were real. He had admitted as much. I doubted she reciprocated. She certainly wasn't thinking about my cousin when she'd been grinding against my cock earlier.

But what kind of person would I be if I betrayed someone I cared about in that way?

"Harry!" I said, shouting as I crossed the threshold into the kitchen. The room was dark, only the dim can-lights illuminating the granite countertops. Ambient color from the Christmas tree filtered in from the living room, reminding me of my distinct lack of holiday cheer.

I caught sight of a familiar, messy scrawl on the blank side of a crumpled receipt.

MEETING EMMA AT MAVEN'S. LOST MY PHONE AGAIN. DON'T WAIT UP.

–H

Motherfucker.

So that was why she was out tonight, despite just having recovered from being sick. Heat burned through my stomach. Harry hadn't even been there for Emma during her illness, yet he still got the reward of being with her, proudly, in public.

Harry could take her out. He could put his arm around her, buy her dinner, even kiss her in front of the whole town.

I ate a soggy grilled cheese and cleaned up the dishes in the sink, going through the motions.

I made my way up to the shower, leaving a trail of clothing as I went. Turning the water temperature as hot as I could handle, I let my head fall forward. The pressure of the water pummeled my shoulder blades as the room filled with hot steam, and I squeezed my eyes shut.

Without effort, my mind wandered to the woman consuming my thoughts. How she tasted on my lips. The warm, wet heat of her tongue gliding against mine. The beat of her pulse and the delicious scent buried where her neck met her shoulder.

What I wouldn't give to have her, naked and wet, with me here and now. If we hadn't been interrupted, if I had held off long enough to get her back to the house, the night could have ended with us right here—her body, warm and wet, pressed against me as I ran my hand down her stomach, straight to the clenching pussy only I could fill.

I reached for my cock, no longer able to resist the temptation to jack off to the thought of my cousin's crush. I'd blown straight past the moral high ground when I almost fucked Emma in my front seat tonight. A little self-pleasure wouldn't make it any worse than it already was. Just enough to get me down off the ledge.

Instead of my callused hand, it was Emma's I imagined now. Smooth and delicate, yet firm and decisive. I would nip at her lip, tug it with my teeth while she jacked me.

God, she felt incredible. I grunted as I thrust into my fist. In my mind, I was thrusting into the pussy I hadn't yet seen or touched but sensed would fit me just right. If we only had five more minutes, I would have known. Would have had my fingers down inside her pants, touching her wetness, making her cream all over my hand.

"Fuck!"

The thought sent me over the edge, and I came, hard, all over the gray-tiled shower wall with a hoarse shout.

When I slid into my cold, empty bed, there was no satisfaction. There would be none. Not now that I'd had a taste of Emma. Not now that I realized that nothing but the real thing would compare.

CHAPTER THIRTY-SEVEN

Emma

I FOLLOWED HARRY OUT of Maven's after spending an obligatory hour and a half with him at the bar. I resisted a glance toward the space where James' truck had been parked, tire impressions still visible in the snowpack.

Harry reached for my hand. My first instinct was to pull away, but I shoved it down before my date noticed. We were still a couple in the public eye, and I needed to maintain that facade.

My clammy hand clasped in his, I allowed him to guide me to my car.

"This beater still running good?" he said, patting the roof above the driver's side door.

"No problems since you got her all fixed up." I gave him a tight, closemouthed smile.

"Glad to hear it." He shoved his fingers in his pockets and shifted from front to back.

The night had been filled with awkward, forced small talk. Despite my lack of interest in Harry on a romantic level, I hoped we were at least friends. We hadn't lacked for conversation until now, not even the evening we met and he had teased me for the naughty Santa audiobook snafu.

Tonight, it had been weird from the beginning, starting with Harry sliding into the booth next to me. I'm sure people who liked to sit on the same side of the booth as their date existed—crazy people—but I was not one of them. He had been polite, asking questions about my day and my plans for the rest of the week. He had even graciously picked up the bill. But it was boring and unnatural, almost like he was trying too hard to be someone he wasn't. And while I wasn't interested in dating the man in truth, I did like him as a person. He didn't need to be anything other than his authentic self.

"Is everything alright with you?" I asked.

"What? Yes! Of course. Why?"

"Slow down. You don't seem yourself, is all."

Harry pulled his hat off to comb his fingers through his hair. "It's all good. It's nothing."

I didn't believe him. "If you say so."

I pressed the fob on my car key. The triple beep echoed through the air when the doors unlocked. "I better get going. I've gotta get some work done since my weekend was pretty much shot."

"Oh, yeah. You were sick, right? James mentioned it."

"Yes. I had a bad flu. He stayed with me overnight on Saturday."

Harry's face scrunched up. "Wasn't that weird for you?"

"No, not at all. Truthfully, he was an enormous help."

Harry scoffed. "I'm not saying he isn't helpful. He just doesn't know when to *stop* helping. I'm only sorry you had to deal with that. I bet he forced you to take medicine, and check your temperature, and eat gross food you didn't want to eat the entire time."

"You know, Harry, I understand that your issues with James are none of my business. They clearly go deep. Hell, you convinced me to date you just to get him off your back. But your cousin did a nice thing for me. More than nice. So you don't get to try to convince me to be mad about it because you're annoyed with him. It isn't fair. James is a good person, and maybe he is the way he is because he's tired of getting no appreciation for the things he does for his family."

I took a gulping inhale as I finished my rant. The man next to me looked shell-shocked.

"I really do need to head home," I said again.

He nodded. "Okay, Emma. But before you go, I have to do this."

I paused in reaching for the door handle. "What's that?"

Cupping my cheeks in his gloved hands, Harry tipped his head forward and planted his lips on mine.

I froze long enough to register that his lips were cold and wind-chapped. With a jerk, I pulled away.

"What the fuck, Harry?"

He kept hold of my cheeks and stared down at me in earnest. "Don't you want to give this a try? A real try? We could be good together. You challenge me. You make me strive to be better. Look at how you just told me off for my attitude about James. You're so fucking sexy I can't stand it."

He leaned in again, but I was ready this time. I brought a hand up as a barrier between my mouth and Harry's. His eyes went wide when he made contact with my palm.

"Guess that's a no, then," he said in a muffled voice.

I couldn't help it. I laughed. "It's a no."

I dropped my hand as he stepped back.

"I hope there are no hard feelings here."

His mouth twisted, considering. "Nope. I won't lie. My ego is a little bruised. But I'll get over it. If you change your mind, I am one hundred percent down for some further Emma and Harry action. What would our couple-name be, do you think? Hemma? Earry? I don't like any of those, do you?"

True to form, he deflected with a joke.

"I'm being serious here. Can you keep up the fake-dating charade if you have actual feelings?"

The lighthearted look fell from his face. "I *have* to keep doing the fake-dating thing. Things are worse than ever with James. Do you realize he got mad at me for not coming to see you when you were sick? I was trying to be responsible for a change. If I caught your bug, then I would have missed work. I've got something special in the works. But he's still pissed at me. I can never win with him."

I sighed. "You have to consider his perspective here too. Having a girlfriend isn't enough to seem like an adult. You have to be a true, supportive partner to that person. Showing up when your partner is sick is part of the deal."

Harry squinted. "Okay. I can see that. See, this is why I like talking to you more than I like talking to James. He never explains stuff in a way I can understand. But you're actually a lot like him in some ways, you know?"

James was a million miles ahead of me when it came to being an adult, but I could somewhat see Harry's point. "You should try talking with him again—when you're not at each other's throats."

"You're right. As usual."

"Not to beat a dead horse here, but are you going to pull a sneak kiss attack when my parents visit? They're coming into town in two days, and they want to do dinner after the holiday parade finishes. I can't have you trying this sort of stunt again while they're visiting."

"Definitely not. And, well...not to be rude, but that was kind of a shit kiss, right?"

"Oh, thank God. It was *terrible*."

He laughed, but I wasn't sure I believed him.

CHAPTER THIRTY-EIGHT

Emma

I RUBBED MY PALMS along the outer thighs of my jeans as my parents stood in the dead center of my cramped living room. They had been here before, though only to help me move in. During this visit, I had to project stability and responsibility, show them Greyport was my home.

Mom turned in a circle, her dark curls quivering as she spun. "It's...cute. I like where you put the Christmas tree, Emma."

"Thanks, Mom." Cute wasn't exactly a ringing endorsement, but it was better than I had expected.

"Keeping warm so far? How is this lock holding up for you?" My father wiggled the handle on the apartment door.

"Lock works fine, Dad."

I didn't say it, but the door was one of the few things that wasn't falling apart. Thank God James had repaired the leaking sink over the weekend when he'd stayed over. My father would have clocked that from a mile away.

"How are you handling all the stairs with your hip, honey? It looks dicey out there. You can't afford to get hurt again." Mom peeked out the window into the small bank of parking spots below the window, as if she was mentally calculating how high up we were and how many stairs I had to navigate daily.

"Stairs have been fine too." I found the shorter the answer I gave, the less space they had to dig.

"It's pretty slick on those steps. Has your landlord been salting and shoveling for you?" Dad asked. He moved to join my mother at the window.

They made an attractive picture there, his gray head bent to her dark one as they schemed up innovative ways to drive me insane.

"I bought a bucket of rock salt a few weeks ago, and I've been laying it down when it gets bad. I don't think I need to bug my landlord with that."

I walked to the couch and made myself cozy under a throw blanket. It seemed my mother and father were going to quiz me on my sub-par apartment survival skills, no matter what I did. I might as well kick back and enjoy the interrogation.

"The last thing you need is to take a spill while laying down salt. That is something you *should* be bugging the landlord about. What's their number? Let me call while we're here. It'll take the task off your plate." Dad marched over to the fridge, searching for any sign of the landlord's contact information.

I slammed my eyes shut, begging some higher power to lend me strength and patience. "Dad. You do not need to call my landlord to sprinkle salt on a two-step entryway."

"There is no need to get snippy when your father is only trying to help. If you injure your hip again, good luck living alone and keeping your full-time job."

I covered my face with the blanket, sending a silent scream into the scratchy wool. I heard my father let out a shout of laughter that was quickly stifled. No doubt Mom had blasted him with a chastising glare.

Calm. Composure. Patience. I had read something once about mantras and manifestation. I probably wasn't doing it correctly, but it couldn't hurt to try. Flipping the embroidered edge of the blanket down, I projected what I hoped was a serene smile at Mom.

"I appreciate your concern, Mother, and I understand where you are coming from. But an injury like that could happen to anyone, at any time. Not just me."

"You aren't just *anyone*. Most people haven't been hit by a car and left with a fractured hip, Emma! It isn't the same, and you know it."

"I am twenty-six years old. Am I supposed to wrap myself in bubble wrap before I do normal, everyday tasks?"

"You're supposed to care about your well-being! You could have died, Emma. Do you not understand that?"

The air was heavy, filled with the sound of Mom's sniffling. I closed my eyes hard against a sheen of tears. Despite our constant bickering, I loved my mom. High stakes emotional conversations were not in my plans for this visit.

"Your mother and I just worry with you being so far away now," Dad said, breaking the silence.

"I get it. I miss you both too. But as I have said, over and over, living at home wasn't helping me heal."

"I don't understand how being around your parents, the people who love you more than anyone in the world, could possibly hold you back."

I had tried to explain, but it was a never-ending cycle. My accident had traumatized my parents too, but I couldn't delay living my life because of it.

"Can we talk about something else? I want to enjoy our time together while you're here."

Mom waited a beat before nodding. A few months ago, she wouldn't have so readily agreed. Maybe she'd been working on herself too.

"To your points, I don't always do the best job taking care of myself, and I'm trying to be better. I shouldn't be taking dumb risks on snow and ice. But I *can* manage to occasionally salt some steps." I put up a hand, as if swearing an oath. "But I solemnly swear I will call a friend if I am having a sore day. Will that do?"

They both agreed.

"Tell us about your friends," Dad prompted.

I perked up, pleased to be moving on to another topic. "So, Jill and Kristi work at the library with me. Kristi is the assistant librarian, and Jill works there a few days a week. They're a lot of fun. It's a bit like the early days at college again, meeting new people." Not that I'd made many college friends, living at home.

"And this boyfriend you mentioned? I assume he would help out if you were in a pickle."

Probably not. Harry wasn't Mr. Reliable, by his own admission. But Mom and Dad didn't need to know that.

And they certainly wouldn't understand that the person I was coming to rely on most in Greyport was my boyfriend's cousin. If I was lucky, I would make it through this visit with nary a mention of James. After all, he wasn't anything to me—hottest make-out session of my life aside—so why would he be anything to my parents?

"Um, yes, Harry is great. Very supportive. Very helpful. The right guy to count on," I said with an enthusiastic thumbs-up.

That sounded one-hundred percent convincing. *Not.*

"You still want to meet him for dinner after the parade tomorrow, right?" I asked.

They exchanged a glance I couldn't interpret.

"We would love to," Mom said after their silent communication was done.

"Okay. Good." Was it good? The thought of Harry and my parents in the same room frayed my nerves. But I was committed. I needed to show them I was settled in Greyport.

"What's the plan for dinner when we meet your beau?"

Plan? I would be lucky if I wasn't falling over, dead tired, after running the parade booth. It would be a casual dinner and bed.

"There's an Italian place in town I've heard positive things about. I was thinking we could eat there. Don't be offended if I'm half asleep at the table."

Mom frowned. "Have you been getting enough sleep? You do look a bit pale."

"Such kind words, Mother Dearest. I've been going for the sickly Victorian child look these days."

Dad snickered from his seat at the bistro table before his wife silenced him with a playful flick on the ear.

"You are beautiful as always, daughter of mine, even if you're sickly. I know when I've overstepped, so I'll stop now." She didn't look like she wanted to stop, but I gave her credit for recognizing when she was pushing the boundary a hair too far.

"As thanks for that, I will share that I was sick with the flu last weekend. But I'm feeling better now."

Mom's eyes got teary again. "I'm so sorry I wasn't here, honey. I should have known you needed me."

How could I tell my mother, who meant well, that my illness wasn't about her?

"A friend helped me. As I said, I'm doing a lot better."

Mom patted my hand. "I'm so happy to hear you had someone looking out for you."

"Me too. It was...really, really nice to have someone there."

It had been more than nice. James had given me safety and comfort at my lowest. He would never know how dark my thoughts had been before he'd shown up. How down I had felt about myself and my ability to maintain my independence. And then he had just...been there. Not pushing but lending me his strength. Even though Harry and Jill resented his meddling, I envied them.

"What do you say we take a walk around Greyport, ladies," Dad said. He hated to be cooped up. "We can see a bit of this town, get a bite to eat. Then your mom and I will scamper off to our hotel room and get out of your hair."

GREYPORT'S MAIN DRAG WAS bustling. Leafless trees glittered with white string lights along the sidewalk. Small shops were open late for last-minute Christmas shoppers. I was proud to show off my new home, proud to be finding my place in a community like this.

We dropped into the local bookstore, Mayfield Books, and I made a beeline for the romance section as Dad checked out the biographies. My mother walked over from where she had been examining a display of children's books, always on the lookout for presents for her best friend's grandchildren.

"Find anything for Beth's little ones?" I asked.

"Some cute stuff. The problem is those kids have so much already. If I get a gift that isn't on their approved list, I'll end up buying something they already have. Beth's daughter goes overboard sometimes."

I hadn't seen Maggie, the daughter of Mom's oldest friend, in a few years, as she too had moved away from our hometown. "I can't believe she has two kids already. She's only a year older than me, and I certainly don't feel responsible enough to raise one human being, let alone two."

Mom flipped over a paperback to read the synopsis. "Everyone moves at their own pace. If you ever decide to become a parent, I know you will be brilliant at it."

I snorted, tucking a new historical romance under my arm to bring to the cash register. "It's not looking likely anytime soon, but I appreciate your confidence in me."

"Does your boyfriend—Harry—like kids?"

I flushed. I had no clue how Harry felt about children. What if I told Mom he wanted to have nineteen kids, like that alarming reality TV family, and then tomorrow at dinner he told them he couldn't stand kids?

"I'm not really sure. It hasn't come up yet." Better to be honest and hope for the best.

"Hmm, alright."

I wasn't prepared to decipher that comment and determinedly ignored it as we moved toward the register to make our purchases. A small line had formed, but it was slow moving as the cashier spent time chatting with each customer about holiday plans and local news—the classic curse of a small town where everyone knew everyone.

I wouldn't trade it for anything.

"I wonder where your father got off to." Mom twisted her head around to look for her husband.

"He'll turn up as soon as we get through the worst of the waiting, just watch."

I felt the slight pressure of more bodies gathering at my back as the line grew longer. Mom turned to the person just behind us, preemptively apologizing. "If a man in a bright-red sweater hops in line, don't worry, he's with us."

Mom always made polite conversation with strangers anywhere she went, much to my eternal dismay. "Mom, please."

"Don't worry about it," the person behind us replied.

Shit. I knew that voice. Intimately. It starred in all my dirtiest fantasies, issuing filthy orders, and leaving my thighs slick.

Pivoting with a smile plastered on my face, I prepared to introduce my mother to James Klein.

CHAPTER THIRTY-NINE

James

I CLOCKED EMMA THE minute I walked into Mayfield Books. I should have turned around and left. The book I was buying for Jill for Christmas could wait. But I was a sick moth to flame with Emma. She drew me in no matter how hard I fought the pull.

The second thing I noticed was what she was wearing. Despite telling me to fuck off, she had listened and worn the winter boots and jacket I had given her.

I looked calm, but inside, I was preening like a peacock.

I flicked a glance down at her feet while she was preoccupied. The boots were the perfect fit. I bit down on a smile.

Harry could claim her in public, but she would wear a piece of me each time she got dressed—at least through the winter. Hopefully, I found a cure for this unflagging obsession by the time spring hit.

"Evening." I cleared my throat, sounding husky even to my own ears. I then gave the stout brunette woman beside her a nod. There was a clear familial resemblance.

I cringed at my rudeness and shoved Jill's hardback under my arm before stretching out my hand in offering.

Emma's mom reached me first, grasping my hand and squeezing. "Linda Hartwell. You must be Harry! I'm so pleased to meet you. What a surprise for it to happen a whole day sooner than we planned."

Well, this was awkward as fuck. I glanced at Emma. She peeked sideways at me. I chewed the inside corner of my lip, reining in a grin.

She unfroze after a beat. "No, Mom! No, no, no. This is not Harry. This is *James*, Harry's cousin. James is definitely not my boyfriend."

The extreme denial wasn't exactly a balm to my ego. I cast her a side glance, catching a flush traveling up her neck and cheeks.

How far would her blush spread if I had her writhing beneath me once more, completely exposed, so I could admire her flawless skin?

I slid my fingers from Linda Hartwell's clutches. Thinking about her daughter naked while I shook the woman's hand added another dimension of fucked up to this scenario.

Linda's eyes traveled between me and her daughter, a crease appearing in the space between her brows.

"There are my girls. I found the ultimate book. It's a memoir from a guy who does Civil War reenactments. He was in a years-long legal battle after he got tied to a cannon and was left behind for days. Doesn't that sound great?"

A thin man of medium height approached. He had a full head of gray hair.

"That sounds...really interesting, Dad."

"You can borrow it as soon as I finish it, honey. Oh, hello there." The man paused when he noticed me. "Let me guess, you're Emma's guy! Larry, right?"

"If a sink hole could just appear under my feet right now, I would not complain," Emma said in a low voice yet still loud enough for me to hear.

"What was that, dear?" her father asked.

"Nothing, Dad, just that, uh—"

"Frank, this isn't Emma's boyfriend. This is his cousin, James," Linda said, cutting in smoothly.

"It's nice to meet you, sir." The older man's grip was firm, but his eyes were warm. I knew those eyes. His daughter had the same ones.

"Call me Frank. It's a pleasure to meet some of our daughter's people here in Greyport. This is a great town you've got. Almost great enough that my wife and I can forgive you for stealing my daughter away from us."

"It isn't like that, Dad." Emma made a half-hearted attempt to pull her parents forward, but they were clearly feeling chatty.

And I was in the mood to irk her, to see the fire in her eyes when she got riled up. I was happy to indulge in this conversation.

"Are you from the area, James?" Linda asked.

I shot her daughter a wicked grin. "I am. Born and raised. I went to school a few hours away but came back to help my mom. Most of my family lives here too."

"How wonderful! And such a devoted son. I'm sure your mother is thrilled to have you so close." There was no mistaking the little jab at Emma in that statement.

"She was. She passed away several years ago, but I know she appreciated our time together." I staved off the potential awkwardness of the dead-mom revelation with a gentle smile.

Linda clasped my upper arm and gave it a little wiggle. "Well then, you *must* come to dinner with us tomorrow after the holiday parade. Your cousin will be there, and we can make it a proper family affair. I insist."

Emma's face went beat red. She shook her head and waved her arms at me in a frantic fashion from behind her parents' backs.

I let loose a shit-eating grin.

"I would love to join you."

CHAPTER FORTY

Emma

I surveyed the Christmas parade crowd for the third time, looking for Kristi. She was running late, and she had the final prize for the auction.

That prize being the James-made drawer insert and spoon set I coveted. Even when he wasn't physically present, the man was on my mind. He had chatted with my parents the entire time we'd waited in line at Mayfield Books, getting all buddy-buddy, even talking business with my father.

Dad was an accountant. He didn't know anything about woodworking or custom furniture. How they had anything to talk about, I had no idea.

I had pointedly ignored James' presence.

He hadn't cared at all. I did not want to see his annoying ass at dinner tonight. Tonight was my opportunity to show Mom and Dad how great my new boyfriend was and how well I was doing in Greyport. It was not supposed to be the *Getting to Know James Hour*.

"Sorry I'm late! Parking off Main Street was insanity." I let out a breath as Kristi emerged around a group of carolers, slipping behind the blue-tent-covered booth.

"No worries. I'm just happy you're here so I can go use the bathroom."

"I've got you, girl. Before you go, where do you want this?" She presented the bow-wrapped spoon set and drawer insert with a flourish.

"I left a spot on the table over here for it," I said, pointing her toward an open space. I had covered the cheap plastic table with a festive red cloth.

Kristi set the bundle down and scanned the booth. "You did a kick-ass job, Emma. Tracy and I ran this event last year, and I promise you, it did not look half this good."

A grin exploded on my face. That recognition felt damn good, especially after so many sleepless nights crafting holiday decorations. My efforts had paid off, and a steady flow of parade-goers had been in and out of the display all evening. It helped that the night was mild for December, not a hint of wind or snow.

"Don't let the whole thing fall apart while I'm in the bathroom, then, okay?"

My friend laughed. "I can handle it. Now, you better get going. There's a long line for the bathrooms around the corner. You might be better off walking farther and just using the one in the library."

I thanked Kristi for the tip and speed-walked through the growing crowd. The tree-lighting ceremony was beginning in a few minutes, and everyone was rushing for Main Square to watch. My parents were somewhere among the cluster of revelers, having arrived early to help set up my space. They hadn't liked the idea of me moving tables on my own, despite my assurances that Tracy had supplied me with a wheeled cart.

As I rounded the block, aiming for the prominent front steps of the Greyport Public Library, a large hand cupped me around the shoulder.

"You okay?" the owner of that hand asked.

It was James. Because of course it was. It seemed I would never get away from him.

"Fine. Why?" I was still steaming mad at him for implying our kiss was a mistake and then crashing my family time.

And now I was even angrier with him for looking seriously hot in a black backward baseball cap. It was honestly unfair.

"You're in a hurry. Wanted to make sure you didn't need help."

"Can't a girl take a break without getting questioned? Get out of my way, please."

His mouth formed an *O* of surprise at my tone, but I wasn't willing to waste my time. If he wanted to talk, then he could follow me. Or he could go kick rocks for all I cared.

I jogged up the library steps at a clip and used my key card to unlock the employee entrance. I took a sharp right toward the staff restroom across from my office.

Once I got inside, I no longer had the urge to pee and, instead, stood statue-like at the sink, taking in my appearance. Wanting to look my best while working in front of the public was human nature, not at all related to James' presence. That was what I told myself as I smoothed down my flyways and wiped away a smudge of eyeliner.

Flinging open the entrance to the restroom, I jolted when I caught sight of the tall man leaning against the wall beside my office. One big, booted foot was propped up behind him, and the top half of his face was covered in the shadow of his ball cap.

I rolled my eyes. "Why did you follow me in here, James? Believe it or not, I can pee on my own, like a big girl."

He said nothing. I was short on patience for his hot and cold nonsense.

I shoved open the door to my office. I was running low on copies of the library activity calendar for the booth. I didn't bother with the light.

The door clicked shut. I turned to see James' big body blocking the door, reminiscent of the first time I saw him.

"What are you doing, James?" I asked.

My voice trembled, not from fear but something far more tempting.

"I need to make you come."

CHAPTER FORTY-ONE

Emma

"**W**HAT?" I SAID, STRUCK stupid.

"You heard me." James stalked closer, his work boots falling heavy on the old, thin carpet.

"Here? Now?" I shuffled backward, retreating to safety behind my desk. I didn't know if I was trying to get away or move closer to the most convenient flat surface—perfect for doing his bidding.

I saw the white flash of his teeth in the dark. A wicked smile.

I turned away from him, unable to take the heat.

"Why do you think I came to the parade at all?"

"Y—your donation to the library booth?"

His breath brushed my ear, his fresh wood scent filling my nostrils as he closed in. My front pressed against the edge of the desk.

"Try again, pretty girl."

I gulped in a breath as his hands bracketed my hips. He hadn't even touched me yet. It was infuriating. Frustrating.

I stretched up on my tiptoes—he was so damn tall—and backed into him with an experimental wiggle, allowing my ass to brush against his lap.

God, he was hard.

He inhaled once—a fleeting glimpse showing he wasn't unaffected—before chuckling and lifting his palms to my waist. He wasn't shy then as he thrust forward in a rocking motion, gentle but with enough force that I could feel every inch.

"You want to feel my cock, huh?"

Fuck, his mouth was dirty. I was out of my depth. I could tease, but he could torture. He gave me another slow, rolling thrust. I returned the favor, backing up into him further.

He pulled away a fraction, still clutching my waist.

"Uh-uh-uh. Answer the question. Tell me what you want."

"I—I want you."

One of his rough hands slid up my midsection, leaving a trail of goosebumps in its wake. He stopped at my collarbone and blanketed my throat in a soft grip. Not applying any pressure, just resting his fingers, as if it belonged in that precise spot, like a favorite necklace.

His callused fingertips stroked the underside of my jaw and tipped my head back, steering me right where he wanted me.

"Be more specific. Say, 'James, I want your cock.'"

I heard myself whine from far off. Like I didn't exist in my body anymore and was watching from a distance.

His breath tickled the fine hairs along my temple as he laughed. "If you don't want to say it, if you don't want to do this, I'll stop touching you and leave. The choice is yours, pretty girl. So, what will it be?"

"If you stop touching me, I think I might die." I twisted in his arms and grabbed his hair, fisting my fingers in the wavy locks. This was a game for two, and I was ready to play.

I tugged him down until our lips were a hair's breadth apart, my smile brushing up against his.

"James," I said in a breathy drawl. "I want your cock."

He closed the scant space between us with a groan, feeding from my mouth as if it was his last source of sustenance. I wanted to keep him fed forever.

Our tongues rubbed in a sensual, twining dance. I gripped his thick strands tight, determined not to let him go this time. But the man kissing me wasn't looking for an out. He blindly reached for the surface of the desk and shoved a towering stack of paperwork down in a fluttering mess. He boosted me up so I was sitting in the space left behind.

"Hope that wasn't important," he said, kissing his way across my jawline in licks and nibbles.

My head lolled to the side. "I'll pick it up tomorrow."

"Emma."

I looked up at him. He was all seriousness as he cupped my cheeks.

"I meant what I said. This is your choice. If there's anything you don't like, just say the word, and I'll stop. I think you can tell I like things rough. I like to hand out orders. But if it's not your thing, all you need to do is tell me to stop. If your mouth is occupied, tap my shoulder. Got it?"

I nodded, but I could somehow tell he needed to hear the word. I held his gaze as I told him, "Yes."

His eyes flashed in satisfaction as he shifted his grip down to cup my backside. "Good. Now, does this little ass want to be slapped?"

I could almost feel his palm on my skin already, like a phantom sensation.

"Uh-huh."

James Klein's signature brand of dirty talk had converted me into an idiot.

"That's my girl. Turn around." He tapped my hip twice in encouragement.

I shot him a teasing look as I lowered down from the desk, making sure he felt every inch of my body on the downslide.

He shook his head from side to side. "You're a brat, aren't you?"

"Sometimes," I said before twirling around.

He paused with his fingers at the waist of my jeans. "Will it mess with your hip to get up here on your hands and knees?" he asked, rapping the surface of the desk with his knuckles.

Oh fuck, that sounded hot. "No." At least, I hoped it wouldn't be a problem. Either way, I was willing to tough it out for this experience. "I've been doing my exercises and staying more mobile."

The last word came out in a sharp exhale as James was already undoing the button and zipper of my pants. In a sharp move, he tugged both my jeans and panties—thankfully a cute pair—to just beneath the arc of my butt, leaving my skin cool and bared to the air.

"Up on the desk. Now." He sounded darker, almost angry. Like he was so turned on he was mad about it.

I longed for nothing more than to do his bidding. Somehow, I knew I could trust him with my body. That he would only push as far as I could take. I crawled onto the desktop as best I could while still constrained at the thigh. A subtle tap between my shoulder blades conveyed James' message. I bent down until I was resting on my forearms.

For a moment, I was too vulnerable, too exposed, until the soft touch of his palm ran along the curve of my ass. I shivered.

"You're so damn pretty," he said reverently. "I can't wait to put my mark on you."

I squirmed in anticipation when his hand lifted, leaving me cold in its absence, and waited for the bite to land.

And waited.

"Do it," I whispered.

Smack.

We groaned in unison. A new gush of wetness built between my legs. I ached to press my thighs together to relieve some of the growing emptiness there, but my position wouldn't allow it.

Smack.

My whimper was loud in the room. James breathed heavily from somewhere behind me.

"Can you take one more, pretty girl?"

I nodded in desperation. Anything for him to keep touching me.

"Good. Next time I'll give you more, but I don't think I can handle it right now. I'm so close, and I've hardly even touched you."

I luxuriated for a moment in the deliciousness of knowing I had as much impact on him as he did on me. There was weight to that. For as much as his stern orders had me desperate to obey, he acknowledged the power I had over him and gave it right back.

It was as intoxicating as it was terrifying.

One last slap, soothed by a gentle rub on what was surely bright-red skin, pulled me from my thoughts. I bit my lip to keep from screaming.

"God fucking damn it. It's too much. Turn around." James' words poured out in a rough grumble.

I scrambled, scooting on the desk's smooth tabletop, making more of a mess as a stapler went tumbling to the floor. James reached out to guide me but only ended up knocking over a mug full of pens.

I snickered, and he let out an answering laugh while I turned front-ward. I smiled up at him so wide my cheeks hurt. My pants were half off, one of my shoes was missing, and my braid was falling out. I didn't care at all.

"Hi," I said into the dark.

"Hi."

Then the soft moment was over as we came together in a brutal kiss. James jerked the thick material of my sweater up as he lowered his lips to my breast. He started with gentle, close-mouthed kisses across the swell of my cleavage before alternating with warm, damp licks. I tried to push his head down, to direct him toward my nipple, but he wouldn't budge, singularly focused on the task in front of him.

I whined, an unintelligible sound, but the meaning was clear.

He looked up, full lips shining. "You're gonna be the death of me, beautiful."

He pounced, dragging the cups of my bra down, not bothering with the clasp. The heat of his mouth encircled one nipple. He sucked and tugged, leaving the tip hard and aching. His left hand came to my other breast, pinching and rolling the stiff peak.

I wanted—needed—to grind on him, but the height difference made it impossible at our current angle.

With a tug in his hair, I captured the tall man's attention, and his mouth lifted off the tight bud. His fingers stayed put, continuing their assault on my other nipple, hardening it to a near painful point.

"What do you need?"

"You're too tall."

"Maybe you're too short."

I pouted. He laughed before boosting me up to sit atop the desk again. I would have to bust out the disinfectant wipes come Monday morning. There were some workplace violations being committed right now.

He yanked my pants and underwear down the rest of the way, cursing when the denim flipped inside out and tightened at my calves. I kicked to help, breathless by the time he was kneeling at my feet.

"Lie back."

I listened, lowering myself until the curve of my spine—exposed where my shirt was hiked up—pressed onto the cool surface of my workspace.

"Fuck." I gasped at the touch of his fingers on the insides of my knees, pressuring them to part.

"Show me how wet you are, Emma."

CHAPTER FORTY-TWO

Emma

THE SLICK, SWEATY SKIN of my thighs stuck to the desktop as I slowly opened myself to James' view. My cheeks heated with embarrassment, but the emotion faded when his wide shoulders were *there,* right at my center, leaving me open for his hungry gaze.

"I knew you would be pretty here too."

I couldn't see him, but I felt every inch of two fingers slicking through the wet cream between my legs, a thick knuckle rubbing at my core, not yet daring to venture inside. He smeared my messy arousal up to my clit before spreading my pussy lips with his fingertips. With the rough pad of his thumb, he strummed little circles on my clit, moving with ease through the dampness.

My hips jogged up and down, and I flung my arms out wide, searching for something to grab onto. Finding nothing but air, I brought a fist to my teeth and bit down. My other hand plucked the delicate bud at the center of my breast.

James' thumb continued to circle my most sensitive place as he pushed a finger inside so gradually I could feel each individual ridge of his knuckle. He added a second digit, twisting and rotating.

"You're soaking my hand right now. It's so fucking sexy. I can't wait to get inside this hot cunt. It's gonna be so tight and warm. But first I need to taste you."

I cried out at the abrupt loss of his hand. But it was worth it when I sat up in time to catch him pulling those wicked fingers from between his lips. His dark beard glistened with moisture. I knew it was from me.

The corner of his mouth twitched when he noticed me watching him. "Delicious."

I almost came on the spot.

With that damp hand, he guided my upper body back down.

"What do you want now, Emma?"

His breath hissed over my inner thighs. The sound of my panting filled the room as I vibrated in eager expectation.

"You have to say it out loud, pretty girl. If you want me to lick it, you have to tell me." With both thumbs, he opened me up again. The heat of his breath hovered above my aching core.

"Please, James." My voice broke.

"Please, what, Emma?"

"Please lick my pussy. I need you."

The end of the sentence came out in a scream as he took my clit in his lips, tongue flicking as he started to suck.

I forced my fist back to my mouth, muffling the moans he coaxed from me. The sounds from his mouth, the messy licking, and sucking, and growls as he feasted were loud in the tiny office. It was dirty and depraved, and I loved it. His tongue dipped down again and swirled around my opening, stealing the wetness there before returning to my distended clit and bringing his fingers back into play, sawing in and out in a steady rhythm.

In a half crunch, I rose to stare at the man who was eating me like I was his last meal. His hazel eyes, fully black, locked on my face, relishing the sight of me falling apart.

Those eyes met mine, and I broke.

The strength of the orgasm hit without warning, my body seizing and back bowing off the desk. I was willing to bet James would have a bald spot from my clawlike grip on his hair. When it was over, I went limp as tremors traveled up my legs.

James kept going with long, smooth licks, eating up every last drop of my arousal. Eventually, I had to drag that naughty mouth away, too sensitive for him to continue.

"You taste better than I imagined," he said, leaning one forearm by my face to make eye contact as I smiled at the ceiling.

"You should take your pants off now," I said, dragging a fingernail in the slight gap between his abs and waistband. I only now noticed he still had on all his clothes. There was something strong in being bare and disheveled while he remained so put together. Like he just had to have me and couldn't spare a second to undo even a single button on his shirt.

Mr. Buttoned Up who never breaks the rules wanted me so bad he was willing to do anything to have me.

"No. This was about you."

I tangled my fingers in the sides of his beard. "But I want to make you come too."

He gave me a sheepish smile. "You did."

"Oh."

"Yeah. Oh. I told you I was close."

"Do you—"

A hollow knock echoed through the dark room. We both froze. "Emma?"

It was Tracy. My boss.

"You in there? Kristi was looking for you."

I'm about to get fired.

CHAPTER FORTY-THREE

James

"So, Harry, what is it that you do for a living?"

I scooted my chair closer to the table to allow a passing server to get through and bumped knees with Emma's father. The tight squeeze reminded me why I didn't come to Carmella's, the local Italian restaurant, very often. I didn't fit. The head of the table—where I currently sat—was the worst spot of all. I had a front-row seat to Emma's parents' interrogation of my cousin.

It was the ultimate fifth-wheel hell, Linda and Frank Hartwell taking up one half of the small table while Harry and Emma shared the other.

Emma sat kitty-corner to me. I could tell she was pretending to pay attention as Harry droned on to Frank about the car repair business.

Since we had arrived, the Hartwells fluttered around their daughter. Linda had even brought some special cushion for Emma's chair, pulling it out of a large, heavy-looking tote bag. Emma had refused to use it, much to her mom's annoyance. Frank was lower key, but I noticed his daughter rolling her eyes at his repeated questions about her landlord making repairs. It was an interesting dynamic, one that I suspected played a role in Emma living several hours away from her parents, despite their apparent love for one another.

Under cover of the red-checkered tablecloth, I slid a boot toward the short brunette and hooked the back of her calf. I wanted to distract her, see those stiff shoulders relax.

If only we were alone, just us two, like earlier.

The woman sent me a subtle side-eye.

She was still annoyed about my reaction to Tracy almost catching us with our pants down—well, Emma's pants down. I'd remained unfortunately clothed.

Apparently, I hadn't appreciated the severity of the situation enough for Emma's liking. I couldn't lie—I kind of enjoyed being accused of not taking something seriously for a change. Still, my quick explanation about helping Emma carry a stack of paperwork to the parade seemed to convince her boss, despite my having been shaking with laughter.

She would get over her annoyance eventually—even if I had to go down on her again.

"*What?*" she mouthed at me.

I dragged a thumb over my lower lip before wetting it with my tongue, as if savoring the taste of something.

And I was. I'd had enough time to run home and change into fresh boxer briefs, but I hadn't bothered washing my mouth or beard. It was filthy, but Emma liked me filthy.

Her blush spread from her cheeks to below the neckline of her sweater.

Fuck, she was fun to mess with.

I was getting hard again at the thought of her responsiveness, how perfectly her kinks lined up with my own. I needed to cool it with that line of thinking—and fast. Christ, I'd already come in my underwear once tonight. If I did it again—in front of the Hartwells, no less—I would never be allowed back in Carmella's, maybe anywhere in town, again.

"How long have you owned your house, James?" Frank asked.

I ripped my gaze away from his daughter, realizing I'd lost track of the discussion, and it had somehow circled back to me.

"Uh, I inherited it from my mom a few years back. Spent some money and elbow grease to fix it up little by little. It's a work in progress."

Emma shot me an incredulous look. "Are you kidding me? Don't let him lie to you, Dad. The house is stunning—far from a work in progress. And you should see James' workshop in the back. It's in an old barn that he adapted for his business. He's done an amazing job."

Now I was the one blushing.

"Thanks," I said, rubbing the nape of my neck. I liked to dole out the praise. Receive it, not so much.

I tucked into my bowl of pasta, hoping it wouldn't leave me lagging at the gym in the morning. A niggling sensation tickled the side of my face, and I glanced up to find my cousin giving me a strange, assessing look from his seat next to his fake girlfriend.

Harry and I had made cursory apologies a few days after Emma's bout with the flu. The kind where we both said sorry for sniping at each other but never addressed the core of the issue. It was what we always did, but something remained off.

I shook him off and took a sip of wine before wading back into the conversation. "Having Harry around to help with the house has been a boon. Never could have done it all without him."

There. He couldn't possibly stay angry with me after that.

The man gave me a brief nod of acknowledgment. I wasn't just blowing smoke up his ass—he had helped with a ton of the manual labor since I'd inherited the Victorian. I wouldn't discount that, no matter how strained things got between us.

A light tap grazed my leg. I flicked my eyes to catch Emma beaming, like she was proud of the way I supported Harry. My whole body loosened. She knew I was making an effort.

The moment broke when Harry flung an arm across her shoulder and pulled her tight to his side.

"Ems, did you tell your mom and dad how we met?" Harry gave a wiggle of his arm, rocking her back and forth. He shot an affable grin at Frank and Linda before sending me a mischievous smirk. What the fuck was that about?

Emma stiffened. It was only a split second, but I saw it. She dabbed her mouth with a green cloth napkin, hiding her face while she gathered her composure. Now that I knew what raw, authentic emotion looked like on her, her tells were obvious.

"No, I don't think she has shared that story yet," Linda said, parsing her words carefully. Was she seeing what I was too?

"Do you want to tell them or should I?"

"Why don't you do it, Hare Bear?" Emma reached up and patted Harry's cheek.

I covered up my snort-laugh with a cough. I doubted I was fooling anyone.

"You good, Jay?" Harry asked.

I hacked once more before answering, "Yep."

My cousin glared. "Getting back to my story, I fixed Emma's car. Then I asked for her phone number, and we went on a date."

A date. If that's what they were calling it these days. More like a one-time romp in the sheets. Not that my meet-cute with Emma was much better: *man scares woman shitless while she's sneaking out of another man's bed.* Five years ago, jealousy and insecurity about the woman I was interested in having slept with my cousin would have kept me up at night, but I was too old for that now. Emma hadn't even known I existed when she'd hooked up with Harry.

Besides, they had been a one-and-done thing. If I had my way, Emma would be coming back for more.

And more.

Who the hell was I kidding? I would be the one begging her for one more moment.

Now, I just needed to figure out what I was going to do about it.

CHAPTER FORTY-FOUR

Emma

T HE CHRISTMAS TREE LIGHTS from the living area illuminated the front entryway of James and Harry's house as I walked in, the two men at my back. At dinner, Harry had proposed—in front of everyone—that I spend the night with him. James had looked ready to put his fist through his cousin's face. But I wasn't sure how to say no, not when my parents believed Harry and I were a couple.

And now here I was, sandwiched between the man my parents thought I was hot and heavy with and his cousin-slash-roommate, the man who was *actually* giving me the most intense orgasms I'd ever experienced.

"Ready to head up to bed?" Harry asked as I toed off my winter boots.

James' fresh wood and cologne scent tickled my nostrils as he reached past me to hang his jacket in the coat closet. "Y—yeah. I just need to wash up first."

I paused to look in the oval mirror after brushing my teeth and washing my face. My feet and back ached from a long, grueling day of parade prep and hours of standing behind a booth. But despite that, my cheeks were flush with energy and my eyes shiny—a picture of health.

I knew precisely who was responsible.

Too bad it wasn't the man whose bed I would be sleeping in.

I was lost on how to handle Harry. I had hoped we had come to an understanding in the Maven's parking lot the other night, after he ambushed me with that kiss. But tonight, he'd had a strange air about him, almost as if he had something to prove. I doubted it had anything to do with Mom and Dad. They had liked Harry just fine and didn't have an intimidating bone in their bodies.

The only logical guess was that his attitude was related to his cousin.

Shutting off the tap, I took a bracing breath in. I'd delayed long enough. When I opened the bathroom door, James stared me down from an open doorway on the other side of the hall. His room. I hadn't seen the master bedroom before, but knowing the man who lived in it, the space would be immaculate, clean, and filled with beautiful handmade furniture.

He took three steps, stalking toward me with the grace of a big cat.

I cleared my throat. "Let me get out of your way. Sorry."

I shifted to the side to let him into the bathroom. He stepped into the doorframe, bringing us face to face, sideways in the narrow space. Close but not touching. The tips of my breasts brushed the lower half of his chest, hardening in an instant.

I couldn't move or speak. He didn't seem to want to either, as caught up in the moment as I was.

The sound of Harry shuffling on the other side of the house made me pull away. I slipped past the tall man and into the safety of the empty hall. Despite wanting nothing more than to walk right into the open door of his bedroom, I resisted.

As I rounded the corner of the hallway that led toward Harry, James' low voice stopped me in my tracks.

"Come to my bed when he falls asleep."

The bathroom door clicked shut behind him.

Chapter Forty-Five

James

I PACED BACK AND forth at the foot of my bed while casting glances at the digital clock on the nightstand. It was almost midnight, and over an hour had passed since my directive to Emma in the hallway. I was even debating a trip to the kitchen under the guise of getting water just to listen at Harry's door.

I was addicted to Emma. I should have been working tonight, not attending holiday parades and eating dinner with Emma's parents. McGuire expected a finished product after Christmas, and though I had been hit with a bout of inspiration at long last, I wasn't making work the priority I should. Fuck, I hadn't even seen Jill in over a week, hadn't checked in on how things were going with Ben and her business.

Instead, here I was, jonesing for my next fix of Emma. And now that she was in my house, now that I knew how she tasted, how she felt on my fingers when she came, I couldn't pass up the opportunity for more—Harry and my lingering guilt be damned.

The red clock numbers flipped to midnight, and I had enough. Striding to my bedroom door, I flung it open, barely catching it before the knob put a hole through my drywall.

Emma stood on the other side, poised to knock.

My mouth dropped open right as she jumped, leaping into my arms and wrapping both legs around my waist. She grinned down, preening at having the upper hand for once.

I couldn't have that. I kissed that smile right off her lips before swiveling with her in my arms, kicking the door shut with my foot. As we turned, I gripped the bare skin of her ass where her pale-pink sleep shorts rode up and squeezed. Soon, those little shorts would be on the floor. In two steps, I had her splayed out on my bed, at my mercy once again.

I didn't bother turning off the lights as I stood above her, taking her in. This time, it wouldn't be dark. I wanted to see her in all her glory, wanted to see every curve and freckle of her skin.

I wanted all of her.

Her dark hair spread out like a halo, contrasting with the light tan of my bedding. Her loose white t-shirt fell off one shoulder. She was a beautiful mess.

She belonged.

If I had the skill, I would paint a picture of her there and hang it just above my headboard. But fuck, even a master artist would never do justice to her beauty in this moment.

Balancing on hands and knees above her, I brought one hand up to cradle her face. She turned into my palm, rubbing on me like a cat. I touched my thumb to her lower lip, pulling down until I could see the pink inside of her mouth, the shining tip of her tongue.

"You're beautiful."

I licked across her lips, dipping into her open mouth, mimicking the way I wanted to lick into her pussy. She moaned, and I knew she was picturing the same thing.

I lowered my hips to hers and let her take my full weight. Our height difference meant we had to shuffle and adjust a bit, but Emma's gasp told me when I'd found the right spot. I gave a gentle nudge, cursing the cotton of my sweatpants. I could practically feel the head of my cock entering her sweet pussy as I thrust again.

"James." Emma twisted the hair at my nape, forcing my eyes up to hers.

"Yeah, pretty girl?"

"Stop wasting time and fuck me. *Please.*"

CHAPTER FORTY-SIX

Emma

I BURIED MY FINGERTIPS into James' hips, working his sweat-pants off while he shimmied my shirt up and over my head. He let loose a vicious growl when he realized I was braless, the sound traveling straight to my clit like a jolt of electricity.

He brought both palms up to my nipples, strumming and playing with the hard tips.

"I want to suck on these all night."

I whined, writhing under his hands. He was taking his sweet-ass time, and I was going insane.

The man laughed. "Don't worry, pretty girl. I'll get to your pussy in due time."

I was going to kill him. But not before he made me come. "Holy fuck, James. Get the condom, please, please, please."

He twisted his torso, leaning over to the nightstand next to his bed. I watched impatiently as he pulled open a drawer and opened an unopened box of condoms.

He looked over and caught me staring. "If you're thinking I bought these today, you'd be right."

That meant he bought them just for me. I wasn't the jealous type—not normally—but something about that sparked a flame in my chest.

I sat up on my elbows as James tugged his loose sweats down below his cock. I had felt the hard shaft earlier, but this was my first true glimpse at it. He was thicker than I had imagined. Long and shiny. The tip of his cock glistened with pre-cum. I wondered how he tasted.

His hand trembled as he rolled down the condom. Was he nervous? I had little time to consider as he quickly secured the thin sheath and shifted my sleep shorts to the side, not bothering to pull them all the way off.

He sent me a smirk when he noticed I wasn't wearing any panties.

"How long have you been bare down here?" He dragged the knuckle of his middle finger up the center of my core.

"Since the library," I said, panting.

My panties had been too wet, too uncomfortable to wear after he had made me come all over my work desk.

"Damn. I should have fingered you under the table at dinner. Next time."

I was still shaking when the filthy-mouthed man thrust home, sending me sliding halfway up the bed. I lifted both hands to the headboard to steady myself, meeting the power of his thrusts with my own.

He bottomed out, filling up the space where I was emptiest. We moved in unison, me bearing down as he moved inside me, the length of his shaft moving with ease through the mess of my wet arousal.

I moaned his name, unable to hold back.

"That's right. Say my name while I'm fucking you. The rest of the world may think you're Harry's girl, but you and I know the truth. In here, you're fucking mine," he said in my ear, catching the lobe in his teeth.

I groaned and thrashed my head with abandon. I couldn't speak. It didn't matter if he was about to come, because I was about to go over the edge too.

James stroked into me, deeper and faster, unevenly. I dug both heels into the thick muscle at the sides of his ass, my body along for the ride. Taking his weight onto one arm, he slid his left hand down my waist to palm my thigh, locking me in place so I could take him in.

I cried out as the new angle hit me in just the right spot, his pelvic bone grinding into my clit. When he took that big, rough palm and smacked my ass, the loud slap echoing, the orgasm moved up my spine.

I was right there.

"Oh, fuck. Fuck, fuck, fuck." I frantically grabbed for one of the pillows behind me, bringing it closer and turning to scream into it. Harry's room was on the other end of the upper level, but I didn't want to chance it.

"That's it, beautiful. Come all over this cock."

Words turned to grunts as his hips jogged, his own orgasm soon following.

With a flop, he slid off and let his body fall to the bed beside me. The mattress rocked with the force of him coming down.

I grabbed my jiggling breasts in my hands, stilling their wild motion. I peeked over to see James watching intently.

His mouth twisted, holding a laugh at bay.

"What?" I said with a smile.

"I just find it amusing. You didn't care your tits were bouncing around while we were fucking, and now they move just the tiniest bit, and you make it seem like they're gonna run away."

I barked out a chuckle before giving him a playful smack on the shoulder.

"First of all"—I held up an index finger—"don't call them *tits* ever again. You sound like a caveman. And second of all, my mind was a little occupied while we were fucking, as you so sentimentally put it. If you had things this big strapped to your chest, you wouldn't want them moving all willy-nilly either. That shit is uncomfortable."

James made no attempt to hide his full grin as he stared at me, propped on one arm and stretched out alongside me on the tan comforter.

"You think you're pretty funny, don't you?"

"Oh, I know I'm funny, James Klein."

He huffed a laugh through his nose. "Yeah. You're right." He reached one hand over and cupped my left breast, running his thumb in circles around the pink areola. The soft skin hardened as I bit my lip.

"These are mine, yeah?" he asked, dark eyes focused.

"Yeah," I breathed out.

He made a satisfied hum before pressing a soft kiss on my lips. When our lips broke apart, he patted me on the hip before curling up to a seated position. "I'm gonna go take care of this condom. You want a washcloth or anything to clean up?"

I raised a brow. "That's thoughtful, but I'll follow you to the bathroom so I can pee. Can't have a girl getting a urinary tract infection now, can we?"

He shook his head in good-humored exasperation. I loved that I made him laugh, even after a serious round of sex. From what I had seen—and from what Jill and Harry had shared—I suspected the man didn't allow himself much room to be silly.

I was far from his perfect match, but fun? That I could manage.

I threw my t-shirt on, straightened my sleep shorts, and trailed him to the hall bathroom.

We made quick work of cleanup, smirking and bumping shoulders playfully as we went through the motions. I couldn't remember when I had last felt so alive.

Not since before the car had hit me, at least.

We landed at the threshold of the master bedroom, and James stepped inside. I paused, unsure where I should end the night.

"Should I stay?" I cast a glance toward Harry's side of the house. Though he'd been fast asleep when I'd left, he might wake up at any moment to find me gone.

"He sleeps like the dead. Don't worry. I'll set an alarm for you."

James reached for me, entwining his thick, rough fingers with my smaller ones. "Besides, I'm not done with you yet."

Should I ask him if he wanted to try something real with me? It wouldn't be serious. I could only handle casual. But I wanted to keep making him laugh, and smile, and come in his pants. I wanted to watch him in his workshop and eat omelets with him. I could end the fake arrangement with Harry and give this a shot.

But if I did that, then James would soon know the real me. And what would he think then? Would he still want me the way he did right now?

Answering his tug on my hand, I allowed James to pull me into the unknown.

Chapter Forty-Seven

James

A DARK LOCK OF Emma's hair tickled the tip of my nose as we lay entwined in bed. I had made her come again, this time with my fingers. I would never get enough of her, of how she felt, and how she tasted, and the sounds she made when her body bucked in pleasure.

It was more than physical. Everything about her drew me in. Her sarcastic wit, her never-ending patience with Harry, how she dove headfirst into life.

I smoothed her hair back down as she blinked up at me with half-closed eyes.

"Tired?"

"A little, yeah. But this is too nice to go to sleep."

"I'm not going anywhere, Emma."

"You can't promise that, though," she said, her tone serious. *What did that mean?*

She sighed and sat up straight. My arm slipped from her shoulder to her hip. "I think I should tell you about my past."

That didn't sound reassuring at all. "Are you on the run from the law? Dodging jury duty?"

My joke earned the smile I'd been hoping for.

"No, you crazy man. I'm talking about how I got injured. Why I came to Greyport and left the only home I ever had. Did I tell you I lived with my parents until I moved here? Never lived anywhere else before—ever."

She glanced down at her twisted hands. I placed a reassuring palm over them, stilling her movement.

"So do a lot of people, Emma, and for a lot of reasons. That's not a failing on your part."

"No, but there *is* a reason it took me so much longer and why I had to go so far to get some independence."

She was confirming what I had noticed at dinner. The way her parents hovered and fussed. Her urge to break away.

Was I doing the same thing to my sister and cousin?

Now wasn't the time to be worried about myself and my problems, though. "When the subject first came up, you said you don't talk about how you got hurt. I don't want you to feel like you have to tell me anything if you aren't ready."

"I wouldn't have brought it up at all if I didn't think I was ready. I feel comfortable telling you."

Damn if her saying that wasn't just as satisfying as making her climax. A nameless emotion ripped through my chest, bright and good mixed with the ugly shame that I was proud to have something from Emma that Harry didn't.

I coughed, clearing the catch in my throat. "Okay. I trust that you understand yourself best. That you know what you can handle. But I need you to hear it: there is no pressure here from me."

Emma drew close to me again, bringing her hands to my cheeks and combing her fingers gently through my beard. "You really need to stop being so perfect, you know that? It's a hopeless task for the rest of us to measure up."

Her palms lifted as my cheeks widened. Me, perfect? That was funny. "Emma. My sister is pissed off and avoids me half the time. My cousin went and found a fake girlfriend because I made him feel so inadequate. I can also think of more than a handful of occasions where I've been a complete dick to you since we met. Perfect is a stretch."

Her gaze grew serious, focused. She gave a tiny squeeze to my face before dropping her hands. "Everyone needs someone who would drop anything to take care of them. And no matter what you say, Jill and Harry will never, ever doubt how much you love them."

I rubbed my temples. "I do love them. But I'm starting to realize that maybe the way I love isn't the best thing for them."

She shrugged, like it was no big deal. "So, find a different way to show your love."

"Like it's that easy?"

"Oh. No. It isn't easy at all. I had to run away from my mom and dad because they haven't been able to do it."

"You still up to telling me your story?"

She blew a raspberry with her lips. "You noticed I deflected there, huh?"

I tipped my chin down, a nod of acknowledgment.

She closed those deep brown eyes, face still pointed straight up at the plaster ceiling. A moment passed, long enough that I wondered if she had drifted off. I leaned over to cover her with the bedspread when her eyes flew open.

"I'm not falling asleep right now. I just have to focus. I'm afraid if I look at you while I tell this story, I'll chicken out. Or you'll distract me with your sex appeal or something."

"Do whatever you need to do. I'm right here."

I meant what I told her. I wasn't going anywhere.

CHAPTER FORTY-EIGHT

Emma

I SETTLED IN, WIGGLING my toes and fingers, allowing my body to feel the contact points on James' plush mattress, hear the sounds of the house settling and the heat kicking on, smell the scent of the fireplace burning downstairs mixed with sawdust and mint toothpaste.

I shuttered my lids once more, cutting off the sense of sight. James breathed in and out, a steady rhythm beside me.

I dabbed my lips with the tip of my tongue and started to speak. "I used to ride my bike to work at home, when the weather was good. The summer before last, it barely rained. I think I biked just about every day."

James slid his hand onto my hip, a calming weight, as if he knew I needed the extra touch to get through the next part.

"It was the last weekend in August, and I was running late. I was coasting, coming up on a small hill before an intersection. But even though I was in a rush, I *was* paying attention to my surroundings. I *was.*"

I swallowed down the wave of defensiveness, irrational shame that shouldn't exist but never failed to surface in hard moments.

"The hill was a blind spot, so when I came up and over, I didn't stand a chance at avoiding the car. It was an older man who'd had a medical emergency at the wheel and crossed into the opposite lane. He didn't make it. And somehow, even after getting hit head on and flying up over the hood of the car, I did."

James was silent, but I didn't need his words. The curl of his fingers in my palm spurred me to continue.

"I was in the hospital for weeks and then had to do therapy in a facility for months after. Luckily, I was still on my parents' health insurance plan, so the debt didn't wipe me out too much. No rent payment helped with that too. One perk of living with Mom and Dad, I guess." I finally looked at him and attempted a smile that I was sure looked closer to a grimace.

"You know you don't need to make light of it to me, yeah? You went through a shitty, traumatic thing, and you're allowed to be mad, and sad, and negative about it if you damn well want to be."

I buried my face in a gray pillow to escape that knowing hazel gaze.

"You need to talk about something else now?"

"Ugh. No. It's okay, actually. I just hate that I've known you for, what, a month? And you understand me better than my parents do when I've known them my entire life. It's like I have to be totally and completely *together* and *positive* about my experience just to appease their worry that I'm fucked up for life. And don't forget, I also have to live in a safe little bubble forever. I know they mean well, but it's exhausting."

James smoothed a palm over my hair. He'd repeated the move a few times tonight, and I liked the new habit. "So, you found a job in a town hours away and moved as soon as you could?"

"Yep. I suck, huh? World's worst daughter. Plaster it across my forehead, right here," I said, poking a pointer finger between my brows.

James chuckled. "Nah, not at all, pretty girl. You're doing what's best for yourself. Have things been better since you've gotten settled here in town?"

"It depends on the day. Like tonight, they were fine for the most part. A little helicopter-ish but nothing too bad. But the night they got into town, we got into it a bit. I'm not sure if they'll ever stop. My mom likes to say that if I have kids, I'll understand. Maybe she's got a point."

"Is that something you want?"

"What? Kids?"

He nodded.

There was no straightforward response. I wasn't ready to explain to James that while I would love to be a mom, my confidence in my ability to care for myself was so lacking that I didn't see a clear path to taking care of a tiny human—not anytime soon, at least.

Instead of answering, I did it again—derailed the conversation with a joke. "Isn't that a rather personal question?"

"Oh, fuck off," he said with a laugh. "I thought that was pretty standard getting-to-know-you conversation when you're seeing someone."

"Oh, are we seeing each other now? Officially?"

"Was hoping it might be headed that way, yeah."

I smiled so hard my face hurt. I owed him a genuine reply. "The answer to your question is yes, I would like to have kids one day. *If* I had a supportive partner to share the load. I've been...struggling on my own, so that's important to me. But if I were with someone who wasn't interested in being a parent, I would be fine with not having kids, as long as the partnership was a good one."

"Sounds reasonable to me. I want to be a father but only with the right person too."

"James Klein, are you saying you want to make babies with me?" I teased. I brought a hand to my chest in the style of a shocked Southern belle.

"Always giving me shit. I might have to spank you for that."

I waggled my eyebrows. "Please do, sir. Please do."

"You're in for it now," James said just before he pounced.

Chapter Forty-Nine

James

T HE RHYTHMIC BEEP-BEEP-BEEP OF the digital alarm clock on my nightstand ripped me out of the best dream. I blinked sleepy eyes and noted the moon was still high in the dark sky—plenty of time for Emma to sneak out before Harry realized she was gone.

Despite being up so late, I couldn't recall the last time I woke so refreshed. Maybe it had something to do with the fact that I had the warm weight of one of Emma's breasts filling my palm. There was no better way to wake up.

We talked late into the night, even after another round of sex had left me drained—Emma playfully mocked my age, and she had a point. But I didn't care about being tired. I would use every minute of every night to learn everything about the woman beside me. If I could open up her brain and step into it, I would.

I dragged my eyes from her spectacular curves to her face. Her eyes blinked open. She smiled when she caught me staring.

"What time is it?"

"Little after four in the morning."

She pulled the down comforter over her head. "Why so early?" she asked, muffled under the fabric.

"You don't want Harry to know you spent most of the night in here, right?"

"Ugh. You're right. But it's so comfy in here with you."

That warmth grew in my chest, growing with every interaction. I tipped my head down and placed a soft kiss on the curve of her shoulder.

"How do you want to handle this, beautiful?" I asked.

"Handle what?"

"The Harry thing. Because I don't want this to be the last time we do this."

Her chest rose and fell with a big breath in and out. "I have to end the arrangement with him. And we have to tell him about you and me."

She didn't sound excited about that prospect.

I wasn't either. I knew Harry would feel betrayed—not by Emma, but by me. Even if I didn't suspect my cousin had feelings for Emma, it would hurt him to find out I knew about the fake-relationship deal and said nothing. He would think I had played along just to mess with him, to make him look like a fool.

I scrubbed a hand down my beard, overgrown bristles scraping against the dry skin. "Maybe we don't do it all at once? You can break it off with him first, and then we give it some time before we tell him about us."

She looked at me sharply. "What do you mean?"

I shrugged. It seemed a simple enough solution. "We do things quietly, and in, say, a few months, we can tell people we're together for real."

Emma sat up, her posture gone rigid. "A few *months*? And I'll be your dirty little secret that entire time?"

My heartbeat roared in my ears. This was going tits up, and I needed to fix it. "That is not what I mean."

She crossed her arms from her perch at the edge of the bed. "You'd better clarify things for me, then. Because that's what it sounded like."

"I don't want to keep you—keep us—a secret. I just want to take this slow, go on dates to see how this goes."

She stared at me, silent, for a beat. Her arms uncrossed, and my inner mascot sent up a cheer.

"Will these dates consist of meeting each other at midnight and fucking? Or dates out in public?"

I slid a hand across the bed and brushed her pinky finger with mine. She didn't pull away. "In public." Her straight spine relaxed the smallest bit. "I want to take you out on a proper date. Not in Greyport yet. I'd like to avoid any gossip. Keep things between you and me for a while."

"It won't stay secret forever, James."

I flipped my palm to grasp her fingers. "I promise I don't want it to. But I don't want to hurt Harry unnecessarily. I mean...what if we go on a few dates, and it doesn't work out?"

Saying that left a foul taste in my mouth. I was committed, but was Emma?

She pulled her hand away and gave me a soft look, like she felt *sorry* for me. "At some point, James, you're going to need to figure out how to live your own life and stop giving up what you want for the sake of others. You deserve better, and so do they."

I watched as she gathered her socks, thin white tee, and pink shorts.

"Okay," I said, swallowing past the lump in my throat as I sank down on the bed. This hurt like a motherfucker.

"But—"

I shot back up. Emma stood at the room's threshold.

"I'll give you one shot. One date. Make it good."

The gentle snick of the door shutting behind her echoed loud in my ears.

Chapter Fifty

James

"Y OU *SLEPT* WITH *EMMA*? What the fuck, James?!" Jill bounced up from the couch and began frantically pacing the living room. "When did this happen?"

"Last night, and could you quiet down? If Harry gets home, he'll hear you screeching like an owl. And it isn't what you think, Jill. I promise."

My sister paused in wearing a tread on the area rug to cast me a burning look. "Are you truly trying me with that cliche? What were you thinking? And what was *Emma* thinking? How could you two do this to Harry?" The pitch of her voice ended on a shrill note.

"They aren't a couple!" I said, shutting her up.

She jumped at my yell, and I felt like a dick. But I would not stand for Emma coming out like the bad guy in this scenario.

Jill narrowed her eyes at me before settling into a perched position at the edge of the coffee table, arms crossed. "Explain what you just said to me."

"Emma and Harry are not actually together. It was a fake-dating arrangement—to convince you and me, apparently, that he's a big boy."

"Fake. Dating. You really expect me to buy that? That doesn't happen outside of T.V. shows and books."

I threw up my hands. "What reason would I have to lie about that? Do you honestly believe I would have slept with the woman my cousin—who I also live with—is dating? I'm not that fucking stupid."

She uncrossed her arms. "Alright. Let's say I believe you. Harry's motivation makes sense, even if his plan was poorly executed. But why the hell would Emma pretend to date him?"

"You would have to ask her that directly. I won't betray her confidence," I said. I doubted I'd be doing myself any favors with Emma if I divulged her worries about making friends to my sister.

"That explanation is not going to cut it. This is fishy."

"Calm down, Sherlock Holmes. I promise you, she had no negative or shady motives here. It was all Harry's plan, and she was along for the ride."

"You know, Jimbo, you should have led with the fake dating bit. Not the 'we slept together' bit that makes the two of you look like scumbags. It would have saved me some anxiety over here."

"I'm a mess, Jill. Show me some grace, would you?" My mouth form into an unwitting pout. I covered my lips to hide it.

My sister hopped up from her seat on the coffee table and scooted over to the couch, her hip pressed to mine.

"Holy fuck, dude. You are in deep shit. So, what happens now that you hooked up with her? Is it an actual thing with you two? Because it would be a pretty bad idea to get in the middle of the Harry and Emma situation just to get your dick wet."

I huffed a heavy breath out through my nose. "It wasn't only *once*."

"Ew. Too much information, Jimbo. I love you, and I like Emma a lot, but no. I do not need details."

"I didn't mean it that way. I meant that it's more than a one-night stand. I have feelings for her, and I hope she feels the same way about me."

"I'm not seeing the problem here, then. If you want a relationship with her, then ask her to be with you. And if she says yes, come clean to Harry. He shouldn't mind since they aren't an actual couple, right?"

"Telling him is the problem. Because I suspect he wants to make it real."

"He doesn't get to call dibs on her, though, James. People don't work that way. Emma is an adult, and she can make her own decisions."

"Harry is pissed enough with me as it is, and now you're advocating for me to swoop in and start something with the girl he's into? I don't know if I can do that."

"I'm not sure I agree about Harry and his feelings for Emma. He ignores her half the time they're together. And this is with him supposedly playing it up for our benefit. That's not the behavior of a man who's invested in a woman."

I shook my head in denial. "He says she makes him better...or makes him strive to be better. Maybe I *should* step aside and let them figure things out."

"Has Emma given any indication she wants to be with Harry, for real? Because sleeping with you doesn't quite give that impression."

"I'm too old and boring for her. I'm sure it's just attraction and chemistry on her end. I'll only wind up being overbearing and driving her away."

"Jimbo, as much as I love that you're asking me for advice, the person you should be talking this through with is *Emma*. It's not your decision as to whether or not she likes you, not your decision on whether or not she considers you a good fit for her. It's her choice. Honestly, the fact that you're so self-aware about your smothering tendencies is scaring me here—in a good way. You're not usually so willing to admit your faults. Are you coming down with some-thing?" Jill pressed a hand to my forehead.

I ducked and dodged, dislodging my sister's icy fingers. "I may have made her kind of mad when I last saw her..."

Jill grinned, rubbing her hands together. "I am *relishing* this. What did you do?"

I winced, already prepared for her reaction. "I maybe, sort of, suggested that we be together in secret for a few months."

"You did not. James. W*hy?* If you're into her, why would you even want that?"

"Because of Harry. I can't hurt him."

"If he likes Emma, he'll have to put on his big-boy pants and accept that she doesn't reciprocate. Simple as that."

"He'll be pissed at me, though."

"You aren't responsible for Harry's feelings, Jimbo. Can I ask you a serious question right now?"

"Yes..."

"When did you last make a decision for yourself? For your own happiness?"

My mouth fell open as I racked my brain for an answer.

"It was starting Klein Custom, wasn't it?" Jill continued in the face of my silence. "Even when you moved back home—not that you wouldn't have come back eventually—it was driven by Mom getting sick. You even kept this house, a huge fucking Victorian, because it had extra rooms for Harry and me to stay in."

"I go to the gym almost every day. That's my self-care, even if you and Harry call me lame for doing it."

"That's like taking a daily vitamin, dude. Try again. Something more recent."

I realized where she was going. "Pursuing Emma was a choice I made for me."

Jill did a slow clap. "See, now you're figuring it out. Emma makes you selfish. And I mean that in the best way. You *need* to be a little selfish sometimes. Otherwise, your life will pass you by while you're so busy trying to dictate mine and Harry's."

I wasn't sure how to feel about this role reversal, where my kid sister dispensed sage advice and left my flaws raw and exposed.

I cleared my throat. "Emma said something pretty similar the other night, actually. That I need to stop giving things up for the sake of others." The words still burned in my brain.

"She's good for you—incredibly good for you, Jimbo. She and Harry never made sense to me. But you and her? You fit."

"She agreed to give me a chance. For one date."

Jill's hands flew around her face in a bizarre fluttering motion. "You're only telling me this now? What are you planning to do? Where are you going to take her? When?"

"Slow your roll. That's why I asked you here. I need your help. I can't remember the last time I took a woman out."

"Ugh, it was probably Laura. She sucked."

"She was alright. Just not the right one for me."

"Didn't she have a phobia of rabbits? And implied she wanted to drop-kick some little girl's pet bunny?"

"That...may have been her."

"Yeah, she was not alright. You better make this the most epic date ever. I can't take another Laura as my sister-in-law."

"I'd like to avoid Greyport at first. Stay out of the line of fire for gossip. I was thinking somewhere in Merlin Heights. They have some nice places that I bet Emma has never been to."

"Yes! You have to go to Three Ring. Here, I'll send you the link to buy tickets to a show. I'm sure they'll have a special event going on this week in the lead up to Christmas. Emma will love it."

"Are you sure? I don't want her to be overwhelmed while her parents are here."

Truth be told, I was terrified. This was my one chance, and if I screwed it up, I might lose the woman of my dreams. Because I was coming to realize that was what Emma was to me. I didn't know how to move forward, but I would figure it out.

"Jimbo, stop being a coward, and do it. You won't regret it."

CHAPTER FIFTY-ONE

Emma

I WAS BEGINNING TO see why the Grinch stole all those Christmas presents. Mom and Dad had filled my minuscule living room with heaps of gift bags and shiny wrapped boxes. Christmas was coming out of my ears, and there were still two days left before the big day.

"Emma, where do you want me to put this one?" my father asked as he dragged a large box in from the landing.

"I really don't care, Dad. Wherever you can find room."

I stole another peek at my phone. Still no word from James. A day and a half had passed. Apparently, now that he'd had me, he wasn't pressed to put in a lick of effort.

"Come on, get into the Christmas spirit!" Mom said, chiming in from where she was washing a stack of dishes.

I smiled wanly. "I'm doing my best."

I had slept like shit. My bed didn't hold a candle to James'. Too lumpy, not enough pillows. Too empty. One night with him and I was acting pathetic.

He would have arranged a date by now if he wanted to. It proved my first instinct was correct. I wasn't cut out for a relationship. He must have sensed it too. He had even said it himself: no point in going public with us when we may not work out after a few dates anyway.

I slammed the phone face down on the cheap wood coffee table, rattling a half-full mug of coffee, and shot up.

"Everything okay?" Dad glanced over from near the tree. He was moving gifts around in a strategic fashion, making room for more.

"Yep. Hunky-dory."

Why the fuck was I talking like someone from the 1950s? Maybe I should call my doctor—James Klein had melted my brain.

"I'm going to do my PT exercises!" I needed to work off this nervous energy, focus on something other than sexy custom furniture builders and my silent cell phone.

"That's a wonderful idea, honey," Mom said. "Frank, move some of that stuff out of the way. Emma has to do her home exercise program!" Suds of dish soap went airborne as my mother gestured wildly at her husband.

Dad parted the sea of presents, and I got to it.

I hit a steady pace, fueled by stress and annoyance, while my parents puttered around the apartment, preparing for our Christmas celebration. Since I was old enough to know the truth about Santa, we always opened gifts on Christmas Eve, saving only our stockings for the next day. Mom and Dad planned to head home early on Christmas morning, hoping to beat the holiday travel rush. I couldn't wait to sleep late and do absolutely nothing.

My thoughts drifted back to a certain woodworker as I squatted and lunged. All my muscles ached from the paces he had put me through. It beat being sore for other reasons, but it also reminded me I might never experience sex like that again.

Great, now I was a horny Grinch.

I was having trouble letting go after the other night. Sure, I had been the one to walk away in an epic girl-boss moment, but it pricked me that he just...gave up. Had just let me walk right back to Harry's bedroom, as if it didn't impact him a bit.

Thankfully, Harry had still been fast asleep when I'd come in. I hadn't been able to stomach lying down with him after everything with James and, instead, woke him to tell him I was heading home. He'd accepted the excuse without question.

My cell phone shook with an alert, dragging me from my reminiscence. As if I conjured him with my thoughts, it was Harry.

Harry: Come over on Xmas morning for brunch? There are presents for u.

I thumped the corner of the device against my forehead. The last thing I wanted was to go back to the scene of my rejection.

But what excuse could I even give Harry? *Sorry, I slept with your cousin and have actual feelings for him, but it turns out he changed his mind because I'm not worth the trouble.*

Not to mention the complicating factor that Harry himself might be carrying a torch for me. I had hoped that the disaster of a kiss he'd placed on me outside Maven's cured him of that, but he had been overly attentive at dinner with my parents—suspiciously so.

Ignoring his message, I navigated to my contact list and pulled up another name.

Emma: Got any time for girl talk? I need your input.

> Kristi: Hey! I wish. I decided last minute to
> go see my sister and nieces. I'm neck deep
> in unicorns and glitter right now. I'll be back
> on the 26th if you want to meet up then?

Well, that was a bust. I could always call, but I hated to be *that* friend who would impose on Kristi's holiday time with her family. I knew she didn't get to see them often.

Jill was not an option, for obvious reasons.

I shot off a brief response, committing to a date when Kristi would be back in Greyport.

> Kristi: You got it! I can't wait to hear all
> about what went down with you and James.
> **wink**

It really, really sucked having a clairvoyant friend sometimes. Nothing was ever a surprise.

"If you keep staring at your phone like that, you'll get a hump in your neck, Emma."

I flicked my eyes up at my mother, reining in the urge to roll them. "Thanks, Mom. I'll keep that in mind."

"What has you so engrossed anyway?"

"Oh, Harry invited me over to his house for brunch on Christmas Day."

I sent off the 'Yes' reply to my fake boyfriend before I could think better of it. I would deal with seeing James. We lived in a small town. There was no avoiding him forever. And this way, I could mentally prepare and better manage my emotions as opposed to being ambushed by seeing him out and about.

If I was already planning my outfit, hair, and makeup to look my best, it didn't mean a damn thing.

"That sounds lovely," Mom said.

It did not sound at all like she found it lovely. I bet she'd much rather I hopped in the car with her and Dad when they left and moved right back home.

Another notification came through. I ignored my mother's frown as I gazed back down at the screen.

James: Hey.

Oh, fuck no. He wasn't getting away with a one-word message. But...

Emma: Hi.

I couldn't resist.

James: Are you busy tomorrow night?

My parents were seeing *The Nutcracker* at a local theater. I had declined out of sheer holiday burnout.

Emma: I'm available.

Emma: Wait. You aren't asking me to see *The Nutcracker* with you, right?

Talk about awkward.

James: No? I have something a little more unique in mind. I'll take note of your aversion to *The Nutcracker*—for future reference.

My belly fluttered as I read the word future.

Emma: I'm game for whatever you've got planned.

James: Good. I'll send you the details.

I pocketed my phone and turned to find my father staring at me. I sent him another smile—a genuine one this time.

"Here, Dad, let me help you find a better spot for that box."

CHAPTER FIFTY-TWO

James

I STOOD OUTSIDE THE entrance to Three Ring, wind cutting through my thick jacket as I waited for Emma to arrive. The imposing building, a popular Merlin Heights attraction, doubled as an event center and bar-restaurant. Jill and I had scoured the website the day before, reviewing the schedule of events before settling on a holiday circus show with a Christmas-themed vegan menu.

Last night, I thought it was the perfect plan. Casual, low stakes, public fun.

I was not having any fun.

I hadn't seen Emma in days. When I had messaged her this afternoon to confirm our plans were still on, she'd agreed. But as I shifted my weight from foot to foot, still waiting, a bolt of insecurity hit.

What if she didn't show up? What if she decided it wasn't worth her time to take things slow with a thirty-five-year-old man who didn't know what he wanted? I was sorely regretting my suggestion that we drive in separate vehicles, but I was trying something new—giving up control.

In my effort to let go, I'd reached out to my former therapist—the one I saw after my mom passed. She was on maternity leave, but another counselor had an opening if I could wait a month to get on the schedule.

I had accepted. I was tired of making the people I loved miserable because of my inability to loosen the reins. It was time to change. For Jill, for Harry, and—I hoped—for Emma too.

An off-key wail from a deafening sound system split the air. The show was starting. I craned my neck to scan the parking lot again.

"James! God, I'm so sorry I'm late."

The weight in my chest lifted as my dream woman walked toward me, loose hair flying behind her. The waiting, the planning...it was all worth it. A short plaid skirt fluttered around her stockinged legs as she booked it across the blacktop.

She must be freezing...

My heart dropped when she went down, legs akimbo and ass to the ice. I rushed over, skidding to a stop at her side.

"Don't stand up too quick."

"I'm trying to maintain some dignity here."

I shouldn't have found her pouting cute, but I did.

"You good to walk the rest of the way?" I asked as I helped her to her feet.

"I'm not going to let you carry me in like an invalid, so yes." Her accompanying wince wasn't reassuring.

A cacophony of shrill guitar ripped through the cold air as I ushered Emma through the double doors. We made eye contact through the glass.

"This sounds very...modern?"

"You sound ancient right now."

"I *am* older than you."

"By what, a few years?"

"Nine. And I'm feeling every last minute of those years at the moment."

She nudged me with an elbow. "Get inside, old man."

We found our seats, and I pulled out the bi-fold program and menu provided at the entry. I placed my other hand just above Emma's knee. Her black wool tights were butter soft, the warmth of her thighs leaking through to my palm. Up top, she wore a loose-cowled black turtleneck. The outfit showed little skin but was somehow sexier for it.

"This alright?" I said, referring to my hand placement.

She nodded.

I paid scant attention to the performers twisting and sliding down red and green silks, my focus intent on the woman beside me. Her hair was shiny and smelled good enough to eat—that coconut scent.

I leaned over to whisper in her ear, to talk to her but also for an excuse to get another hit of that smell. "You look beautiful."

She blushed.

Okay. Cheesy compliments were a go.

I made it through the full performance and dinner without popping a boner, but it was a challenge.

We walked out of Three Ring hand in hand, the crowd surging around us as we lingered.

"Do you want—"

"—let's go get coffee."

I checked the time. "At almost ten at night? Not sure if any places are still open."

She sighed. "Ugh. Okay, you're right."

"I don't want tonight to end either."

"Is Harry at your house?"

"Yep." I'd had to make up a lame story to explain where I was going. I don't know how well he'd bought it.

"My apartment is empty. Mom and Dad are in a hotel."

"My truck will stick out like a sore thumb in the middle of Market Street." I cursed the Klein Custom vinyl wrap emblazoned on the side.

Great for advertising, shitty for clandestine dates.

"Could we just...sit in your truck for a bit? And talk?"

I short-circuited. The last time Emma had been in my truck, we hadn't done much talking. "Uh, yeah. Yes. We can."

She shot me a cheeky grin as she sauntered toward my pickup. "I'll lead the way."

I was helpless not to follow.

CHAPTER FIFTY-THREE

James

I CRANKED THE HEAT in the pickup as I navigated the vehicle to a more private section of the parking lot. It was high school all over again, trying to snatch any spare bit of privacy possible.

Emma reached her hands out to warm them at the heat vent, and I angled my body toward her, damning the oversized center console that kept her so far from me. A decent sized truck was a necessity in my line of work, but right now it was a goddamn nuisance.

"So, what did you think of the show?" she asked.

"It was...strange," I said with a wince. "I'm sorry. I should probably be more open-minded. The performers were talented, though. Did you like it? That's what matters most."

She smiled, a flash of white in the dim cab. "Not every piece of art is for every person. I enjoyed it a lot. Thank you for inviting me."

"The food was fucking amazing."

"Oh my God, yes! That vegan roast with the cranberry sauce was unexpectedly good. I would try making it myself if my kitchen wasn't so miserable."

"I'll let you borrow mine."

A dimple appeared in Emma's left cheek. I couldn't resist brushing the backs of my fingers over it, feeling the smooth skin dip. "I didn't realize you had one of these."

Emma turned her face into my hand. "I have to be ridiculously smiley in order for it to pop out."

My other life achievements paled in comparison to this moment. If I could spend every day of the rest of my life making this woman smile the way she was now, I would die happy.

I wanted to kiss her so badly, but I couldn't get carried away. I already knew sex with Emma was mind blowing, but I wanted to know all of her, know her mind and her habits, what made her tick.

I slid my palm from her cheekbone, along the cap of her shoulder, down her forearm, before taking hold of her warm fingers.

"Did you have any pets growing up?"

She snorted. "That was a rapid change in topic."

I grinned. "Just answer the question, smart ass."

"We had a chocolate lab with the very creative name of Brownie. The first few years of my life, I thought her name was Little Bastard because my mom called her that every time she peed in the house. What about you? I'm shocked you don't have a dog. You seem the type."

I cracked my neck. It wasn't the first time I'd heard that. Maybe it was because of the baseball cap and the truck.

"I'm actually allergic to dogs. Like, break-out-in-severe-hives-level allergic."

"That sucks."

"Is that a deal-breaker for you? Have you always longed for a dog and I ruined the dream? I can do allergy shots!"

That damn dimple deepened as she grinned cheekily. "I *have* been considering a dog lately. But I could make an exception. How do you feel about felines?"

"Never had a problem with them."

"Good."

"Great."

I followed the path of her eyes. She was looking at my lips. Fuck, now I couldn't stop thinking about kissing her, fucking her, eating her pussy until she came all over my beard...

I shook it off. "Quick, what's your favorite food?"

She giggled. "Is this Twenty Questions? And I can't tell you."

"Why not?"

"That's like asking me to choose a favorite book or a favorite child—if I had one. I can't pick."

"Narrow it down to your top five, then. You're not wiggling out of this one."

"Fine, but only if you go first."

"I don't need a top five. It's pizza."

"Pizza. James, that's the most basic, boring answer to the favorite-food question if I've ever heard one."

"It isn't a cop out, I promise! I have a very valid reason for it. Pizza is adaptable. There are endless limits to how you can customize it. The classic cheese-and-pepperoni combo. A breakfast pizza. Hell, I've even had pizza that tasted like a dill pickle."

"That is cheating. You can't pick a singular favorite food and then list a multitude of different versions of that food."

"Hey, at least I named something, Miss I Can't Possibly Pick One."

"If you must know, my favorite food is the taco. Want to know why?"

"Why's that?" I said, leaning in. We'd scooted closer and closer to each other without realizing, leaning across the console, caught up in our banter. I hadn't had this much fun in...well, ever.

"Because I can customize a taco however I want," she whispered.

I kissed the smile off her face.

I pulled back. Her eyes broad cast disappointment, but I didn't stray far.

"Keep talking. How do you customize them?"

"The classic Mexican taco."

Kiss.

"Breakfast tacos."

Another kiss, longer this time.

"Fish tacos," Emma said as I trailed my lips down her neck.

"I even made..." she said with a gasp when I nibbled the delicate skin behind her ear, "mac and cheese tacos once."

I reared up. "That is a crime against humanity."

She burst into laughter, the joyous sound filling the truck.

"They were awful. Never again."

We quieted, all noise inside and outside of the pickup fading as the last few concert-goers peeled out of the lot.

"I like you a lot, Emma."

I wouldn't hide it anymore, wouldn't act the coward. No more pretending I needed months to decide she was it for me.

"I like you too, James."

"When can I see you again?"

"I'll be busy with my parents most of the day tomorrow. They're leaving on Christmas Day, so we're celebrating the night before."

"After that?"

She gave me a soft, teasing smile. "We'll see."

"Still giving me a hard time, huh?"

"The deal was one date, right?"

So that was how she wanted to play it. I cocked my head. "C'mere."

"Where?"

I widened my legs as much as the bucket seat would allow and tapped my thigh. The perfect spot for her to sit. "Right here."

"James, you're, like, seven feet tall. I won't fit."

I didn't mention the many creative imaginings I'd done regarding Emma and me and this truck. I had the logistics covered.

"You scared?"

Her spine went ramrod straight.

"Not scared. Practical."

"Sounds like a delaying tactic to me. I was told I had to make my one date count. Now, come on. Sit on my lap. Don't make me ask twice."

I heard the exhalation, the stuttering breath she tried to hide.

Yeah, I knew how to get her going.

She crawled over the console, that little checked skirt riding up as she moved to throw one leg over my hip. I stopped her.

"Face the steering wheel."

I had plans.

"Uh, okay."

I shook my head when she settled sideways on my right thigh.

"Like this."

Both hands gripping her ass, I shifted her until she sat in the middle of my lap, legs draped over my thighs, spread out atop the stiff rod of my cock, and splayed open just to my liking.

"James?"

"Yeah?"

"Is this a Santa kink?"

I choked. "Are you into that?" I wasn't sure if I was, but fuck it. With Emma, it might be fun.

"I could be."

"That wasn't the plan, but...we can see where this takes us, yeah?"

"Okay."

"Relax, baby."

She listened, eager and trusting as her body melted onto mine. I brought a hand up to blanket the base of her throat and felt her swallow under my grip.

"Same thing I told you the other night applies here. If there's anything you don't like, say the word. Or tap my shoulder. I'll stop no matter what. Understand?"

"Uh-huh."

"Say it."

"I understand."

"You have to be quiet. Don't want to attract unwanted attention. We are in public after all."

I'd never thought of myself as an exhibitionist before—not until Emma. I never deviated, never made trouble, but here I was, taking part in the riskiest of play, baring myself to this woman and to the world.

I would eat up every minute.

The material of Emma's wool tights caught on my fingertips as I trailed them from her kneecap to her inner thigh. I paused at the juncture of her groin, absorbing her body's shivers.

She cried out when I reversed the process and repeated it another time.

"Shh," I said, taking the hand at her throat up to her mouth. "You've got to be quiet, remember? Otherwise, I might have to put you on the naughty list."

From her reaction, she didn't hate the Santa thing. She mumbled something incoherent against my palm. But fuck, I needed her out of control, clawing and biting.

I kept on trailing my fingers along the inside of her leg, drunk on the sensation of her squirming against me. At last, I relented, cupping her hot center.

"How attached are you to these tights?" I asked, speaking low in her ear and uncovering her mouth.

"Not at all. They were only—"

Rip.

The flimsy fabric tore like tissue paper along the center seam. From there, it was quick work to tug her lace panties to the side, exposing that glistening pink skin to the cool air. Like unwrapping the most delicious present.

She shivered in my arms.

"Are you turned on, or are you cold?"

"Both."

I smiled against her hairline.

"Don't worry, pretty girl. I'm gonna take care of you so good."

I dragged my middle finger through her center, coating the thick digit in her wetness. With my ring and index fingers, I opened her up, brushing her clit once before lifting off and hovering just above it.

"Tell me how you want it."

"Just touch me," she said, bucking to make contact. I brought the palm circling her neck down to her leg, stilling her with a firm touch to the thigh.

"I'll make it easy for you. Multiple choice. Do you like little circles?" I traced the pattern on her tight bundle of nerves. "Or side to side?"

"Circles," she said, arching up.

"Fast or slow?"

God, this was fun.

"Fast. Fuck, James, stop torturing me."

I gave in to her demand because, really, all I wanted was to make her happy.

With hard, quick whorls, I drove her to the edge, her body tense and quivering against me. She reached an arm up over her head, grasping at my hair.

Just when I could tell she was about to go off that cliff, I tugged her dark locks and brought her mouth to mine, swallowing her keening moans.

The truck windows were steaming. Anyone around could tell what we were doing. I was lucky there wasn't a soul in sight.

I placed a possessive hand over my girl's pussy, eating up the aftershock of her climax.

"What do you say, did I earn that second date?"

"Jury is still out," she gasped.

A guttural sound tore up my windpipe. God, this girl was fucking incredible.

"Reach into the glove box."

"Huh?"

"Just do it."

She leaned over, and I seized the opportunity to smack her tight little ass. Her giggling shriek was a reward in itself.

I shimmied my black pants and boxer briefs down my hips while she was occupied.

She slapped the foil packet into my hand. I ripped the condom open with my teeth, tossing the wrapper into the backseat. I'd have to remember to clean it up tomorrow.

I rolled the condom on and tugged Emma toward me until her back touched my chest.

"C'mon, pretty girl. Hop on."

She sank down until my cock was seated all the way inside her. I bit my inner cheek—hard—to stop myself from coming on the spot.

"One day soon, I'm gonna fuck you raw. Feel every last inch of this hot cunt on my dick. Would you like that?"

"Yes," she said. It was more breath than words.

"We'll do it safe. I would never do anything to hurt you. Because this body was made for me. Do you understand?"

She nodded.

"Good. Now, ride this cock. Because you own it now."

Her moan was loud, all attempts at discretion out the window. I fisted those little lace panties in one hand, locking her in place as she heeded my command.

"Fuck, Emma, I'm close. Are you gonna come again for me? Be a good girl for Santa?"

"Uh-huh."

"Give me your hand." I grabbed it before she had a chance to respond. Sucking her middle three fingers into my mouth, I laved my tongue in the curve of her knuckles, leaving them dripping with saliva when I released them.

"Rub that clit in those little circles you like. Get yourself there."

I didn't have to tell her twice, and it wasn't long before her movements grew erratic. Her panties dug into her flesh as I twisted them around my fist, losing control before following her over the edge.

I collapsed into the seat. She fell back onto me.

"I think you might have killed me," she said.

"*I* killed *you*? I'm the old man here. If anyone is gonna die from sex, it's me. I mean, fuck, you turned me into Santa Claus for a minute there."

Her inner muscles clenched around me as she laughed.

"Hey." She twisted around so she was sitting sideways across my legs.

"Yeah?"

"I'll go out with you again—if you're still interested, that is."

"Of course I'm fucking interested."

"If you're ever...not interested anymore, you'll tell me, right?"

I didn't know where this was going, but I sensed this was important to her.

"I promise to tell you. But I don't see that happening, just so you know."

"There are no guarantees in life, James. Anything could happen."

CHAPTER FIFTY-FOUR

Emma

MY APARTMENT WAS A mess, and I didn't even care. I was floating on air, and not even a Christmas Eve lecture from my parents could get me down. I'd convinced James to come back to my place after our date. It had taken some inventive maneuvering to hide his truck—down the street and in a corner near a dumpster—but we'd been determined and horny.

And then we'd done each other...all night long.

We'd talked too, about so many things. Like how challenging it had been for James to take on a parenting role to Harry and Jill right after his mom passed away. How his friendship with Ben Till had started back when James had been a tall, lanky teen, Ben shielding him from childhood bullies until James had bulked up doing sports.

For me, I'd shared stories of writing grad school papers with my childhood stuffed animals piled on shelves behind me. How romance novels got me through the stress of writing endless papers. The disappointment of missing my favorite folk singer in concert because I'd been laid up in the hospital during her last tour.

James didn't mind that I was a hot mess. In fact, he seemed to embrace it. Despite his overbearing tendencies with his family members, he hadn't once treated me with kid gloves. He'd even taken my weird, melancholy turn in the truck in stride, reassuring me with words and actions.

The morning had come too soon, though, and he was rushing out. My parents called to tell me a water main broke at their hotel, and they wanted to come over—right that minute—to wash up and start our holiday festivities.

James stopped at the threshold of the door as I held it open. I wore his royal-blue college sweatshirt—and nothing else. I could tell from the gleam in his eyes he would rather stay and fuck me while I was wearing it. Truth be told, I wanted that too.

"I'll call you later tonight," he said, pressing a slow, deep kiss to my lips. "We're doing this again."

I could only nod, giddy as I watched him stumble his way down the stairs to exit the building. I hadn't told him Harry invited me for brunch, hadn't wanted to ruin the moment by mentioning my fictitious connection to his cousin. Not when things were only beginning with us.

When I heard the outer door slam shut, I raced to my bedroom to throw on something more presentable. I tossed my hair up in a messy bun and brushed my teeth, all while kicking dirty clothes under my bed so Mom wouldn't see. The sight of my ripped tights sent a thrill up my spine, goosebumps prickling my arms as I remembered what James had done to me in his pickup, how he'd driven me insane with wanting. I had teased him about only having one date, but the minute I had seen him in that Merlin Heights parking lot, black dress pants straining those thick thighs as he paced with nerves, I would have accepted a second, third, and twenty-third date if he had asked.

"Knock, knock!"

Only my mother and father would say, '*Knock, knock,*' instead of simply knocking on the door.

"Coming!" I said, tossing the tights into the recesses of my drawer.

I was breathless by the time I greeted them.

"Good morning! You look...very nice, Emma," Mom said.

I smoothed a hand over my crooked bun. "I wasn't expecting you so early. Sorry, I didn't have much time to get things in order."

"I wasn't being sarcastic," she said, moving toward the bathroom with her floral toiletry bag. "Yes, the place is messy, but you seem healthy. Happy. I haven't seen you like this in a long time."

I was glowing from all the orgasms, but no way in hell would I tell my parents that.

"Hope you don't mind, but I brought over one last gift for under the tree. We passed by that bookstore on the way here, and I couldn't resist."

"Dad, there's barely any room as it is." Still, I had to laugh as he produced a small wrapped box with a flourish.

Time moved in a whirl as Mom and Dad buzzed around me, prepping breakfast while I drank a much-needed cup of coffee on the couch. It was hectic, but...nice.

Had James Klein given me a lobotomy with his dick?

"Honey?"

I looked up to see my mother and father staring at me.

"Yeah?"

"You okay? I said your name about three times," Dad asked.

"Good. Great. I'm a little tired. Didn't sleep well last night."

I could see Mom biting her tongue, but she restrained herself. "Breakfast is ready."

The three of us sat around my wobbly bistro table—James had hit me with a wordless look when he'd seen the shoddy workmanship, and I suspected a custom-made kitchen table was in my future.

"So..."

"Yes, Mother?" I knew she wouldn't be able to hold in her curiosity for long.

"Things seem to be going well with Harry, then?"

I choked on a bite of scrambled eggs. "Um, yes. Very well."

"Well, I can't say I'm enthusiastic to see you settling so far from us, but you deserve someone who brings you joy. And his family seems wonderful too. They'll look out for you when your father and I can't."

Yeah, Harry's family was great. Namely, one family member in particular who excelled at taking care of me in all the ways.

"I liked that cousin of his. James. I looked at the website for his business, and I was impressed, let me tell you. Talk about talented. Too bad you didn't meet him first, eh?" Dad jabbed me with a playful elbow.

My coffee went down the wrong pipe, triggering a coughing fit.

"Are you okay, honey? You've been coughing a lot today. Are you getting sick again?"

I flapped my hands in denial as Dad gave me a jarring slap on the back. "Just swallowed wrong."

My mother looked skeptical, but we continued on with the meal, blessedly free of all mention of my fake boyfriend and his cousin.

I spent the rest of the morning surrounded by food, wrapping paper, and my own thoughts of James. Even Mom's most passive-aggressive gift—a framed sign for my desk at work with small pink hearts and *Call Your Mom* emblazoned across it—didn't bring me down. Granted, she and Dad also gifted me a new welcome mat along with a heartfelt note about making my new home my own. They were trying.

I realized, as the time with my parents wound to a close, that Christmas was about to end. I'd spent so much of my energy anticipating the day, worrying and building things up in my head, that I'd forgotten just how fast it all moved.

One more day, and then Christmas would be over. My arrangement with Harry would be over. But maybe I could step into a new season with James by my side.

CHAPTER FIFTY-FIVE

James

HARRY WAS WAITING FOR me, arms crossed and toes tapping, when I got home from Emma's house.

"My, my, my, someone is getting home late. Or should I say early? That is...very interesting. Anything you care to share with the class, Jay?"

"Nope," I said, hanging up my jacket in the front closet and stowing my dressy, non-work boots. My black pants were visibly wrinkled. It was obvious I'd been on a date, but I hoped to deter Harry from probing for details.

I saw my sister seated on the brown leather couch as I walked farther into the living room.

"What are you doing here?" She'd told me her retail job had her scheduled until mid-day on Christmas Eve to account for all the last-minute shoppers.

She made an *I don't know* gesture with her hands. "I called out sick. My boss is pissed, but I'm hoping I won't need that job much longer. Harry said we needed an emergency planning session."

I looked down at my phone. Sure enough, I had missed several messages in a string from my cousin and sister. Too caught up in Emma. I couldn't bring myself to regret it, even in the face of an irritated Harry.

I slammed into the kitchen, avoiding my cousin's narrowed gaze. He followed me, a dog with a goddamn bone.

The sink was chock-full of dishes.

"Are you kidding me, Harry? I was gone for less than twelve hours. How the fuck did you eat so much? And you couldn't even wash up after?"

He walked over to the sink and washed one bowl. One.

"Better now, Dad?" he said, turning to give me an infuriating smirk.

"You're such an ass, Harry," Jill said, hopping to my defense.

The man's blue gaze cut away from me. "Why are you even here, Jill?"

"Uh, because you invited me, you dipshit."

"Alright, you two, cut it out. Glad to see you're both acting like adults this morning."

"Is it a grown-up thing to sneak around and not tell your loved ones you're staying out all night? I know I get distracted, but I'm not overlooking that one."

"Maybe Jimbo was buying a gift for you," Jill said. She was aware I'd been with Emma and was trying to cover.

Harry looked from me to my sister. It was clear he still didn't buy it, but he gave a brief nod, accepting the explanation for now.

"What is the deal with this emergency meeting?" I asked. Best to move the conversation forward before Harry started in again with the questions about where I'd spent the night.

"I invited Emma for Christmas brunch tomorrow. I need help planning."

What the fuck? "Since when do we do brunch on Christmas? And when did you invite her?"

"Yesterday afternoon."

"And you decided not to tell me until today?" And more importantly, why hadn't Emma mentioned it to me either?

"Yeah, sorry, I forgot. Do you think you can make those thin pancake kinda things? I bought a shit-ton of eggs the other day to add to my smoothies, but I haven't used many."

"Are you talking about crepes?" I hadn't made them in years—not since Mom had found them to be one of the few foods she could stomach toward the end of her illness. I'd spent hours getting the consistency down.

"Yeah. I think Emma would like them. Don't you?" Harry looked at me pointedly.

"You would know better than I would."

"Yep. I would know. Since she's my girlfriend."

"Right..." I crossed my arms and leaned back against the counter. If he wanted to be a little shit, then I wasn't in any kind of rush to assist with his stupid, last-minute plan to impress Emma.

"Well, do we have the ingredients or not? I need to know. Now."

"Why don't you find a recipe yourself? The internet exists. You could even open up a few cupboards while you're at it."

"You're such—"

Jill clapped her hands together three times and grinned when both Harry and I shut up and looked toward her.

"I do that at the library with the kids. Always wanted to see if it worked on adults too. It does. Cool."

"This is none of your business, Jill," Harry said with a snarl.

I straightened to full height, not saying a word.

He got the message, standing down. "Sorry, Jill. Sorry."

"Whatever, Harrison," my sister said will an eye roll. "My comment is for you, anyway, and you won't like it. You're the one who wants to do this brunch, but you're asking James to cook for you. Really, dude?"

He had the good sense to look contrite, putting me in mind of a sad, lost puppy.

"I can't cook, guys. I'll poison Emma." He steepled his hands together. "Please help?"

"And you didn't think to order something?"

There went Jill with the logic.

Harry threw up his hands in defense. "It's Christmas Eve. How am I going to get anything now? Besides, it's not exactly impressive if it isn't homemade, right?"

"Who is supposed to be impressing Emma, Harry? You? Or James? Because it's not a point in your favor if you have someone else do all the work for you. Last I checked, James wasn't Emma's boyfriend."

Damn, Jill was on a roll tonight. She hadn't come to bat for me like this in ages, and I certainly wasn't upset about it. But she was getting too close to home with that last comment.

"Why did you even bother coming over if you were just going to shit on me the entire time? You sound just like James with the nit-picking It's getting really fucking old."

"First off, I came over because you asked me to, asshole. Only to hear you trying to pawn everything off on my brother. Like you always do. I'm not in the mood for this."

"Jill. Harry. That's enough."

"I'm only trying to help—"

"She's totally out of li—"

"Stop. Jill, I don't need you to fight my battles for me. I'm a grown adult. And Harry, Jill is right. You can't put this all on me. But I will help—mostly because I don't want to starve tomorrow."

My cousin's mouth opened, but I cut him off with a pointed finger.

"Go count how many eggs are in the fridge. Jill, go check the pantry and see what we have for bread and spices. Powdered sugar too. I'm not making crepes. Too much work." And too many painful memories. "We can make French toast casserole."

I would take care of the planning, as usual, but I'd be damned if Harry wasn't at least going to crack a few eggs.

Chapter Fifty-Six

James

"Would you turn that fucking music down? I'm trying to listen for the door." I watched from my stool at the kitchen island as Harry whisked a bowl of eggs and shouted orders at Jill.

"Still crabby, Harrison?" my sister snapped. Tensions were still high over the brunch-planning fiasco.

"Nope. But I'd rather not have shitty Christmas music blasting my eardrums while I'm making breakfast for my girlfriend."

I clenched my fist where it rested atop my thigh below the countertop. I hated him referring to Emma as his girlfriend. Even if I hadn't wanted her for myself—and I very much did—I was growing more and more bothered by the ease with which Harry was carrying out his lie.

"I'll take over with the eggs. Go sit in the other room and watch for Emma's car." I stepped over to my cousin and gently shouldered the shorter man out of the way.

He dropped the whisk with a clatter and clapped me on the nape of the neck. "Thanks, bro. I thought my wrist was about to snap off. You would think I would be used to it from...you know...but apparently not."

"You're disgusting," Jill said as Harry left the room, eager to be rid of his part of the meal prep. He sent her a raised middle finger as he skipped backward out of the kitchen.

My sister turned to me once we were alone. "Please tell me your date went well, and Emma is breaking things off with him soon. I cannot take another minute of this weird version of Harry where he acts all ambitious but retains his slacker-like tendencies. He's driving me nuts."

"The date was amazing, but I don't know how she'll want to handle things. I had to rush out this morning because her parents were coming over. I'll try to talk with her today, but I need you to keep Harry distracted."

"Don't you worry, Jimbo. I have a brilliant plan in mind." Jill made a gesture with her fingers near her temple, as if noting her brilliance.

"I can't wait," I said deadpan. I couldn't help but worry she would go overboard into unbelievable territory. But I was putting my trust in my little sister, who, so far, had offered solid advice in the situation. Funny, given that Jill seldom spoke about going on dates, let alone serious relationships. She was perpetually single. But I wasn't planning to question her about it now, not when it seemed we were getting back on an even keel. I would just have to keep humbling myself to her as much as my pride could handle. That had seemed to do the trick.

If the way my heart leapt out of my chest when I heard a knock on the heavy front door was any sign, I would be plenty humbled again—and soon. Emma kept me on my toes.

As a distraction, I added a few spices to the egg mixture, all the while pretending not to pay attention to the voices coming from the entryway. I was suddenly struck by an uproar of butterflies in my stomach.

Jill raised her eyebrows at me. "Are you going to hide in here and not say hi?"

"Someone has to make breakfast."

She cast her eyes to the ceiling. "You're hopeless, you know that?"

I kept my focus on cooking as I heard her light footsteps carry her away.

Once the casserole was in the oven, I no longer had an excuse to hide, not without drawing extra attention. Working in the barn wasn't an option. I'd completed every outstanding order, even the ones for McGuire, in the last few days, fueled by the high of my interactions with a certain brunette.

I wouldn't quite call her my muse, but...

On socked feet, I ventured to the living room where Jill, Harry, and Emma's bright chatter competed with the sound of the Christmas playlist.

I cleared my throat before wading in. "Food is baking. Should be ready in about thirty or forty minutes."

It was all I could do not to step up to Emma and gather her in my arms. Her feet were curled up under her, where she sat on the couch next to Harry.

My cousin's arm stretched out along the back of the brown sofa, tucking her in close. My short fingernails bit into my palms as I squeezed them shut. I wanted to leap across the room and launch Harry into the corner—not to hurt him but to get him as far from Emma as possible.

On second thought, hurling him across the room wouldn't be sufficient. Across town would be better.

They looked good—right—together, and it infuriated me. Harry was younger, closer to Emma's age. He was fun and spontaneous, while I was boring and set in my ways. He had a large friend group and social life—something I knew was important to Emma. I would only bring her down.

And was I risking fucking up my relationship with my cousin permanently to pursue something with a woman who might not want me long-term?

"Merry Christmas, Emma," I said finally, because what else was left to say?

"Merry Christmas, James." A tremulous smile—and that damn dimple—wreathed her face.

That made this all worth it. Putting myself and my feelings on the line was worth the risk if only I got to see more of that dimple. Whatever was happening with Harry, he and I would work it out. Because Emma and Jill were right. I couldn't continue putting my happiness on hold. Not when it was sitting directly in front of me in my own house.

"James," Harry said, rising from the couch and marching toward me.

"Yeah?"

"I want to open gifts now."

"Okay… What crawled up your ass all of a sudden?" He was acting strange again. Curt and rude, like I was intruding. I lived here too, damn it.

"I just don't want the entire focus to be on the food. It's Emma's first Christmas with us. It needs to be special."

I bit my tongue so hard I tasted iron. Harry had been panicking the night before over the food, and now he was bitching at me for making it a priority. I couldn't win.

"Just get the presents."

I sat in my recliner while Harry bustled about with armfuls of reflective, green-wrapped boxes. I refused to help him, on principle alone.

"Alright, that's everything, I think."

"Holy shit, did you buy out an entire store?"

"No, Jill, I did not. And kindly keep the commentary to yourself."

Harry made quick work of dividing up the gifts, leaving small piles for each recipient. I used my foot to slide over the packages I'd bought for him along the hardwood.

In a mass rush, we ripped into boxes and tissue paper. I glanced to my left, where Emma sat stiff and wide-eyed.

"We don't take turns. Go for it."

She looked at me and paused, then nodded before digging into her own pile.

A sea of cardboard and torn paper surrounded us when we finished. I had amassed thick gloves for shoveling snow, a new portable speaker for my workshop, and a few gift cards to local stores in town. Jill appeared pleased with the set of hand creams I had purchased for her, along with a sweater from her wish list.

I purposely didn't look at Emma. I had already given her my purchase for her—the new coat and boots—but I hadn't been able to resist getting her a biography of a famous community organizer.

"I can't believe you got this for me, bro," Harry said, clutching the mountable camera I'd ordered him. He had been talking about wanting something like it to use when doing all his various sports.

"You're welcome."

"No, really. If I'd known, I would have upped my game from gloves and a gift card to the hardware store."

I shrugged off the praise. "The oven is beeping. I'll be back." I strode purposefully into the kitchen and jabbed the button to power off the oven. Thirty seconds remained on the timer, but it was close enough.

The steam from the casserole warmed my face as I set the dish on a hot plate. With a heavy sigh, I turned and relaxed, the small of my back biting into the hard countertop.

Emma's warm brown eyes met mine from the other side of the island.

Chapter Fifty-Seven

Emma

I HAD DEBATED IGNORING James' presence altogether—not entirely, not so much that Harry and Jill would notice something amiss—but I didn't trust myself not to fall into his arms, not to stare at him too long or pour out the depths of my feelings for him in front of everyone.

That was the truth of what I was dealing with for James...feelings. The very thing I wanted to avoid. If I felt something for someone, I gave them the power to hurt me when they finally realized I wasn't worth the hassle, that I was too much of a burden with my messy life and shitty, half-broken body.

The instant James had entered the room and wished me a Merry Christmas, my plan to ignore him flew out the window.

After waiting for what I hoped was an appropriate amount of time, I followed him to the kitchen. As usual, he was the person leading all efforts to host and cook. He was a caretaker, through and through, and it was attractive as hell. But he was self-destructive about it, and a relationship with him would never work if he couldn't draw boundaries.

He didn't even want to be open about dating me if it meant pricking his cousin's pride.

That was all it was, really…pride. Harry would be fine once his crush on me receded and he found a better match.

I tried—and failed miserably—not to check out James' ass as he removed a delicious-smelling dish from the oven—I would need to get the recipe—and then slipped off a pair of ridiculous Santa oven mitts. I could only berate myself so much for my failure. The man had an excellent ass. It looked good in jeans, but I knew firsthand it felt even better in my hands when he was thrusting his hips.

My cheeks burned when he turned, and we locked eyes, my brown and his hazel.

"Um. Hi."

I was eloquence personified.

He bit down on a smile, and it outshone any gift I'd opened in the living room.

"Do you need help with anything?"

"No."

Did he want me to leave him alone? I couldn't get a read on him this morning. "Okay, then. I'll—"

"Come here."

I was on the other side of the island in five steps before I stopped a pace in front of him, unsure of my next move. My fake boyfriend was only feet away.

James took the choice out of my hands, sliding one muscular arm around my waist and the other behind the cascade of my hair. He pressed me into a hug. The warmth of his breath on my collarbone triggered a trail of goosebumps up my neck.

"I missed you." His words tickled my ear, and I couldn't hold in a giggle.

"It's been twenty-four hours."

"Doesn't matter. I miss you anytime you're not right here." The slight squeeze he gave me made his meaning clear.

"I missed you too," I whispered.

I felt the loss of his heat as he pulled away, separating our upper bodies. He didn't let me go far, cupping my elbows in his steady grip.

"We should talk about how to approach Harry."

I nodded. "Yes, I agree. We can—"

"We have one more present!" Jill's shrill voice cut through the scant space between me and her brother.

I was a pace away, smoothing down my hair when Harry strolled into the kitchen.

"What the hell, Jill?" Harry mumbled, half turning to shoot a scowl at the woman. "I can tell her myself. No need to give everyone on the street a permanent headache with your screeching."

Had Jill's outburst been to warn us that Harry was coming? But that wouldn't make any sense—not unless she suspected my connection to James.

I was still slow-breathing, working to calm the racing of my heart, as Harry grabbed my hand to drag me back toward the Christmas tree. His palm was slick and sweaty.

I dared a glance at James. His jaw was set, frustrated yet determined. I felt his eyes on me long after I turned away.

Harry hustled me over to the couch. He was a ball of chaotic energy—more so than usual.

"Sit here, okay? I have another thing for you to unwrap, but I left it upstairs." He ran to the staircase and started up, taking each step two at a time.

"What the hell is going on? Didn't we already finish this shit?"

"I don't know!" Jill said to James in a rushed whisper. "He started getting jumpy out of nowhere and said he had something he forgot to give Emma."

A cold bead of sweat dripped down my temple. My chest grew tighter and tighter, and no amount of measured breathing offered relief.

"Uh, guys, I'm freaking out a little here." I looked frantically from James to Jill and back again.

"Emma," James said. His commanding tone somehow sent a wave of calm through me. "Just…sit. Breathe. Focus on your feet on the floor. I'll go find out what he's doing." He stalked in the direction his cousin had gone, only to come up short when Harry bolted down the flight of stairs, sliding on the wood floor when he reached the bottom.

"Slow down before you fall on your ass."

Harry was panting as he walked to me, carrying a small, shoddily wrapped rectangular package under an arm.

"Ems," he said as he crouched down. I pressed my knees together—hard—to hide the shaking.

What the fuck, what the fuck, what the *fuck* was in that box? And why did he sound so serious?

"This last month with you has been amazing."

I made eye contact with Jill above Harry's head, broadcasting a desperate *'Help me'* plea. The blonde was pale, her mouth agape.

I wouldn't—couldn't—look at James.

"I need to show you how serious I am about you, how committed I am to doing this. Together."

He handed me the wrapped gift. I held it in delicate fingers, like handling a grenade.

At Harry's eager expression, I slipped a finger under the crooked tape holding the wrapping paper in place. A clock ticked as "Have Yourself a Merry Little Christmas" echoed through the Victorian.

My mouth grew dry when I unveiled a small, white jewelry box. Harry, tired of waiting, reached over and lifted the lid. Inside was a shimmering opal strung on a dainty gold chain.

"Do you like it?" he asked as he held the necklace up to the light, looking as excited and earnest as a dog from one of those videos where the owner comes home from a deployment.

"Y—yes," I said in the face of his questioning gaze.

"Let me put it on you."

I kept my eyes pinned straight ahead, looking at nothing and no one, while Harry moved my hair and fumbled with the tiny chain. The opal settled like ice into the hollow of my throat.

The back door slammed, and I knew James was gone.

CHAPTER FIFTY-EIGHT

James

I KICKED A MOCK-UP table leg halfway across the workshop, splinters flying. The tabletop resting on it tilted at an extreme angle, taking out boxes of hardware stacked on a shelf.

I shot out a harsh breath in the aftermath, puffs of condensation visible in the cold air.

As soon as I saw that damn necklace, I stopped breathing. Even now, after crossing the yard and destroying a quarter of my shop, I wasn't sure whether to cry or punch Harry in the nose.

What had he been thinking? Not only to put Emma on the spot the way he had, but to use the opal, of all things? He had no fucking right.

The barn door clattered open, slamming to a halt at the end of the upper track. I looked up to find a red-faced Emma standing on the other side.

She shivered in the snow. No jacket, no shoes. Nothing but a flimsy sweater, jeans, and reindeer-print socks.

"Get the fuck in the shop before you freeze to death." I could barely make out my own words over the sound of my heartbeat. I must have sounded like a lunatic.

She shouldered through the open door and rushed to me. I kept my hands planted on my hips. If I reached for her, touched her, I would fall apart.

"Are you okay?"

I should have been asking her that question. She looked as pale now as when she'd been sick with the flu.

She placed her chilled palms on either side of my face.

I shook her off.

"James, please talk to me."

I tore away, stalking over to the workbench. I gave her my back and set to righting the fallen hardware.

"You should leave. You're not wearing shoes. There's shit you could step on."

"I'm not going anywhere until you tell me what is wrong. This is all confusing, and I can't make heads or tails of it."

I whipped around to face her. "This isn't about you, Emma! Not everything in my life is about you!"

I regretted it the instant I said it—the instant she withdrew from me, shrinking back.

"Okay, you're right. I'll leave. But before I do, I need you to know that I returned the necklace to Harry, told him I couldn't accept it. I hope he can return it to wherever he bought it from."

I laughed, but there was no humor in it. "He didn't buy it."

"What?"

"I said, he didn't buy it. He took it."

"I don't understand," she said in a small voice. I thought I might hate myself forever for the way her voice sounded now. Like she was afraid of me. I would rather she despised me than be scared of me.

I coughed and softened my tone. "The opal was my mom's. She wore it almost every day. It was never officially willed to anyone, but we've kept it in a safe ever since. The three of us—me, Jill, and Harry—agreed we would discuss if any of us had the desire to wear it or give it to someone else to wear."

"And Harry didn't ask you or Jill about this?"

"What do you think?"

"I'm sorry, James. I'm sorry Harry did that to you and Jill. That's a betrayal. And I'm sorry for any grief that brought up, especially during the holidays. Seeing the necklace like that must have been really, really hard."

I shook my head in disbelief. It baffled me how Emma could articulate in so few words how I was feeling.

"I am sorry for snapping at you."

Her eyes, wet with a sheen of tears—because my Emma experienced everything deeply—rose to meet mine head on.

"I understand. I have a better idea of the reasoning for it now. But that doesn't make it okay for us to be cruel to each other."

"I'm afraid I'm gonna blow it with you. You're too good for me." Might as well confess all my fears while she had me bleeding out on the table.

The little brat laughed. "You're joking, right?"

I crossed my arms. "Nope."

"I feel like an imposter most of the time. Meanwhile, you're successful, and driven, beloved in this town. You're an artist, even if you won't admit it. You can cook. You own a house. And you make my ovaries go boom."

"I'm also uptight and don't know how to let shit go. You're brave, and funny, and smart, and so damn beautiful it hurts."

Emma nodded, but I wasn't positive she believed me. I would work on that, on getting her to see herself the way I saw her. I hoped for a lifetime to do so.

"It sounds like we both like each other," she said after a moment.

"I'd say so."

"What do we intend to do about it, then? Should we go on more clandestine dates while you decide if I'm worth upsetting your cousin?"

I groaned. "I knew that was going to come back to bite me in the ass and should have never said it. It was idiotic, and I don't feel that way. I *know* we're good together. Two dates or twenty dates…I won't change my mind. I'm sorry for suggesting it in the first place." It seemed all I was doing tonight was apologizing.

"I accept your apology, James. I think I knew you didn't mean it the other night, not really. But the problem isn't whether or not you meant it. It's *why* you said it in the first place. You value taking care of Jill, and Harry, and your friends so much. And I love that about you. I do. But where do I fit in? Would I be a priority in your life or just another responsibility? I've been enough of a burden the last year and a half, and I'm not eager to repeat the experience."

I swallowed past the lump in my throat. This was my issue, and I was ready to change. I recognized it, logically. But the change itself was hard as hell.

"Can I come over to you?" I wouldn't ask her to close the distance I had placed between us. It was my job to do that.

She agreed, and I took the opening, not wasting another moment. With my arms wrapped around her, I bent my lips to her ear and asked, "Is this okay?"

I felt her head bob up and down where it nestled against my chest.

"I want to talk to you, if you have a few minutes."

Truth be told, I didn't just want to talk to Emma. I needed her and her steady bravery to keep me in one piece. For once, I would allow someone else to take care of me.

She pulled away to look me in the eye. "Yes. I will always make time."

"I still don't think I deserve you."

She scoffed. "You're off to a pretty good start in convincing me to give you a shot. Now, sit down and start talking." She tipped her chin to the metal stool where she'd sat when I removed her splinter.

"You are going to be mine. Trust me on that, Emma." I wasn't accepting anything less.

But I listened, and I sat down, pulling her onto my lap. In my little workshop, separated from Harry, and Jill, and the rest of Greyport, my life was perfect. I only hoped this would last when we stepped back into the real world.

CHAPTER FIFTY-NINE

Emma

I PRESSED MY COLD nose into James' neck and smiled at his full-body shiver. He felt nice—better than nice—as I straddled him, inhaling his clean sawdust scent.

It was sexual—undeniably so—but it was also more. There was intimacy there, a closeness I hadn't experienced in a long time. Maybe not ever. I wanted to stay wrapped up in him for as long as possible, to feel the steady thumping of his heartbeat against my ear forever.

It was hard for me to wrap my mind around James' perception of me—smart, and capable, and not at all how I saw myself. I couldn't quite shake the worry that he would find me out eventually, but I was too far gone to go back now. James had wormed his way into my heart, and I was growing ever more comfortable keeping him there.

"Are you too cold?" he asked. I knew his caretaking nature would never go away, nor did I want it to. But I hoped he could meet the challenge I'd set before him. To make room for his own happiness, with or without me.

"Not right now."

"Good."

My eyes drifted shut as he rubbed big circles on my back with the flat of his palm.

His voice was rusty when he spoke again. "I told you I was young when I moved home to Greyport, yeah?" He paused, and I felt the force of his swallow. "My mom didn't ask me to do it, but I knew I was the only one who could handle it. Jill was still in high school, and Harry's mom—my mom's sister—wasn't reliable. *Still* isn't reliable. I did everything after that. Went to all Jill's track meets, started a fund for Harry to go to trade school, met with every doctor and social worker for my mom. Harry and Jill have been annoyed with me for a while, but I don't know how to back off. They've always needed me. And I wonder if I'm addicted to that, to being needed."

I shifted up, smoothing a hand down the side of his beard. His cheek rose under my palm. "You're an amazing person, James. What you've done for your family is beautiful. The last thing I want is to change that."

He gave me a little shake at my hips. "I do need to get my priorities straight, though. I talked with Jill too. She pointed out that every decision I've made since I started my business was made based on helping my family. I haven't made a choice solely for my benefit in ages, haven't been selfish for longer than that. And you—being with you—is a hard choice to make because of it."

"Because I'm for you and you alone?"

"God, I fucking hope so, Emma."

It was only natural for my lips to melt into his after that. I opened my mouth on his, and our tongues brushed together slowly, like we had all the time in the world.

He nipped my lower lip and then soothed the bite with a soft lick. I moaned, rocking over the thick erection hardening in his jeans.

The metal stool wobbled sharply to the left.

"Whoa." He withdrew with a laugh.

I bit my lip, grinning.

"Probably not a wise idea to get too carried away, anyway. I don't have any condoms out here. Not to mention, it's fucking freezing."

"Oh, did you think you were about to get lucky, James Klein?"

His lips raised in a sexy smirk that only proved him right. "You tell me."

I flopped my forehead into the curve of his shoulder. "I hate to say this, but I should get inside. Jill took Harry on a walk after I gave him back the necklace, but I'm sure they're almost home. There's a long-overdue conversation I should have with him."

James' grip on my waist tightened. "What are you planning to talk about? Do you want me there with you?"

I shook my head. "No, I'll be fine talking with him on my own. I need to clarify to him that this fake-dating thing is just that—fake. I thought we were on the same page after he kissed me, but that Christmas gift threw me for a loop."

"Hold up. Harry *kissed* you? When was this?"

"Um. The same night you and I first kissed. Outside Maven's."

A muscle in his cheek clenched. "Okay. I'm trying not to be pissed off because I know I have no right to be, but I fucking *hate* that he kissed you."

I rested my hands on his shoulders, steadying him. "It was little more than a peck. He caught me by surprise, and it was super awkward. We agreed afterward—or so I thought—that there was no romantic connection there."

James caught the nape of my neck and brought my mouth back down to his, dragging me under in a tangle of lips and teeth and tongues. When I resurfaced, we were both panting.

"Just reminding you that things with us are far from awkward."

I rolled my eyes. "Now that you're finished pissing in a circle around me, I have to ask if you're really okay with the fact that I slept with

Harry—*not* recently, but the night you and I first met. We can't have that hanging over us. Not if we're going to move forward."

Assertive was my new middle name. I could do this, step out on a limb and be vulnerable with James. If he broke me, I would rebuild. I'd done it once before.

"I won't lie and say I like that you were with him. Won't ever want the details. But I won't hold something that happened before you and I even met against you. I don't own you, and the things you've done and people you've been with before me are none of my business. You have to know going forward that I don't share. If you're my girl, you're mine only. And the same goes for me. I want to be your man, Emma."

A door slamming outside doused the warmth growing in my chest.

"Sounds like Harry and Jill are back from their walk. I better head in." I slipped off James' lap and started toward the barn door.

"Wait, wait, one more."

He tugged me in for one last kiss, and I went easily. There was no sense resisting the inevitable.

"Alright, gotta go." I shoved off and ran to the house, socked feet freezing the entire way up the stone path to the Victorian.

CHAPTER SIXTY

Emma

I TAPPED ON THE frame of Harry's open bedroom door. "How was the walk?"

He lifted his head from where he sat on the edge of his bed. With a sheepish smile, he patted a spot on the comforter next to him.

This conversation was going to suck. I liked Harry as a person and didn't want to hurt him. Who would want to hurt a golden retriever, after all? Even if they made a mess of your house, they were lovable and loyal.

"I shouldn't have put you in an uncomfortable position with the necklace. Jill ripped me a new one while we were out. I wasn't thinking."

"Are you sure you weren't thinking? Because it sort of seemed like you planned the whole thing out."

"I really didn't, Ems. I promise you." He turned his upper body in my direction and gathered my left hand into both of his. "It was a spur-of-the-moment idea. I got carried away. James and Jill *still* aren't treating me like an adult, and I panicked. I thought if I took a bigger step forward in our relationship, then it would help."

"Look, Harry, I can relate to your frustration over being treated like a kid. My parents do it to me too. But you totally violated the agreement we made when we started this relationship—this *fake* relationship," I stressed. "I already told you at the start, and again at Maven's, that this doesn't go further for me. And I'm sorry if you don't feel the same way, but I won't force something that isn't there."

He gave my fingers a light squeeze. "Okay. I get it. I'll do better with respecting your boundaries. So—" He stood up from the bed and paced back and forth in front of his dresser. The curves and craftsmanship of the large piece momentarily distracted me, and I knew without asking who had made it. God, the man was skilled with his hands.

"—what do you think about that?"

"Huh?" I shook off my distraction. "I'm a little tired from all the holiday stuff. Can you repeat that?"

Harry bounced on his heels. "My friends, Landon and Mark, have a party every New Year's Eve. We can attend as a couple—and yes, I know we will be playing pretend. I won't even kiss you at midnight. It still aligns with our plan because James usually comes if I drag him there. It's his one night a year to remove the stick lodged up his ass."

I saw red. Harry had some nerve, speaking about James that way after the stunt he had pulled with the necklace. "Would you stop fucking insulting him? It's rude. Your cousin does a lot for you."

Harry's brows came down, dark slashes above his blue eyes. "Last I checked, James was a dick to you nine times out of ten. What business is it of yours if I insult him or not?"

"You're acting ugly. It's disappointing." I rose to stand. This conversation was going nowhere.

Harry hung his head in shame. "You're right. That was a shitty thing to say. Sorry."

"I'm not the one you should be apologizing to. I hoped we could be friends, but I don't think it'll work if you make a habit of talking about others that way."

He pressed his palms together in a prayer-like gesture. "My cousin and I have some shit to work out. But from now on, I won't bring that kind of talk around you. Is that better?"

"For now. We'll see."

I crossed my arms and waited for him to continue.

"God damn, you're a tough nut to crack, and it's hot as fuck. I wish we shared some actual chemistry, you know?"

I rolled my eyes. "I'm gonna head out now, okay?"

"Before you go, will you answer my question? Yes or no to the party?"

"The arrangement was that we would end this after Christmas. It's done, Harry. No more fake girlfriend and boyfriend. If you didn't get what you wanted from it, maybe you need to take a closer look at your own actions."

He shoved his hands in his pockets. "How about we go to the party as friends, then? It'll be the perfect opportunity to tell people we broke up. To show we're on good terms."

He had a point. And it *would* be preferable to spending the New Year alone. And if James attended, we might steal a midnight kiss or two.

"Alright. I'll go with you." I narrowed my gaze at Harry. "But no funny business, do you understand?"

CHAPTER SIXTY-ONE

James

I SLAMMED THE TAILGATE of my truck shut as I unloaded the final piece for McGuire. The job was done. Things were coming together at last—on both the personal and professional sides.

I hadn't seen Emma in a few days, not since the Christmas brunch necklace debacle, but I sent her daily messages about my day, asking about her community events, even a goofy photo or two of me in the workshop. Enough to show she was on my mind. That she could fit into my life. I could tell she wasn't completely sold yet, but I wasn't giving up.

As much as I wanted to see her and move forward, wanted to solidify this thing we were doing, I had to take it slow. Every time I saw her, I had the urge to tear her clothes off and eat her up. I wanted her to understand that this was more than just sex for me, but I didn't want to reveal too much too soon and scare her away.

Harry told me Emma had ended their relationship, still maintaining the lie that they had been an actual couple in the first place. I wouldn't push. I made it known that I wasn't happy about Harry's actions with the necklace, but to my cousin's credit, he had offered a heartfelt apology. Once the stress of the holidays was over, I would speak with him about moving out. It was the right time. For both of us.

Hopping behind the wheel of the truck and heading for home, I made the last-minute turnoff toward Greyport Grinds. Emma was busy hosting an event at the library, but I hoped to surprise her with a mid-day cup of coffee.

Grinds was bustling when I walked in, not unusual for the lunch hour as they served an array of sandwiches and salads along with coffee.

I perused the menu before stepping up to give my order to the young, tattooed barista behind the counter. A sandwich, black coffee, and one with light cream and two sugars for Emma—how she'd taken it the morning she woke up at my place after the club.

Right as I was about to exit, I collided with Harry.

"Jay! This is destiny. I was going to call you to meet up for lunch. How did it go with McGuire? Did they like the final product? Let's get a table. I'll buy."

Before I knew what hit me, I was crammed into a tiny chair at a low metal table, watching Harry navigate the space of the small café, carrying his own plate of food.

"Thanks for getting me something, man," he said as he snatched the drink I bought for Emma and took a big swig.

"Uhhh."

"Oh, shit! This was for someone else, wasn't it? My bad, dude. I'll replace it before we go because, holy shit, that is delicious."

Harry dug into his salad, shoving the lettuce into his mouth with alarming speed. If I didn't know better, I would have guessed the man hadn't eaten all week.

"So," he said while I bit into my turkey sandwich. "Who was the coffee for? You know, before I stole it."

I choked. Coughing, I washed down the food with a sip of my piping-hot drink.

I planned on telling Harry about Emma and me...eventually. But not when I was unprepared, especially in public. And not without the green light from Emma first.

"Just a friend." I swiped my lips with a napkin.

Harry gave me a sly look. "Are you blushing? Was this drink for a lady friend? James, you dirty dog! Who is she?"

Grasping at straws, I became the worst sort of hypocrite and lied through my teeth. "Nobody you would know. It's not serious at all."

"Wait...is it the woman who works at McGuire? Anna something? She's super cute, dude!"

There *was* a woman named Anna who I'd been in contact with at McGuire. Beyond her name and that she was professional and skilled at her job, I hadn't even noticed her. I must have mentioned her at some point, and Harry clearly knew her well enough to think she was cute.

My cousin continued to chatter on at a mile a minute, not giving me a chance to deny his assumption. He went on and on about how cute Anna was and how good his salad tasted. Before long, he moved on to talk about his friends' annual New Year's Eve party kicking off the next night. As usual, they'd invited me, but I was skipping out this year.

"I convinced Emma to come."

"Huh? Aren't you two broken up?" God help me if Harry planned to mount a campaign to win her back.

"We are. She's coming as a friend. There are no hard feelings there, and she doesn't have any other plans for the New Year since Kristi and Jill will be at Mark and Landon's too."

"When does the party start, and what should I bring?" No way in hell was I missing this party now.

"At about eight, over at Mark and Landon's place. Landon got a keg, but if you want anything other than what's on tap, you may want to grab a six-pack. You still like that one IPA?"

The last time I bought a case of that one IPA, Harry had drunk all but a single bottle. "Yep. I'll get that if it's what you want."

His face lit up. "I can always count on you, Jay."

"Yeah, yeah, that's what I'm here for." It felt nice to banter again with Harry, to step back from the edge we'd been balancing on for so long now.

If all it took was buying a six-pack, I would do it anytime.

"You know what you should also bring with you..." Harry trailed off with an exaggerated eyebrow wiggle.

I waited him out.

"Bring your new girl with you! Now, I better run. Ross has me working on something cool. Gonna get my hands all greasy!"

"Harry, wait. I'm not gonna—"

But he was already pushing up from the table and jogging out the door, full steam ahead, before I could say I wasn't bringing anyone to the party. If I was lucky, I'd be leaving with Emma, but I would arrive alone.

"Call me, Jay. I gotta go!" The jingling bell above the door signaled my cousin's exit.

And I was left wondering how my already messy situation had grown even messier.

Chapter Sixty-Two

Emma

I ROTATED THE WINE bottle on the shelf to better see the price sticker.

Within budget. And a decent brand too. The last thing I wanted was to show up to this New Year's Eve party empty-handed or with some cheap, glorified grape juice.

Mom had forwarded me a bundle of mail earlier this week. Several credit card offers—instantly trashed—but the kicker had been an outstanding medical bill, one that I hadn't factored into my monthly budget. Naturally, Mom had gotten on my case for how it had slipped through the cracks, and I'd ended up hanging up on her. It was a sore subject, not only because of the money but because it reminded me of what I most wanted to forget—that I was a twenty-six-year-old woman who relied on her parents to remind her to pay bills. James would never.

It didn't help that my hip was acting up as well. No amount of mobility exercises and alternating ice and heat had gotten rid of the ache. I'd learned through experience that some days were just like that, but it didn't make it any easier to live through.

"Getting drinks for the party tonight?"

I jumped as Kristi sidled up to me, silent as a ghost. She steadied me with a hand on my shoulder, ensuring I didn't topple into a stack of mini-liquor bottles arranged as a Christmas tree.

"Whoa! Sorry to startle you. Thought you spotted me when I was over near the whiskey display. Did you see they set it up to look like a fireplace? Complete with beer cozies in the shape of stockings. Nobody tell them Christmas is already over. The person in charge of making the displays might quit in protest."

I threw my arms around Kristi in a hug, and it was her turn to jerk in surprise. I instantly let go, not wanting to crowd her.

"Is everything okay with you?" she asked, brows furrowed.

I released the heavy sigh that had been building all day, sitting like a weight on my chest. "It's been an awful day, to be honest with you. I hope I didn't overstep there. We haven't established our hugging boundaries yet. But I feel so much better seeing you and knowing I get to hang out with you and Jill later."

"Oh, don't you worry. I'm a hugger, girl. You might regret opening up that dimension of our friendship. And I'm not going to say I could tell you were off today, but...I could tell."

"The psychic thing, right?"

"That's what Jill calls it. I don't call it anything other than being myself. Every woman in my family has been similar, so it's never seemed strange to me."

"Whatever it is, I appreciate it. And you."

Kristi's brown eyes warmed. "Do you mean that? Jill feels that way too, but a lot of people say I'm weird."

If she hadn't looked so earnest, I wouldn't have believed her. Kristi fit into Greyport so well I would have guessed she'd lived there her whole life. I hadn't ever seen anyone acting oddly toward her either.

She projected such confidence. I couldn't imagine she had any insecurities. Perhaps, unlike me, she was just skilled at hiding them.

I placed a gentle hand on Kristi's upper arm. "I don't think you're weird. Well, no, I do think you're weird. But a nice weird. One that matches up with my weirdness, which is why I'm glad we're friends." I paused and collected my thoughts. "Wow, I'm not very good at the whole comforting thing, am I?"

Kristi laughed and hooked her arm into mine, dragging us toward the cash register.

"You're not bad at it at all. I understand what you mean. And thanks. I'm in kind of a funk today too. Trying to shake it off."

"Did something happen?" I'd been busy running an event all afternoon and had seen little of Kristi at work.

"Just an annoying comment from a library patron about my 'personal style,'" she said with finger quotes. "Whatever that means. I was wearing a gauzy shirt and spider-web earrings. It's not the norm, but it wasn't over-the-top offensive. Plus, this guy was dressed like an absolute slob, so what the fuck does he know?"

I stepped up to the register to purchase my bottle of wine. Once I paid, I turned back to Kristi. "I'm sorry you had to deal with that. It's no one else's business what you choose to wear, especially at work."

"Well, someone should tell this guy that."

"Who was it?"

She waved a dismissive hand before taking my place at the cashier's counter. "No one important."

I recognized a dismissal when I heard one. I wouldn't push it. She would me tell when she was ready.

"It's a wonderful thing we've got wine and a party tonight, huh?"

Kristi grinned. "You are one hundred percent right about that."

We parted ways outside, Kristi hopping into her dark-red hybrid SUV and heading for the opposite end of town. Harry had offered to give me a ride to Landon and Mark's house, but I had declined.

I wanted to send the message that we were friends and friends only. Arriving at the party separately was the ideal place to start.

I spent the rest of the day wasting time around my apartment, reorganizing my junk drawer, before doing my makeup and slipping into a short, black sequined dress. My dark hair fell in loose waves down my back, and the bodice of the dress emphasized my cleavage. I was eager to see James, and I wasn't ashamed to admit to leveling up my usual style in the hopes his jaw would drop to the floor.

Harry's friends lived a few streets over from Harry and James' place. Their house was another older Victorian home, though in rougher shape. It was bustling with music and people going in and out by the time I pulled up. Parking on a side street, I hopped out of my car and maneuvered around piles of slush and snow to the front porch.

Someone came up on my left, a gust of fast-moving wind lifting the hem of my dress. I turned to greet a smiling, dolled-up version of Jill.

"Hey! You look *amazing*. My brother won't know what hit him."

Hold up.

"Wait," I said, stopping Jill before she reached the door. "Do you...know about me and James?"

The blonde leveled me with a flat look. "It's pretty obvious. And yes, I also know you and Harry were never an actual couple."

Aside from my parents, who exactly had Harry and I been faking things for? "Oh. Um. Are you okay with it?"

"Honestly? I love it, and I hope you and James can make something work. I think you're good for each other."

My insides grew warm. I was far from perfect. But despite all the hiccups of my experience in Greyport so far, maybe I had found a home after all.

"Ready to head in?" Jill nodded toward the bustling house.

"Ready."

CHAPTER SIXTY-THREE

Emma

I SCANNED THE LIVING room for what felt like the thousandth time as Jill and Kristi continued their conversation around me. It had been an hour since we arrived, and though I was enjoying time with my friends, the person I wanted to see most was nowhere to be found.

I hadn't seen James since Christmas Day. He had reached out daily, sending me cute messages and a brief video call to show me his finished product for the McGuire Restaurant group. He'd even left a fresh coffee at my work desk the other day.

But I wanted more. I was *ready* for more.

A dripping wet ping-pong ball bounced at my feet, a casualty from a nearby round of beer pong.

"Toss it back, Ems?" Harry waited on the other side of the table.

My now-former fake boyfriend had been pleasant and thoughtful. A perfect friend. He had made it known when I walked in that we were no longer a couple, but his friendly behavior kept things civil.

And he was certainly using that new singlehood to his advantage, as he had been flirting with an auburn-haired woman most of the evening.

Bending at the knees, I grabbed the white ball and sent it Harry's way.

"Does that bother you at all?" Kristi asked, her gaze directed toward Harry and his lady friend.

"No. You know what the deal was between me and Harry. I'm glad he's happy and moving on. She's pretty too."

Kristi nodded. "If you're sure."

"Positive."

"Well, I, for one, am only a little annoyed that Kristi knew about this fake-dating thing well before I did. And I had to hear it from my brother, of all people."

"Oh please, Jill," Kristi said. "Like you don't keep your own vault of secrets?"

The blonde shimmied her shoulders. "I pride myself on being a woman of mystery."

"Speaking of secrets...am I allowed to mention a certain brother's best friend and what may or may not be going on there?"

Jill stiffened. "I thought we'd already established that topic is off-limits."

Kristi didn't press again. "I learned my lesson from last time. But don't forget we're here to talk about anything."

"I'll tell you eventually, but...not now. He's so...ugh. I don't even know. Lately I've been having fantasies about punching him. Is that normal?"

"Doesn't sound normal to me."

Jill's white wine went airborne at the deep voice—one I didn't recognize—that sounded behind us.

"Careful, Jilly Bean."

That voice, I knew. Intimately.

We turned to the two tall, handsome men standing behind us.

"Hey, Jimbo." Jill flicked her eyes momentarily to the man beside her brother. "Ben."

"Jill."

Kristi offered her own greetings, her tone far lighter than Jill's had been. Then it was my turn to meet James' best friend—and the apparent bane of Jill's existence.

Ben was just a touch shorter than James. His light hair, which he kept clipped in a close crop, cast an almost intimidating air that was belied by the warmth in his pale-blue eyes.

He gripped my hand in his as we shook. "Nice to finally meet you." He smiled, his left incisor a tad crooked.

"Likewise." I stole a peek at James, only to catch him staring at me, unabashed.

"What?" I mouthed at him.

He didn't respond, but one side of his mouth quirked up. My cheeks grew hot.

"This is getting uncomfortable, you two. Jimbo, go socialize. This is one of the rare nights of the year you leave the house. You can steal her later."

"It was good to meet you, Emma. I'm sure I'll be seeing more of you," Ben said before moving on.

James shot me a scorching look full of promise before following Ben back into the crowd of party-goers.

I was tittering inside. The man was being far from subtle, and my lingering worry that he might want to push hold on our relationship for Harry's sake was eased.

"I think I just got pregnant," Kristi said.

I coughed as I inhaled a gulp of wine.

"Girl, you better prepare yourself, because I suspect you're going to be choking on something else tonight."

Jill whirled on her friend. "What the fuck, Kristi? Can we move on from this before I vomit everywhere?"

I opened my mouth to speak, but Jill placed a light palm over my lips.

"No more talking about my brother. We are going to dance, and drink wine, and have fun until that giant disco ball drops. After that, you can go find James. I'm happy for you, don't get me wrong, but I do. Not. Need. Details. Understand?"

I could only nod before the blonde removed her hand.

"Thank you. And ladies, don't let Ben within ten feet of me. I don't want to see his smarmy face again. He's killing my New Year's vibe."

"He seemed nice enough to me," I said with a shrug. He'd been polite, almost gentlemanly.

"Less talking, Emma. More wine and dancing."

❦ ❦ ❦ ❦ ❦ ❦ ❦ ❦

AN HOUR LATER, I was ready to stomp across the room and throw the blaring speaker out the window. I was posted up at the corner of the makeshift dance floor, watching as an unfamiliar woman traced her long, pink fingernails down James' forearm. To his credit, he didn't seem to welcome the attention, but he wasn't pulling away either.

My stomach dropped, and I crunched the red Solo cup in my grip. Had I waited too long to approach him? Had he already decided my crap wasn't worth the hassle? Maybe the new-and-improved version of me was as much a coward as the old, familiar Emma, after all.

"Taking a break from all the dancing?" I looked up to meet Ben Till's silver eyes.

"Yep. I'm getting tired. I woke up early today." Filled with nerves about the party and the fight with my mom.

"I don't know how those two do it," he said, gesturing toward Jill and Kristi, who were bouncing around, belting out the lyrics to a peppy pop song. "I'm working my way up to heading home. I'm too old for this."

I let out a little laugh. No wonder Ben got along with James. "I'm debating calling it an early night myself." My hip and head were screaming.

And my heart—and pride—were a tad bit bruised.

"You know that doesn't mean anything, right?"

"Huh?"

Ben tipped his cropped head toward the other side of the dance floor. "James. Over there, talking to that woman. You're pretending not to notice. He came here for you. All you have to do is take one look in his direction, and he'll be over here in a second."

My mouth twisted. "Would he? There's still a lot I don't know about him."

"I bet if you think about it, you have a better understanding of who he is as a person than you realize. You may not know his favorite color or first job. But his values and needs? Those you get. Otherwise, you wouldn't be here."

The memory of that night in James' truck, him quizzing me about my childhood pets and favorite food, flashed behind my eyes.

"Maybe so."

"You'll figure it out eventually," Ben said with a firm nod.

"How do you know? You just met me tonight."

He shrugged his shoulders. "Because I trust James' judgment. He wouldn't waste a minute on someone who didn't deserve it. See you around, Emma."

I turned to my left, but the space Ben had occupied was empty. What a strange man.

"Ten! Nine! Eight!" The countdown to the New Year began around me, loud voices and party poppers sounding off.

Craning my neck, I glanced back to the place I had last seen James and Pink Nails.

They were gone.

I froze when a heavy hand landed at my elbow and dragged me backward.

Chapter Sixty-Four

James

I muffled Emma's scream under my palm as I tugged her into the pantry and cinched the heavy door closed.

I'd been waiting to touch her all night. My patience had run out.

The bite of her teeth on my inner palm forced me to pull away and tug on the string-light above us. The harsh fluorescent light blinded me in the small space.

"What the hell, James? You scared the shit out of me. You're lucky I didn't kick you in the balls. And you would deserve it for—"

Four. Three. Two.

One.

"Happy New Year, Emma," I said against her lips before kissing away her words.

She opened to me without hesitation, her hands twisting and tangling in the coarse hair of my beard, dragging me closer.

A sound brushed across the outer door, and I stepped back.

My girl's smile was more blinding than the naked lightbulb floating above us.

"I forgive you for manhandling me, because that was a great kiss. Happy New Year, James."

"I didn't want to wait another minute."

"I thought you left."

What? "Where would I have gone?"

"I didn't know. You were there one minute and gone the next. I thought maybe you stepped out with the person you were talking to."

I didn't recall talking to anyone. I'd spent most of the evening pretending not to watch Emma dancing and scowling about the fact that I had to keep waiting to touch her.

I shook my head once to clear it. "I don't even remember who I was talking to. I wouldn't have left without seeing you."

"Well, okay, then." She stepped into my chest and encircled my waist with both arms.

"You give the best hugs, you know that? I didn't even think I liked hugs."

She smiled up at me, her soft, pointed chin resting at my sternum. "It's a special hug I've reserved just for you."

"Better be just for me, or I might have to take you over my knee."

I felt her lower body clench, almost imperceptibly, and I couldn't stop the inward smile from growing.

"You like the sound of that, don't you?"

"Don't turn me on when we can't do anything about it, James Klein. We're in a—wait, where are we right now?"

"It's the pantry."

Emma's head darted from side to side. "Why is it so much nicer than the rest of the house? I'm surprised the shelves aren't falling off the wall."

"Because I fixed it for them last year. And you're not far off on what it looked like before that."

"So...are the shelves sturdy?"

Did she even have to ask? "Don't insult me."

She spun in a little circle, the hem of her dress fluttering against my legs. "What I hear you saying—and please correct me if I'm wrong—is that these are high-quality shelves that can most definitely hold the weight of one average-sized adult woman?"

"Are you the adult woman in question?"

"Maybe."

Her words went straight to my cock. My Emma was getting sassy. "Are you trying to call the shots here, Emma?"

She bit down on her lip. I ached to be that lip, to take that bite.

"Hop up on the shelf. And lose the panties."

In a hurry, Emma shimmied her underwear from under her dress and scooted up onto the shelf. I caught the scrap of pink lace she tossed at my chest, tucking it into my jeans pocket.

"How is it? Sturdy enough for you?"

She shifted around. I couldn't wait to get my hands on her, but I was enjoying the sight and sound of her eager anticipation.

"Seems alright to me. Only the highest quality shelf for my ass. Why are you still so far away? And still wearing pants?"

"First, I know you've been drinking tonight. Are you okay to go here with me? Because I'll always be patient for you."

"I am absolutely, one hundred percent okay. Enthusiastically consenting with all faculties. I've had two glasses of wine since I got here."

"That being the case..."

I stepped up into her space, relishing the shiver that thrummed down her body when I bent close to her ear. "This is about you. You wanted to take control. Now you get to tell me what to do."

Her eyes lit up. "Holy shit. Really?"

I chuckled under my breath. This hadn't been the plan when I brought her into the pantry, but I was going with the flow. Adapting.

I dragged my tongue up the length of her throat, stopping to nibble the underside of her jaw. Her breathy moans had my cock straining against the zipper of my dark jeans, but I kept both hands in place on either side of her hips.

"You have to promise to be quiet, yeah?"

She bobbed her head up and down. "I'll try."

"What do you want me to do next? Should I get up under this skirt?" God, I hoped that was what she wanted.

"Yes, please. I need that."

"Say it, then. Say, 'James, finger my pussy.'"

She kept up that moaning, pressing against my front as I continued the onslaught of licks and kisses along her delicate neck. She smelled delicious there, but I knew she would smell—and taste—even better below her skirt.

"I'm dying here, Emma. Tell me what you want before I come in my pants like a damn high school boy."

Her giggle had my shaft growing harder, if that were possible. She gripped my beard, twisting just the smallest bit, and looked me right in the eye.

"Fuck my pussy with your fingers. *Now.*"

Thank fucking Christ.

Not skipping a beat, I slid one palm under her short black dress, the fabric brushing my knuckles. The skin of her inner thigh on my thumb was softer than the smoothest wood grain.

Lingering there for a moment, I gave the thigh in my grip a squeeze. There had been a change in her gait, a tightness earlier, and I suspected her hip was bothering her. The slight hitch in her breathing as I rubbed told me the hunch was correct.

"I'll go easy on you."

"Don't you dare," she said with a snarl.

"If you say so."

I tilted up her chin before taking my middle and pointer finger between my lips, savoring the flavor of her sharp exhalation. I kept eye contact with her as I sucked.

"Hurry, James." She drew her arms down from around my neck and struggled to drag up her skirt, her hips jogging along the surface of the shelf as she fought with the fabric.

"I've got you, Emma. Haven't you figured out by now that I always take care of you?"

I figured I'd tortured her long enough. I flipped that flimsy skirt up, feasting on the sight of her wet, pink pussy shining under the bright light.

All for me.

I brushed a fingertip through her hot slit, taking the wetness up to her belly button. Powerless to resist, I crouched down and stole it with my tongue, lapping up her exquisite taste.

I wanted to tear my shirt off, throw her over my shoulder, and take her to my bed before making her sit on my face all fucking night. I would die happy, like the fucking caveman I was.

But that could wait. This minute, I needed to get my girl off before she killed me. If her grip on my wrist was any sign, I would be left with claw marks either way.

Bringing my mouth back up to hers, I ceased my teasing and slid my palm between her thighs. I gathered up more moisture from her core, taking it up to her clit, where I dragged those little circles she liked around and around. I groaned into her mouth as her damp heat coated me before traveling back down to her center and sliding in up to my knuckle.

"Does my finger feel good filling you up?"

Her nod was desperate.

"Think you can take more?"

"Yes, yes, yes. More."

I almost laughed at her breathless pleas, but I was too busy feeling her fuck my hand. Too busy loving the way her inner walls squeezed my fingers as I circled her clit with my thumb. Too busy letting her screams fill my mouth as I swallowed them down.

Her body jerked, her thighs pressing around my wrist like a vise.

My eyes rolled in ecstasy as I brought my hand up and licked it clean. If I had anything to say about it, Emma was spending the night in my bed. I was dying to eat that cream straight from the source.

"That was fucking amazing," she said, readjusting her dress. "Can I have my panties back now?"

"Nope. Mine."

"You're lucky you just finger-fucked me into oblivion and I'm too weak to argue. Those are nice panties, James."

"I'm going to start a collection. You can have a drawer at my house."

"That's a pretty big step there, don't you think? A girl might read into that, wonder what it means."

"And what do you think it means?"

Her throat bobbed. "I'm scared to say it."

"Don't be. Ask me how I feel about you."

"How do you feel about me, James?" she whispered.

"Like I'm falling in love with you."

It didn't hurt to say, not like I'd thought it might. Instead, it was a weight lifted. Open and freeing, like I could finally take a full breath.

"I think I might be falling in love with you too."

If I thought I was weightless before, now I had wings.

"Come home with me?" I needed more time with her. No amount of time would ever be enough, but I would accept small doses. In a few months, we could talk about her moving in, getting married, and even some kids.

But I could start with tonight.

"Won't Harry notice my car? I assume he doesn't know. He didn't mention anything to me earlier."

"He doesn't. I wouldn't tell him without giving you a heads up. He's staying the night here. I'd like to tell him in the morning, though. I'm sick of waiting. It isn't fair to any of us."

She intertwined our hands. "We'll do it together."

"Harry is my issue to deal with, Emma. I don't want you to put yourself in an awkward position for my sake. If you want to tell him together, I'm all for it—but only if you're sure."

"It impacts both of us, and I want to support you. You'd better get used to someone else taking care of you right back, James Klein."

God, I fucking loved this woman. I pulled her close again and pressed my lips to hers, willing that she felt the depth of my feelings in the gesture.

"What the fuck, bro?"

The pantry filled with noise as the door flew open. Harry stood on the other side with a room full of people behind him.

CHAPTER SIXTY-FIVE

Emma

M Y HEAD SPUN AS I looked into the eyes of the party guests. It was as if all of Greyport was staring, judging—finding me lacking. I scanned the room for Jill and Kristi, for any friendly face, but James stepped in front of me, partially obscuring my view.

"Dude, isn't that Harry's girlfriend?" came a voice from Harry's right. The stocky, pale-skinned man with freckles was Mark, one of Harry's best friends and owner of said pantry James and I had just hooked up in. I met him at trivia night at Maven's a few weeks back and wasn't impressed.

"No, no, they're not dating anymore—as of, like, yesterday, I think?" This from Landon, Harry's other best friend—a tall, handsome Black man and the other party host.

"Still, that's pretty shitty, don't you think? Bros before hoes and all that, right?" Mark gave Harry what was likely meant to be an encouraging slap on the shoulder.

"You want to repeat that, Mark?" James said.

I peeked around his broad frame to witness Landon pulling Mark a short distance away.

Mark threw up his hands. "Hey, I call it how I see it, man. What kind of woman jumps from one guy to another so fast? Might as well go down the entire family tree while she's at it."

My stomach dropped.

"Shut the fuck up, Mark."

It was Harry who said it. Meanwhile, James coiled up like he was about to explode. I laid a soft hand on his back, but he shrugged it off.

"What the hell, dude? I'm only looking out for you," Mark said.

"Emma didn't do anything wrong. She was never my girlfriend."

"Wait, what?"

"You heard me. It was fake the whole time. She wanted to meet some people in town, and I wanted to seem like less of a screw-up, so she agreed to pose as my girlfriend. It didn't work, we broke up, and now we're here—where my cousin is hooking up with her."

"Oh. Whatever. Sorry, Emma. I didn't know."

Despite the apology, Mark and his sour, misogynistic comments could fuck all the way off.

"You'd best do better with that apology if you don't want me to split your fucking lip. And after that, I never want to see you speak to Emma again," James said. His voice was nearly inaudible, but the anger blistering under the surface was evident.

Mark's face paled under his freckles.

"Um, uh, yeah. I'm very sorry, Emma." He paused but continued on when he took in James' glower. "I shouldn't have talked about you that way, especially without knowing the full story. It wasn't cool."

I acknowledged Mark with a nod before James shifted a half step toward the shorter man.

"Don't even look at her."

"I can defend myself, James," I said in a low voice. He was pissing me off with the protective shit.

Landon—reading the room—grabbed Mark by the arm and pulled him into another part of the house. A few people still lingered in the kitchen, but their attention had moved elsewhere. Only James, Harry, and I remained in a strange huddle near the wide-open pantry door.

Beyond his admonition of Mark, Harry was silent—suspiciously so. But I knew James was attuned to every beat of his cousin's silence.

"Harry, I—"

"Save it, Jay. I'm not mad at Emma, but *you?* That's a different fucking story. See, she knew we were faking, but you didn't."

"It wasn't like that, Harry," I said, shouldering past James.

"Don't, Emma," James said. "This is between me and him."

Well, that was a slap in the face. We had decided to do this together—not like this, but I was prepared to roll with the punches. James not so much.

Harry laughed, but there was no humor in the sound. It sounded...wrong...coming from his jovial self.

"I think it's also between someone else, isn't it?"

"What the fuck are you talking about?" James asked.

"I'm talking about Anna, motherfucker. You know, your girlfriend?"

H ARRY STORMED OUT OF the kitchen, and James followed. He didn't look at me once and left.

Prickles began in my fingers and toes. My coat was somewhere. It didn't matter. I had to get out of here.

Did James have a girlfriend? Surely Jill would have mentioned if he did. But what was Harry talking about, then?

And did it matter? Did I even want the man when his first move was jumping to Harry's side at the soonest possible second, leaving me alone and vulnerable in front of the prying eyes of Greyport?

Perhaps moving here was a mistake, after all. It wasn't about James—not entirely. But the town was small. Jill was tied to James, and Kristi was tied to Jill. I worked with them every day.

I sucked in a breath when someone threw an arm over my shoulder. Turning, I saw it was Kristi. Would she still associate with me if I were the town pariah?

"What is going on? I heard some shit when down in the kitchen with James and Harry? And James looked like he wanted to kick Mark's ass? Which would be well deserved, let me tell you."

"I don't want to talk about it," I said through numb lips.

"Are you alright? Jill and I are hanging out in the basement where it's a little less crowded. Why don't you come down there with us and relax?"

"I need to go."

The space between Kristi's brows scrunched, and her dark eyes radiated concern.

"I'll drive you."

I shook my head and moved back, stepping toward the front door. "No. I can drive. I only had two drinks." It had been well over three hours.

"Emma, I'm not offering because I'm worried about you driving drunk. I'm offering because I care, and you look rattled. Whatever happened tonight, I'm your friend. And I'm positive Jill feels the same."

The image of Kristi blurred. I wanted to believe her—I really did—but I couldn't process anything beyond getting away from this party.

"I'm at least walking you to your car." Kristi pointed her finger at me. "Don't try to argue. I won't say a word. This is so I feel better right now. I'm being selfish, and you can't deny me."

"Okay." I had no willpower left to fight.

We walked in silence. Enough snow had fallen in our few hours inside to leave a coating on my windshield. Kristi insisted on brushing it off while I sat in the driver's seat with the defroster on full blast.

It took maybe five minutes, but to me, it was an eternity.

I startled in my seat when Kristi opened the back passenger side door, letting in a draft of icy air. She poked her head into the vehicle, and we made eye contact in the rearview mirror.

"All set. Here's your snow brush. I won't bug you again about driving you home, but shoot me a message when you get there. Other drivers out there are crazy, especially the G-State students."

"Thanks."

As I pulled away from the curb, I caught the blur of James' form exiting the house at a clip.

I kept driving. My phone rang in my purse, but I didn't bother reaching for it.

It rang twice more while I navigated the side streets to my apartment. Once I parked, I took it out of my bag and braved a peek at the screen.

Three missed calls. All from James.

The device vibrated in my hand as a message from him popped up. More rolled through in rapid succession.

> James: Why did you leave? I thought we were staying at my place.

> James: If it was too much, too soon, that's okay. But please tell me when you make it home.

James: Kristi said you were crying. I was trying to get back to the kitchen to find you.
Please don't shut me out.

Had I been crying? I tapped the corner of the phone against my lip, closing my eyes as the vehicle lost heat in the quiet of the night.

Emma: I got home safe.

I sent the same to Kristi, another notification from James appearing as I typed the second message.

James: Thank God. I was worried. Can I call you? I'll come over if you want me to.

Emma: Not tonight. I need to sleep and think things through.

When I didn't get an immediate response, I slid out of the car with all the grace of a lumbering bear. I made the slow trek over the slick sidewalk and up the stairs, my hip nagging at me all the way.

I took my time changing into a pair of raggedy pajamas, leaving my cell phone face down on the nightstand and doing everything I could to avoid flipping it over.

I tossed my shimmery dress into the hamper. There were no panties to go with it. A certain bearded man had those. It only served to remind of that buzzing feeling I experienced not even an hour ago. How swiftly the night had changed.

Sliding into clean sheets, I reached for the electronic elephant in the room.

James: That's fair. I'll give you that space tonight. But I'm not giving up, Emma.

James: I'll leave you alone after this, but I have to say one thing first. I DO NOT have a girlfriend.

James: No. That's not right. *You* are my girlfriend. I hope. There's no one else. Harry was confused.

James: I'm rambling. Goodnight, Emma.

I wished him a silent goodnight before powering down the device.

I rolled over and slid open the uneven drawer of the nightstand, searching for the crumpled piece of paper buried under the medical bill Mom sent me.

My list. I hadn't looked at it—hadn't even thought about it—in weeks. Not since things with James started in earnest. The list had been my security blanket for so long, and I'd somehow forgotten it. When I first applied for the job at the library, when I found the posting for this shitty little apartment, when I embarked on the long drive to Greyport...the list had kept me going.

As much as I hated to admit it, meeting James had changed me. I stopped living to check tasks off a list and started living in the moment. Even when I thought I couldn't stand him, he unlocked something inside me.

Tracing my finger down the smeared rows of ink, I stopped on the last line.

Say YES to everything.

That was what had gotten me into trouble. If I had never said yes to going home with Harry, I never would have met James. If I had never agreed to pose as Harry's girlfriend, I wouldn't have gotten to know his cousins, and even Kristi, as well as I had.

If I hadn't said yes to kissing James in the Maven's parking lot, to being with him in offices, and beds, and closets, I wouldn't be in this mess.

I trusted James to give me space, but I knew I would have to talk to him eventually. I promised him I wouldn't run away.

But I didn't know if I had the courage to keep saying yes.

Chapter Sixty-Six

James

I'D NEVER UNDERSTOOD PEOPLE who got destructive when they were upset, but I was starting to get it as I stared a hole through my cell phone lock screen. I was half tempted to launch the thing across the workshop as I waited for it to give me anything but silence. Tolerance for people and social activities wasn't my strong suit on a good day, so waiting by my phone was a novel—and unwelcome—experience. I hardly tolerated it on my work phone, the old brick I kept turned on strictly during business hours.

I would wait forever for Emma if I had to, but I really hoped it wouldn't take that long.

The New Year's Eve party had been an unmitigated disaster—so promising when I'd stolen that midnight kiss from Emma, only to end in shambles.

Now, it was two in the morning, and I was working off a layer of adrenaline, creating half-parts of furniture I never intended to complete.

I could tell that Emma was angry at me. She hadn't said it, but I could read her now. I'd messed up by chasing after Harry, and then I hadn't even been able to find him. Someone said they saw him leave with a redhead he'd been flirting with earlier in the night.

Funny how Mark hadn't said jack shit to Harry about moving on, but he'd made that comment to Emma. If I never saw his miserable face again, it would be too soon.

I needed to talk to Emma to set things straight. It had looked bad when I left her alone in that kitchen. The second I stepped out of the room, I knew I screwed up by leaving. When I'd tried to return to her, the party crowd slowed me down. While I was sifting through drunk, dancing bodies, she was driving off.

She had asked for space, but I could see what she was doing—running away. And if I couldn't convince her to switch directions, I didn't know what I would do.

I'd told her in that pantry that I was falling for her, but that wasn't true. Not anymore. I loved her. Full stop. No falling about it. If she didn't want to be with me...I couldn't even finish the thought. It wasn't an option I was willing to entertain.

The barn door rattled open. I glanced over my shoulder to see the glowering face of my cousin, looking worse for wear in an inside-out shirt with his wavy hair frizzing up.

"Are you drunk?" The fucker better not have driven a car that way.

"Nope. Thanks for asking, though, Dad."

I grunted. "You want to talk?"

"I'm here, aren't I?"

So that was how this was going to go.

I set down the power drill I was white-knuckling. "I'll start. I'm sorry you found out about me and Emma the way you did."

Harry crossed his arms. "But not sorry you hooked up with her in the first place?"

"I love her, Harry. It wasn't just a hook-up. Not like it was for you."

He stalked across the barn to lean into my space, baring his teeth. "She wasn't just a hook-up for me either, asshole! She was my girl-friend!"

I breathed—in for four beats, hold for four, and out again.

"She was never your girlfriend, Harry."

"Yes, but *you* only found that out tonight," he said, pointing an accusatory finger at me. "It's good to know you're the type of guy to betray your family—more than family. Your best friend. I thought you were better than that."

"I've known it was fake for a while. Emma slipped and told me the night she was sick. For the record, I didn't touch her until after I knew. I wouldn't do that to you, despite what you believe."

He laughed bitterly. "Great. Who else knows?"

"Jill and Kristi too."

He threw his hands up. "So, were you all laughing at me, then? About how stupid and useless I am? So useless I had to ask a woman to pretend to date me so people would take me seriously?"

My right temple throbbed. "I never laughed at you, Harry. If any-thing, I felt awful that you thought I wouldn't respect you without you resorting to some ridiculous farce."

Harry sank into a spineless lean against my tool bench, head hanging down below his shoulders.

"I made it worse, didn't it?" he said. "With the fake-dating thing?"

"Made it worse by telling a lie in order to look more responsible?" I pinched my thumb and forefinger close together. "Little bit, yeah."

His head popped up. "Lay off with the sarcasm, would you, asshole? Can't you see I'm struggling here?" He placed his clasped hands over his heart.

I took a chance and stepped a fraction closer to him, sideways scooting along the edge of the tool bench. I treaded lightly, unwilling to risk catching a stray punch. "Trying to lighten the mood, that's all."

He blew a breath out between his lips in a trumpeting noise. "I kinda hate you even more, because it's working. But hating you is dumb too, isn't it? I'm not supposed to hate you for doing what you always do."

"What do I always do?"

"Make everything easy for me. I'm coming to the conclusion that I need to struggle on my own a bit. To help me grow up. Because despite knowing that you, and Emma, and Jill are right about me needing to make changes, I try and still can't figure out how to make those changes stick. It's like I'm stuck."

I shuffled nearer to my cousin, hesitated a second, then slung an arm over his shoulders. A sigh of relief puffed out of my lungs when I felt him relax into me.

"What do you need from me, then? Or should I say, what do you *not* need from me?"

He shrugged. "I think I need to move out."

"Yeah. I think so too."

He stepped back and quirked a brow. "You're not going to offer your advice on how to budget for an apartment? Or the safest neighborhoods in town?"

"Nope." I bit my tongue. I *wanted* to do everything he'd just mentioned. "I've got some growing to do here too."

He rolled his scapulae a few times, like he was prepping for battle. "Okay. I'm doing this." He paused, looked at me, and tilted his head. "Say, you wouldn't happen to know if Emma is moving out of her apartment, would you?"

I froze, my body going cold. "What? Why? Is she leaving town? Have you heard something in the last two hours that I haven't?"

All my fatigue washed away, and I started frantically stowing the various tools I had strewn around the shop in anger. Once I got this junk cleaned up, I'd come up with a game plan. There wasn't much time if Emma was moving.

Harry placed a firm hand on my arm. "Chill, Jay. She isn't going anywhere. I was thinking more along the lines of her moving in here—with you."

The whiplash hit like a ton of bricks. "Let me get this straight. You walked in here, heated about me getting with Emma—the woman you have feelings for. And now you're encouraging me to ask her to move in with me?"

"You said you love her, bro. I mean, she's hot as fuck, and I admire the hell out of her. If she wanted to date for real, I would go for it. But I don't love her. Love is...not in my wheelhouse. And she isn't interested in me either. I think I got caught up in the idea of her, you know what I mean?"

I didn't know what he meant at all. Moving on from Emma was unfathomable to me.

"What brought this on? Not that I don't appreciate the support, because honestly, I'm going to be with her regardless of whether or not you approve."

If she still wanted me.

"Eh. It's not that fast a change. That girl I was talking to at the party was cool, and I didn't miss Emma at all. After I saw you two at Mark and Landon's—oh, *fuck Mark*, by the way—I realized she was always looking at you when the three of us were together. You guys fit. You're more fun with her, and it gets you off my case too. Who would have thought my strait-laced, rule-following cousin would get caught in the act in public at thirty-five years old? I'm happy to accept Emma as my cousin-in-law if it helps you chill out."

"Slow down, dude. We're not getting married. Not yet. Things are new still," I cautioned Harry, but damn if I didn't enjoy the thought of living with Emma and making her my family. Cooking her omelets every morning. Prepping her daily dose of caffeine before she left for work. Ending the day with her falling asleep in my arms.

"Okay, sure, that dreamy look on your face *definitely* sells me on you wanting to 'take things slow.' If you have your way, she'll be moved in with a ring on her finger by next Christmas."

"Well, she's pretty pissed at me at the moment, so who knows."

"Why is she mad?"

I lifted a finger to flick him in the forehead. "It might have something to do with the fact that you announced to her—and everyone else—that I have a girlfriend."

"That fucking hurt, dude," Harry said as he rubbed the space below his hairline. "And yeah. That was pretty stupid, wasn't it? I realized you never actually said you were dating Anna about two seconds after I said it. It was Emma all along."

"Yep."

"You told her I was full of shit, though, yeah? She won't be that angry when she realizes I got confused. Do you want me to call her and clear the air?"

The sensation in my temple had progressed from a dull throb to a sharp stabbing. "I'd better talk to her first."

"Didn't you talk before you left the party?"

"I tried to. But I made the mistake of going after you. By the time I turned back around, she was already leaving. Now she won't answer my calls."

"Dude."

"What? Don't make me feel like an even bigger idiot than I already do. I'm out of my element here."

"Well, you have to fix this, because walking away from Emma in a moment like that must have made her feel terrible. Being the new kid in Greyport is, like, her biggest hangup."

"I figured that out right after I walked away. I'm usually better than this at taking care of people, but the stakes are higher with Emma. I want to do it the right way with her."

"You're good at taking care of practical stuff. This is taking care of emotions. It's different."

"When the fuck did you get so smart?"

A serene smile grew on Harry's face. "I started meditating. It helps me focus when I'm bowling too. If you want tips, I can pass them along."

That...wasn't the worst idea I'd ever heard. "I may take you up on that offer."

"The student has become the teacher. Now, what's the plan for you to get out of the doghouse and back on track to get me a new cousin-in-law?"

Chapter Sixty-Seven

Emma

The bench—my bench—was gone.

Coffee sloshed up over the rim of my travel mug as I came to a dead stop in the center of the walking path. The space where my broken down, peeling bench typically sat was empty. Four divots in the wet grass were the only clues that the patch of lawn had once been occupied.

"Hey, Emma!"

I turned at the voice, spotting Tracy and Scott taking a brisk power-walk around the loop. Tracy shot me a quick wave as they continued their workout. It was unseasonably warm, and Greyport residents were out in full swing, enjoying the day before another round of snow hit.

I licked a drip of spilled coffee from my hand and continued down the pathway until I found another place to sit.

This bench was sleek and modern, made of metal with some sort of weird plastic coating. Hesitantly, I sat down.

I hated it. There was no give, no warped wood made smooth from countless bench-sitters throughout the years, no question-able wobble when first settling. Worst of all, the chill of the metal seeped through my jeans. I was basically sitting on an ice cube tray.

A pair of worn work boots appeared in my line of sight.

"Emma."

"Hey, James. You found me."

"You told me this was where you would be." He gestured to the margin of space next to me. "May I?"

"Sure." I scooted over to make as much room as possible. I didn't trust myself to touch him. I had to hold firm.

His face scrunched as he lowered onto the plastic-coated metal. "I'm not going to lie, I was expecting a different sort of bench from how you described it."

"That's because they *took* my bench! Can you believe that? It was worn down and falling apart, but it was mine. Now I'm left with this weird, uncomfortable thing. It looks like it belongs on a spaceship, not in Fair Street Park."

"You're gonna hurt New Bench's feelings, Emma."

The laugh shot out of me like a cannon. I slammed my lips closed and pressed them into a straight line.

"I'm supposed to be mad at you. Now I'm just mad you made me laugh when I want to stew."

"You can be mad at me. But never stop laughing, Emma, please. It's my favorite sound in the world."

"I thought your favorite sound in the world was me moaning your name?"

His cheeks lifted, and he scooted closer until his hip pressed against mine. "You're a fucking smartass."

"And you love it."

"Yeah. I do."

We sat in silence, me sipping on my coffee while James watched groups of walkers make a loop around the pond.

"Morning, Emma. Morning, James!" a pair of regulars from the library greeted us before running off after a fast-moving toddler.

"So," I said.

"So."

"Will you explain why Harry seems to think you have a girlfriend?"

"He made some assumptions after he caught me sneaking in the house after our date. And he saw me buying you a latte from Greyport Grinds the other day. The woman he thought I was dating works for McGuire, and I've interacted with her a handful of times for my job. I'm not interested in anything beyond a professional relationship with her, just so you know."

Wasn't that just like Harry to go off half-cocked? "Okay. Having that explanation makes me feel better. But I'm still hung up on how you just...left me standing there at the party. You went after Harry, and I was alone. I needed you."

"I know, Emma. I fucked up. Figured it out pretty quick too. I turned back around maybe a minute later, but by the time I got through the crowd, you were already gone."

I nodded, processing. "You have to understand how that felt for me. How that highlighted what I've been most worried about all along. That you would have a tough time balancing your priorities."

"You're right. I need to work on it, and I'm taking steps to do that. I can't promise I'll be perfect, but I will try. I scheduled an appointment with a therapist next month. There's a lot I need to address so I can be a better brother, and cousin, and partner. I'd like to be your partner, if you'll have me."

I reached over and grabbed his hand. "I'm proud of you, James. That's a big step. I also sent an email to my counselor this morning to ask about getting some regular video visits booked again. Moving here and adjusting has been a lot for me."

"You're not leaving, though, are you?"

I swallowed. "That's a hard question to answer. I haven't accomplished a fraction of the things I've wanted to do since I arrived. I've been struggling and too proud to admit it. I should be confident enough to ask my boss for a special chair for my hip. Or say no to ice-skating. And Greyport might not be the best place for me to figure out how to do that."

He was shaking his head before I even finished. "Respectfully, I disagree. You were strong enough to take a chance and come here. Fuck, Emma, you're strong enough that you could be stranded in the middle of a desert and find a way to power through. It's not about Greyport."

How could he have so much more faith in me than I had in myself? "I don't know, James."

"So, where does this leave us?"

"I don't think I can do this right now. With you. With us." I was all wrong, still, and I couldn't be the person James needed—not when I was failing myself.

He looked forward, sights set straight out across the duck pond. He squeezed his eyes shut, crow's feet crinkling.

"I'm sorry," I said.

He responded with a single nod.

"I'm not making any decisions about leaving anytime soon. I'll be around. But I'll keep to myself and avoid Maven's and the like."

His eyes flew open. "Fuck that."

"W—what?"

"No. I won't have this conversation where you tell me all the ways you plan on running away and hiding. What's your plan here, Emma? Become a hermit in your rundown apartment every day after work? Will you go to work, or will even that feel too much like living a real life?"

I pulled up like he'd slapped me. In a way, he had. "You don't get to tell me how to process my feelings, James."

"No, but I sure as hell can tell you what I'm going to do with the bullshit you're giving me right now," he continued, ignoring my mouth hanging open. "Because that's what this is: bullshit. You're scared, and you're reacting out of fear. But I won't give up, because I know this is the real deal. *You* are the real deal. So, I'll give you time and distance for now. But don't take too long, Emma."

He stood up and walked away, abandoning me on my alien bench.

CHAPTER SIXTY-EIGHT

Emma

I PULLED THE BEDSHEET over my eyes and pretended not to hear the pounding at my door. It had been going on for a minute, and whoever was out there hadn't gotten the memo to go away.

I shuffled into a pair of hard-sole slippers and dragged the comforter with me, ambling over to peer out the peephole.

"Open up! We know you're in there. We see the shadow of your feet!"

Groaning, I tugged open the door and stepped aside, allowing Kristi and Jill to enter.

I didn't speak, only plodded over to my lumpy couch and threw myself onto the cushion, blanket up over my head. If they were going to be rude and show up uninvited, I wouldn't bother acting the hostess.

"How goes it, Blanket Queen? We haven't seen you at work much lately," Kristi said.

I had ended things with James three days ago. "I've been there. Just busy in my office. Working."

"With the door closed and locked, which isn't normal for you. You're hiding."

Kristi wasn't wrong. I had been getting to work early and leaving late, staying holed up at my desk all day. It was the coward's way out, and damn, it made me even angrier that I was doing the exact thing James had said I would.

It was almost like he understood me.

Jill came over to the couch, perching a butt cheek on the plaid arm. "You can talk to us, Emma. We aren't here to judge you."

Would she say the same if I told her I broke her brother's heart? That I was toying with the idea of moving back to Mom and Dad's and leaving Greyport behind?

"Have you talked with your brother recently?" I asked. It was no use acting like I wasn't dying to know.

"I did. He was useless. He said I should come speak to you."

"Did he seem...okay?"

"Oh no, you don't." Jill gave a chiding finger wag. "If you want to know anything, you'd best give us more than crumbs in return. We heard Harry caught you and James at the party. Rotten timing, but he had to find out some time, I guess. But the two of them talked it out, and things seem better than ever between them. So, why are you and my brother both so miserable and mopey?"

"And why are you ignoring us? We're your friends, Emma. We aren't going to hold anything that happened with James against you," Kristi said.

I appreciated the effort, but...

"You're his friend and his sister. I don't want to make things awkward for anyone. It's better if I'm the one to step back."

"Emma, Kristi and I have wanted to get to know you since we met you on your first day at the library. We became friends with you independent of your relationships with James or Harry. Now, unless you did something egregious to my brother, like, I don't know, kidnapped his dog, or—"

"James doesn't have a dog," Kristi chimed in.

"He's allergic to them," I said. I'd already mentally stricken that task from the list the minute he'd told me.

"It was a hypothetical scenario," Jill said. "Again, unless you did something unforgiveable, we are still your friends. That's how friendships work. Now, will you tell us what happened? Please?"

I rubbed my face, letting the blanket shield drop below my shoulders. "The morning after the party, I told him I couldn't be with him. I—I don't think I'm the kind of person he deserves. He's so confident in me, and us, and I'm so...not. I mean, look, I've barely accomplished anything on my list, and he's got a business and a house and a whole town of people who love him! Meanwhile, I have a broken-down car, and a crappy apartment, and—"

"I'm going to stop you there before you spiral down further. What list?"

"It—it's nothing, really. Only something I wrote up when I first moved to Greyport. Tasks to help me fit in and get settled. It's part of the reason I agreed to that stupid plan with Harry."

"Give it here," Kristi said with a waggle of her fingers.

"It's in my bedroom."

"Well, go get it. We'll wait."

"I'll pour us each a glass of wine!" Jill said as she hopped up and scurried into the kitchen.

Less than a minute later, we squeezed close together on the sofa, me clutching that worn piece of paper and Jill divvying out glasses of red.

"Here it is." I handed the lined paper to Kristi, who read it silently before passing it on. I focused on chugging down my cup of liquid courage.

"Uh, Kristi?" Jill said first.

I didn't look up, but I knew they could tell I was listening.

"Yes, Jill?"

"Is it just me, or has our wonderful friend Emma already done almost everything on this list?"

I stood up, flinging off my comforter cape.

"That isn't true! I haven't done any of those things. I can't remember to pay my bills. I'm a hot mess. James doesn't need that in his life, not when he's so busy and focused on his family and his company. I refuse to be the type of partner who *needs* him all the time without giving anything in return. If I can't manage to finish a dumb set of tasks, how can I be an adult in a relationship?"

Kristi held up the page at eye level. "Point one: *befriend your coworkers*. Check. You've done that, and there will be no more debate. I'll try not to take it too personally that you didn't already cross it off. Two: *Join a group*. I mean, you've gone out with the library group a few times, right? And trivia night with Harry and those doofuses. That counts."

I crossed my arms but acknowledged the point with a tight nod.

Jill snatched the list with a swoop of her arm and took over. "Skipping over the gym and the sports league tasks—because that's not you and let's not pretend otherwise. I hope you're prepared to ditch the dog idea. James' allergy is fierce—swollen eyes and everything. *Stroll local market*. I'm counting the Christmas parade for that one. *Go on a hike*. It's the dead of winter, but I say ice-skating counts. What do you say, Kris?"

"Absolutely."

"*Say YES to everything*. That one I do like. How's that going, Emma?" Jill said.

I gritted my teeth. "Not great. It was the impetus for the whole Harry-and-James disaster."

"But look where it got you. I mean, if the whole purpose of this list was to make friends, then haven't you done that? We're here, aren't we?"

I watched as my friends—and they *were* my friends—took lines of blue ink through the list I had so thoughtfully curated months ago. It was almost...liberating, in a way.

"Emma, if you break it down, what does this piece of paper and what you do or don't accomplish from it say about who you are as a person?" Jill asked. "It's a starting point, and I can see it motivated you when you needed it, but this isn't really personalized to you. It's, like, generic life advice that we've now established you did in your own time. You're a normal twenty-six-year-old who recently finished her MBA and is adjusting to a new town. You're not defective. You don't need a list, and you certainly didn't need Harry, to be worth something."

"Jill is right. I had trouble when I first got here too. I'm a little strange, a little different, but I found my people. And it seems—I hope—you've found your people too. Can I ask you a question?"

"Okay," I said, my voice raw.

"Do you feel bad about yourself when you're around James? Because if you do, Jill and I will shut up, and we won't say another word about him."

I shook my head in a flurry of denial. "No. No. I feel confident, and funny, and safe with him. But I want him to feel that way about himself when he's with me, and I'm not sure I can give him that."

"Emma, I hate to bring this up, because James is my brother, and *ew*, but he had a spontaneous hook-up with you in a closet. Normally, the man is a robot with three factory settings. He worries, works, and works out. That's *it*. You honestly think he doesn't feel confident or fun with you?"

"I—I—that's just sex, though."

"So, if I give you one of those monster dildos I sell, that will be the same, yes?"

"Well...no."

"So, it isn't *just* sex, then."

"No," I whispered. "He told me he's falling in love with me."

"Of course he's falling in love with you! You're *incredible!* Now, it's up to you to believe him."

"It sounds so easy when you say it like that."

Kristi shrugged. "Maybe it could be easy. Do you think everybody has their shit together when they meet their person? Or is it a work in progress for all of us?"

"You're right. I just... I need some time." The way they'd dissected my comfort blanket—the list—in less than ten minutes had me reeling.

"Well, don't take too long. If I know James, once he's made up his mind, he doesn't deviate."

My eyes flicked up to meet Jill's. "What do you mean?" That sounded vaguely...threatening.

She smiled, all sharp angles and teeth. "Why don't you talk to him and find out for yourself?"

"I'll...consider it."

"He's pretty awesome, huh?"

I gave a watery smile. The wine was making me sentimental. "So awesome."

Jill reached over to take my hand. Kristi grabbed the other, sandwiching me in.

"Thank you both."

"That's what friends are for."

"Kris, that was so cliche," Jill said.

"Yeah, but it's true! Cliches are cliches for a reason."

I laughed for the first time in days. "Can I tell you two a story? It's a little sad, but maybe it has an okay ending, after all."

CHAPTER SIXTY-NINE

Emma

I CURSED JILL AND Kristi as I trudged down the stairs to Greyport Grinds, regretting that last glass of wine. But I had needed the liquid courage, especially when it came to sharing the story of my accident and recovery. To my shock, it had grown easier to tell since that first time with James, like my body now knew that exposing myself to the raw reality of my past in a safe setting was manageable.

My friends had been supportive, understanding, empathetic. They hadn't tried to downplay my experience, nor had they looked at me with pity, as I'd so feared. We had ended the night in fits of giggles as Kristi played the role of Tracy while I practiced asking for a new desk chair. When the two women had left around midnight, Jill had squeezed me into a hug with a whispered reminder not to underestimate myself.

With that in mind, I paused at the threshold of the cafe and opened up the contacts list on my phone. I navigated to the message thread I needed.

> Emma: I didn't like how we ended things the other day. Would you be interested in attending my next session with Talisa?

The reply was instantaneous.

> Mom: I would love to, honey. I love you.

I sent over the information for my upcoming virtual appointment with my therapist before entering the busy cafe. Talking about things with Mom would be good. And I also needed to work on the negative thoughts I had about myself.

A coffee grinder whirred as I stepped up to the counter, sending a stab of pressure into my already aching head. Gritting my teeth, I gave my order to the barista—a G-State student outfitted in a shirt with *Brew Me Daddy* emblazoned across the chest. The young woman gave me a startled look, so I put forth my best effort to smile. The speed with which she sent me to wait at the end of the counter told me the attempt failed.

The door clanged open, and a cold draft whipped through the cafe as I waited for my coffee. I pulled the open ends of my coat closer together.

My beautiful, warm, expensive coat. Purchased for me by a certain someone I couldn't stop thinking about. Couldn't stop missing even after less than a week apart.

Was he throwing himself into work, sticking to the same rigid routine? Was he remembering to have fun and live a little?

"Order for Emma!" I stepped up to grab my latte and aimed for the door. I looked forward to another day of hibernating in my office at work, though this time it was less about hiding and more about my nagging hangover.

"Hey."

I froze. "Hey, Harry."

"How are you doing?"

"Um. Not great, to be honest." I shifted to the left, staring down the fluorescent exit sign.

Harry continued to stand directly in my way. He wasn't reading my body language—not like James would have. "I'm really sorry if I ruined anything for you at the party. James does not have a girlfriend."

"Yep. I know."

We both nodded in the empty air. "Well, I'll see you around."

I managed to make it out the door and partway down the sidewalk before his heavy footsteps shuffled behind me.

"Emma, wait!" I drew to a halt but didn't bother turning around.

"What is it, Harry? I have to get to work."

"I just want to tell you one thing, and then I'll get out of your hair."

I finally turned to him. "Alright," I said, crossing my arms over my chest.

"You should come to James' workshop tonight at six."

"Why?" I didn't trust Harry farther than I could throw him. And he was way bigger than me. I couldn't throw him far.

"He won't even be there! I promise. There's something you need to see."

"Harry, not to be rude here, but you've been lying about one thing or another since I met you. You're not exactly trustworthy."

"That's...well, it's actually incredibly fair. And okay. It was a ploy. But it's for good reason! Anyway, how about—oh, shit, sorry, I better take this call."

I almost took the opening to leave while he was preoccupied with the phone, but I saw his face pale and heard the frantic, garbled voice on the other side of the line.

Was this how my parents felt the day they'd gotten the call about my accident?

"Okay. Okay. I'll be there as soon as I can." Harry hung up his phone and looked up, dazed.

"What's wrong, Harry?" My lips were numb.

"That was Ben. James got hurt. I have to get to the hospital."

CHAPTER SEVENTY

James

I STOOD NEAR THE front desk in the waiting room, tapping my toe as I looked around for Harry. The asshole was taking forever to get here, and the nurse had told me I needed someone to pick me up.

What the nurse didn't understand was that I *needed* to get home, needed to finish an important project.

Instead of working, I was stuck at Canal Town Hospital with stitches up and down the base of my thumb. I had been careless when operating my table saw—not for the first time—and had the patchwork to show for it. They'd given me some pain meds while fixing me up and didn't want me driving.

It had been two hours, and I felt fine. I was lucky enough to avoid any major damage and wouldn't need further intervention. My biggest problem was my slow-ass cousin and the derailment of my schedule. My hand wouldn't be much of a hindrance with what I had left, not if I bandaged it well and wore my largest size gloves.

I was regretting not insisting Ben pick me up, but he'd had a client meeting.

A sneaker squeaked on the yellowed tile floor, and I looked up to find Harry barreling around the corner of the vestibule that filtered into the room.

"What took so long? I've been waiting here forever."

"What? Ben called me, like, twenty minutes ago. I got here as fast as I could."

"Let's just go."

"Harry! You walk too damn fast. I've never been here before."

I pulled up. That was Emma's voice, preceding her appearance.

"Dude! Why didn't you warn me she was here?" I said to Harry, panicking. I wanted to see Emma. I always wanted to see her. But I had *plans* that didn't include hospital lighting and the sound of someone hacking up a lung.

"She insisted—like, to a scary degree. I was with her when Ben called, and she pretty much took over."

Sure enough, Emma whipped into the room at a near march, her pale, freckled face set and determined.

I'd never seen her more beautiful.

I didn't regret Harry being the one to pick me up anymore.

She looked up, and we made eye contact. I could have sworn her lips trembled once before she started running.

I let out an *oof* as she barreled into me, burying her nose in my chest.

"You're okay," she said, patting up and down my back, like she was assuring herself that I was still in one piece. And was she crying?

"Yeah. I'm okay. Only some stitches."

She lifted her head—she *was* crying—and I tightened my hold on her just the smallest bit. I wasn't letting her go now that I had her again.

"Stitches?"

I lifted my bandaged hand to her eye level. "Yep."

I watched in fascination as she rounded on my cousin. "You didn't think it was pertinent to tell me James' injury was stitches in his hand, Harry?" She sounded disturbingly polite.

"Uh, no?"

"You made it seem like he was seriously injured!"

"I mean, it could have been bad, right? He could have lost a lot of blood or something."

"Harry, go bring the car closer so James doesn't have to walk so far."

"He doesn't have stitches in his feet."

"Harrison. Car. Now." She threw a black key fob on a fuzzy purple keychain at his head. He managed to catch it a split second before it smacked him in the face.

"Ugh. Fine."

We were alone—well, as alone as it got in a hospital waiting room.

I rocked back and forth in my work boots, opened my mouth to talk, to confess how much I'd missed her, how lovely she was, how the light shining in through the wall of windows made her look like an angel.

Maybe the drugs they'd given me had been stronger than I'd thought.

"We can talk later. Did you get your discharge paperwork?"

I held up empty hands. "Nope."

She stalked over to the registration desk. Two minutes and some aggressive pointing in my direction later, she returned with a stapled sheet of paper.

"There's a prescription antibiotic waiting for you at Magritte's Pharmacy. We'll grab it before I drop you off at your house."

I stared at her, struck dumb and possibly still a little high. She shook her head at me.

"Right now, we are walking. Here, hold onto my arm. You look a little pale, and we both know I'm not big enough to catch you if you go down."

"Emma, wait. Give me a second," I said, keeping a grip on her with my uninjured hand.

She glanced back and waited for me to continue.

"When you drop me off, will you stay? I have something to show you."

I wasn't done with my project, but I realized, looking at her standing in front of me with that light beaming down, that it didn't matter if things were perfect and finished. I wanted her to be there for the progress. I wanted to be there for her progress too.

"This thing you want to show me…" Her mouth quirked. "That isn't code for your dick, is it?"

I roared with laughter, somehow, here with my hand throbbing and a screaming kid going past in his father's arms.

I placed my heart in her hands. "Fuck, Emma. Will you? Come home with me?"

CHAPTER SEVENTY-ONE

Emma

THE ANSWER HAD BEEN easy, after all.

Say YES to everything. Wasn't that the whole point of this?

I trailed after James, who tugged me by the hand, over the flagstones in his backyard and down the path to his workshop, where he poured his heart into his craft.

We had dropped Harry off at his new apartment, with me paying little attention, before finishing the rest of the drive to the blue Victorian in silence. Later, we would talk about Harry moving out at long last. But we both knew that talk could wait.

James paused at the door to the converted barn. "I was trying to think of something profound to say, but I think it's if better I show you."

My lips shook as I gave him a small smile. "You're making me nervous."

"No need for that. Trust me."

The workshop was dark as the door rolled open. The familiar shapes of worktables and tools became visible as my eyes adjusted to the low light.

"It's in the back, over here."

He guided me toward a smaller section in the barn's rear, where he stored finished projects. He flicked on the overhead lamp.

Whoosh.

That was the sound of my heart falling straight out of my chest and into James Klein's lap.

It was the missing bench. *My* bench. Still worn and discolored but now reinforced, patched together.

I glanced at James, where he leaned against the wall, one shoulder posted up. So cool and casual. "How? When? It was gone."

He rubbed the back of his neck. "I, uh…reached out to the village parks department. Ben's mom knows someone there. They were going to take all the old benches apart and recycle the wood. It wasn't that hard to get it."

"But—but I ended things with you. You went to all the trouble of tracking this down and fixing it up, even after I did that?"

The heat in his eyes belied his relaxed posture. His throat bobbed. "I told you I wasn't giving up. Did you think I didn't mean it?"

Had I thought that? That insecure and self-pitying part of me had. But James was trustworthy. He was loyal. He was stalwart and never, ever let go of what was important to him. There wasn't a doubt in my mind about that. But somehow, I'd gotten lost in my head along the way.

I straightened from where I bent, peering down to inspect his handiwork. James held my gaze, waiting as I took one step toward him. "I know you meant it."

He cleared his throat, moving past me to crouch by the side of the bench. "So, over here is where I still want to do some work. You said you liked that it was more worn, so I'm not doing too much to it, just a few repairs and patches where things are—"

"James?" I stole a peek at him, grinning at the flushed skin that appeared above the line of his dark beard. "Are you nervous?"

He stood, towering over me, bandaged fist tight to his chest. "Nervous is an understatement. I've never been more terrified in my entire fucking life. It isn't perfect, but you have to know what this bench means, Emma. You have to. I can't get over the fact that the first time I told you I loved you, it all went to shit and you walked away. I'm looking at you, right here in front of me, and I can't even believe you're real. I never want to watch you walk away again. So yeah, I'll drag out a conversation about bench repairs. I'll tell you about different colors of wood stain. Fuck, I'll make you help me organize my hardware drawers, as long as it keeps you here with me."

I rested a shaking hand against James' warm cheek. A hot trail of saltwater dripped past my lip. "I was going to tell you I wanted to try again the minute I saw you at the hospital. Because when Harry told me something had happened to you, it made me realize I didn't want to waste another second. Greyport *is* home. *You* are my home. So, yes, I understand what the bench means, and I love it. But mostly, I just love you."

He grabbed me by the hips—as much as his injured hand would allow—and boosted me up. I wrapped my legs around his strong waist and clasped my arms behind his neck. I pressed a kiss to each of his closed eyelids before tracing soft kisses down his face and, at last, on his lips.

His groan filled the barn as I licked into his mouth.

"Holy hell, woman, you are torturing me. Although I'd love to get you naked right here and now, I'm a little hopped up on painkillers."

I tugged gently, chiding, on his beard hair. "Why didn't you say anything? You should be in bed, resting!"

He only smiled, wide and proud. "I've got exactly what I need."

Chapter Seventy-Two

James

O NE NAP LATER, I was sitting at my kitchen island, ass on a stool, as I watched Emma cook me lunch. I couldn't recall the last time someone had cooked for me, but with her, it didn't seem strange. It was just right.

"Do you have to go in to work?" I asked. The selfish part of me hoped she didn't, but it was midday on a Wednesday. I didn't expect her to take a whole day off to tend to me.

She glanced up from the burner where she was flipping a grilled cheese sandwich. "Nope. I called Tracy when Harry and I were on the way to the hospital. Told her I'd be out for the day. I figured I'd be pretty useless at work, no matter what state you were in."

"Huh. Sounds to me like you may like me a little."

"Don't get cocky on me, Klein. Here, eat your food." She set a plate in front of me at the counter.

"Might need you to feed it to me. It's so cheesy, and I've only got one functioning hand." I made a show of cradling my bandaged palm against my heart.

It had the desired effect of making my girl laugh. But she went ahead and did it anyway, alternating bites of gooey grilled cheese for me with nibbles of her own sandwich.

When we finished, Emma's hands and my beard were a mess. She got close and stuck her tongue out, pretending to lick a drop of melted cheddar from my face before she changed direction and wiped it with a napkin.

"I love you, but not enough to lick food off your face."

"Want something else in your mouth?" I said as I scooped her off her chair and fireman-carried her into the living room.

"Oh my God. You did not say that," she said between fits of giggles as we settled onto the couch.

"Hey, I'm not always uptight."

She stilled. "I don't think you're uptight. You do know that, don't you?"

I cleared the catch in my throat. This was the hard part of being a work in progress, admitting to an insecurity and simply…trusting her to accept it.

"Part of me may forever be worried people will think that of me. Or that they'll only want me around for the things I do for them and not for me. I'll never be the fun, spontaneous life of the party with interesting hobbies." Not like Harry. "I like my job and working. Going to the gym and cooking. There isn't much more to me than that. I'm boring."

She moved over to straddle my lap. "You are brilliant and caring." She feathered a kiss across my brow. "Creative." Another kiss on my cheekbone. "Secretly funny as hell." Another at the corner of my mouth. "Devastatingly sexy." She pulled back to meet my eyes, brown bleeding into golden edges. "And I am in love with exactly who you are. You don't need to be a wild, fun-loving person to make me happy. Just be you."

"How did I get this lucky?" I said, half to myself.

"I'm scared too, James. I might always be afraid I won't live up to your level of having it all together. That you'll figure out I'm too much of a mess to be with you. That…that my injuries could get worse as time goes on and I'll be a burden to you."

"Hey," I said, drawing my hands up to cradle her neck. "Just how you're in love with who I am, right here and now, I feel the same way about you. You did something—moving here—that I was never brave enough to do. You took charge today, ordered Harry around like a boss, made sure I slept and ate. No one's ever done that for me before, not since my mom."

I paused, the heaviness of the moment hitting as hard as a ton of bricks. "Emma, your worries about your health… Those are real, and we don't know what the future holds. But I think… I think caring for my mom in her hardest days showed me I can do that. Be a caregiver. I'm *good* at it. So, if we ever have to cross that road, we'll do it together, and we'll talk about it and make decisions, and talk about it again if we have to. But you're never alone, and you're never a burden. My eyes are wide open. *You* are what I want. For as long as you'll have me."

She leaned down and touched her forehead to mine. A tear spilled from her cheek onto my wrist. "And you say you don't have a way with words."

A chuckle rumbled up from within me. "I guess you bring out a different side of me."

She smiled, looking sleepy and happy. "James?"

"Yeah?"

"How out of it are you right now?"

My ears got hot. "Not at all since the nap. The meds wore off. Why?"

A sparking hint of mischief floated below the surface of her gaze. "Can I make you feel good?"

My brain short-circuited. "Huh?"

Emma's tinkling laughter echoed in the room as she hopped off my lap, placed a hand on my chest, and pushed me down until my shoulder blades met the back of the couch.

"Relax," I heard her whisper.

After that, it was the clink of my belt buckle, the unzipping of my fly, a shift of the hips, and Emma's lips and tongue. Everything else was a distant memory.

CHAPTER SEVENTY-THREE

Emma

"Y OUR BED IS FUCKING amazing."

I rolled around back and forth on the mattress, rocking like a wobbly canoe as I snuggled deeper into James' blankets.

We'd napped again after I'd blown his brains out. He had been pretty non-functional afterward, a byproduct of the day's events and my stellar oral skills.

He grinned down at me as he pulled a pair of gray sweats—sweet, blessed gray sweats—over the tight muscle of his ass—commando. I would never voice a single complaint about James' rigid gym schedule.

Especially given his ridiculous stamina.

"That's because you're used to a tiny bed."

"It's not that small. You're just a giant."

"I'm six foot five. A California king is the only way to go for me."

"Well, I hope you don't mind a frequent guest. I know you just got Harry out of here and into his own place."

He sat and tucked a strand of my hair behind my ear with his good hand. "You better be here every fucking night of the week."

"My lease isn't up for another few months. And my apartment has a coffee shop under it."

"I'll buy you a latte maker. When is your birthday, by the way? It'll be one of your presents."

"James! I'm being serious. I can't move in right away."

"I'm joking—kind of. But if you need me to, I'll slow it down. But don't think I won't jump at the opportunity to have you with me every night as soon as you're ready. For now, we'll alternate. C'mon, when do you turn twenty-seven?" he asked as he ran his knuckles under my chin.

I scooted out from under the covers and sat next to him. "Um. Next week?"

"Is that a question?"

"Nope."

"In that case, I'd better get moving on your gift."

"No, no, no. You're not getting me anything. You went overboard for Christmas with the coat and boots. And the book and the bench on top of it. What I really want for my birthday is for you to take one week off from work. Rest your hand. Let me spoil you."

"Will this spoiling involve any more of the treatment I got on the couch?"

I leaned up and kissed him on the cheek, right above the line of his beard. "It could—if you behave yourself. Starting now. Go turn on the TV and relax. I'm making dinner."

"We can order takeout."

I was already up and sliding out of the room in my fuzzy socks. "I'm itching to use your fancy kitchen. You can't stop me."

"Yeah, yeah, yeah. Keep it up, brat. Once I have two working hands again, that ass is mine."

"I'm counting on it."

❦ ❦ ❦ ❦ ❦ ❦ ❦ ❦

"A LRIGHT, I CAN'T EAT another bite."

"So, how were they?" I asked as I gazed at James, chin propped on my fist, as he polished off the last bite of a hard-shell taco.

"They're good as hell. What did you use to season the meat?"

As requested, James had kicked back on his brown leather couch to watch...the Food Network. He'd trusted me to take care of dinner without hovering.

"Just a combo of stuff I found in the pantry."

"You need any help cleaning up? Not sure how useful I'll be washing dishes with this bandage, but I can try."

"Nope. I like to clean as I cook so things don't get unmanageable. Will you sit down and talk with me while I put the leftovers away?"

"As long as you don't mind me staring at you like a pervert."

"Stare away."

I scooped leftover taco fixings into glass containers—James had the nice meal prep stuff—while we talked about mundane, everyday topics. He smiled the whole time, ear to ear.

I put that smile on his face. Me.

I made him safe and took care of him. I marched into a hospital today, trauma and fear of blood be-damned, and managed my shit.

I was a Grade A badass.

My phone chimed from where it sat charging by the fridge. It was the tone reserved for video chats from my parents.

"You need to get that?"

"It's my mom and dad. You mind being on a video call?"

"Do you? I don't want you to worry about their thoughts on us. You know, you being with your ex-boyfriend's cousin."

I strode over to the phone, wiggling out the charging cable. "I realized when I bumped into Harry at Greyport Grinds that zero people in town care that we're dating. Mark's lame reaction and my insecurity just threw me for a momentary loop."

"Mark is a chode."

"You won't hear me arguing." I swiped to answer the incoming alert. "Hey, Mom. Hey, Dad."

"Hi, honey! It looks like you're not at home. Want to call us back at a better time?" Mom asked. I was impressed by her offering me an out and not giving me the third degree about my current location.

"It's an okay time to talk. Here, say hi to James." I slid into a seat beside him, our shoulders bumping.

"Hello...James?"

Dad's eyes darted to Mom's, and I laughed at their bugged-out expressions. I wasn't above fucking with my parents from time to time.

"Surprise! You know how I told you things with Harry didn't work out..."

My mother emitted an uncharacteristic screech and smacked my father on the upper arm.

"I hope that was a good noise," James muttered, out of the camera's view.

I bit my lip on a grin. It was definitely a good sign.

I gave Mom and Dad the abbreviated tale of how James and I got together, leaving off the part about my relationship with Harry being fake. We had always purported that it was nothing serious between us, so the natural shift to James after getting to know him made sense. In reality, that wasn't far from the truth. Maybe one day I would divulge the full story, but I wasn't quite ready yet.

James' injury naturally drew questions. On screen, my parents, huddled together at their oval dining table, mirrored James and me at the kitchen island. Never once did James monopolize the conversation, allowing me to lead. At the same time, he didn't leave me alone to carry the call. I doubted he even knew what he was doing. He wore the role of boyfriend like a second skin.

When I ended the call, I placed gentle fingers atop his white bandage.

"Thank you for that."

"You're welcome. It was easy. I only wish you could have met my mom too."

I lifted my hand to his cheek. "You can tell me all about her."

"I will. We have all the time in the world."

Epilogue

Six Months Later

Emma

"Harry! Hurry up! He's going to be here any minute, and you need to be gone." I paced at the top of the stairs of the Victorian while Harry took his sweet time in the upstairs bathroom.

"Alright already. I really had to pee. I've been holding it for three hours. I promise I'll be out of here before he gets home." Harry stopped to look at me as he stepped into the hallway. "Hold up. Are you nervous?"

A strangled sound erupted out of me as I mimed a choking motion in front of his face. "Nope. Not at all."

His brows rose. "Uh, yeah, because you sound totally normal and not at all insane right now. You know he's going to be obnoxiously happy about this, right?"

"Has he said anything to you about it? Do you think he suspects? You don't think it's too soon, is it?"

"I don't know, I'm not a weird detective like Kristi."

"She prefers *intuitive*."

"Well, whatever you call it, I'm not it. He's been acting his usual self as far as I can tell. You're better off asking Jill. She mentioned asking him to stop by to help with that sticky cabinet at her building."

Jill had purchased a rundown building several months ago. It was a sore spot with her and her brother as it was riddled with problems. I steered well clear of the mess and was letting the two of them work through it in their own time.

"Did you get everything in place for me?" I asked.

"You're all set. That thing was heavy as hell, and I expect you and James to be at my next bowling tournament to say thank you."

"Harry, if this goes well, we will be there with signs and shirts, don't you worry."

A silly, puppy-dog grin wreathed his face. "In all seriousness, I'm really excited for you two."

I gave him an answering smile. We had settled easily from fake dating to real friendship. "I appreciate that, Harry. Now, please leave."

"Alright, alright, I'm going." He skipped down the stairs of his former home, pausing at the last step to glance over his shoulder at me. "And don't be nervous. He'll say yes."

A flutter rose up from my stomach into my chest as the door closed behind him.

James

My HAND SHOOK AS I fumbled with the key in the lock. It had been six months since Emma and I made our relationship official, and she wanted to celebrate together. So, of course I wound up having to make a last-minute delivery to a client in Merlin Heights. Then, Jill ran into an issue at her building, so I had to make an emergency stop. I'd planned to be home an hour earlier to celebrate spending half a year with the love of my life.

There had been hard times certainly, moments when we bickered or when our insecurities cropped up. But we'd gotten through those moments together. Never once had one of our disagreements left me thinking the relationship itself was at risk. I kept up my monthly therapy sessions, and Emma continued to meet regularly over video with her own therapist as well.

Our first real test came a few months back when Emma's parents had been in town, kicking her anxiety into a swirl. But she'd held firm to her boundaries, and I could see the more time Linda and Frank spent in Greyport, the more they were coming to love it here too. By the time they'd turned the corner to head for home, Emma had even admitted she was looking forward to their next visit. It was progress.

I was hoping for even more progress tonight. I planned on asking Emma to move in—officially. She spent practically every night at my place, anyway, only sleeping at the apartment above Greyport Grinds if she had a late night at work.

My bed was a lonely place to be on those nights.

"Emma?" I called as I stepped out of my work boots, stowing them in the hall closet. Emma had a penchant for tripping over shoes in the entryway, and I didn't like the idea of her getting hurt. She'd been diligent about her therapy exercises lately, and she was feeling more fluid. I hated the thought of her taking a spill and getting set back, and I knew she would hate it too.

I peeked into the kitchen and living room, but she wasn't on the lower level. We had planned on having a relaxing night in front of the fireplace with plates of Thai food.

Starting up the stairs, I heard soft music coming from my room. I recognized it as Emma's favorite playlist to unwind from the workday—a mix of pop-punk and folk songs.

Halfway to the top of the steps, the track rolled into the song that had been playing in Emma's apartment the day I'd found her sick on the floor. I smiled at the memory. That was the first night I had allowed myself to think of her, of making her mine, without an ounce of guilt.

I tapped on the bedroom door as I pushed it open, the smell of a floral candle tickling my nostrils. My girl had gone all out, it seemed.

"Hi."

Whoa. The sight of Emma in a deep-purple dress hit me straight in the gut as the door opened fully.

"Should I shower and get changed? Because you look...sexy as fuck." I had on dirty work clothes, and the sweats I planned to change into weren't going to cut it next to her.

"Thank you. And no. You're just right, just like that."

"Are you sure? You look incredible, and I look—"

"Fine! You look fine. Can you come into the room now?"

"Uh, yeah?" She was being weird, but I stepped through the threshold, unbuckling my belt.

I decided to get the hard question out of the way and ask, "Hey, so with your lease—"

"James, stop talking."

What the fuck?

I paused in unbuckling my belt and studied her, moving beyond the cleavage and sexy dress. "You're shaking."

"That's because I'm nervous, you dipshit."

"Why? I'm just asking you to move in with me. You basically live here anyway."

"James! Look around you right now. What's different about this room?"

I did a full spin, not noticing anything out of the ordinary. "My brain kind of malfunctioned when I saw you. All the blood rushed to my dick. Sorry."

Maybe she'd let me eat her out to make up for it.

She rolled her eyes. "By the foot of the bed."

"Oh. *Oh.*" The bench. But why was it inside? We usually kept it out in the backyard on the covered porch.

"How'd you get it inside? It's heavy as hell."

"That's not important. It's a gesture. And you're stealing my thunder here with the whole moving in thing too."

"So, do you not want to move in?"

"No!"

"No?"

"I mean, yes, I want to move in, but that's not what I'm talking about. I want to marry you!"

Holy shit. "What?"

She walked toward me, padding on bare feet across my bedroom. *Our* bedroom.

"I had a whole thing planned. I asked Harry to move the bench inside for me. I even bought a ring."

My heart was beating too fast. I was only thirty-six and in good physical shape. I ate well and tried to keep up with that meditating stuff Harry got me into. A heart attack was unlikely. But I could have sworn my dream girl was proposing to me.

"I can see you're surprised." She gave me an indulgent smile, her eyes warm. "James, I love you more today than I did six months ago. I'll love you more in twenty years than I do today. From the minute I met you and thought you were a serial-killing home invader, you've been challenging me, and encouraging me, and turning me on. I want that forever. I want to be imperfect with you for the rest of our lives."

My heart gave out as I watched Emma lower down to the floor on both knees, pulling a shiny silver band from the cup of her bra.

"Sorry, this dress doesn't have pockets."

My view of her went blurry as I laughed. She was everything I had never known I needed.

"Will you marry me?" she asked, that damn dimple shining through.

"Get up off the floor," I said, tugging her by the shoulders and into my arms. I lifted her until she wrapped her legs around my waist, the skirt of her purple dress hiked up. "Fuck yes, I'll marry you."

Her smiling lips met mine as we spun in a slow circle. "You're my fiancé," she said as she pulled back.

I let her slide the ring onto my left ring finger. "Yeah. I am."

What she didn't know was I had a ring for her too, waiting in my dresser drawer for the perfect moment.

THE END

Not ready for Emma and James' story to end? Sign up for Rachel Kaye's newsletter or scan the QR code below to receive access to a free bonus epilogue.

Coming Next

If you're in the mood for more Greyport, you're in luck! Jill's book, *The Velvet Fix*, will be in Kindle Unlimited and paperback in April 2025!

Curious about Merlin Heights? Check out Jennifer Aline's, *The Ex Project* to learn more!

About the Author

Rachel writes small town romantic comedies with plenty of steam and twice the heart. She is a reader first, writer second, and holds the principle of happily ever after as sacred. Rachel lives in Western New York with her bearded husband, two rambunctious children, snuggly cat, and a one-eyed Chihuahua.

If you loved hanging out in
Greyport, you'll love
visiting Merlin Heights!